"In true Kathi Macias fashion, *The Deliverer* draws the reader deep into the lives of women and children subjected to mankind's cruelty—in this instance, sexual slavery. One would expect such a novel to fill the reader with sadness. And it does. But the joy of *The Deliverer* is knowing there are people, some of them former victims themselves, who devote their lives to righting this wrong. This is a novel of pain, forgiveness, salvation, and hope."

—TRISH PERRY, author of *Love Finds You on Christmas Morning* and *Tea for Two*; trishperry.com

"With well-defined characters we have come to know, Kathi Macias brings a satisfying conclusion to the story of Mara and the other girls in the story. Both heartwarming and heartrending, *The Deliverer* is a story and characters you will long remember after turning the last page. Don't miss this final chapter in this timely series on human trafficking."

—MARTHA ROGERS, Touching Hearts, Changing Lives; marthawrogers.com; marthasbooks.blogspot.com

"*The Deliverer* is a book about choices. Though we may not have a choice about our circumstances in life—hurts, challenges, and sometimes tragic injustice like human trafficking—we all have the same option. We can choose to love and forgive. Kathi captures this truth in every chapter with every character. Whether it's dealing with the pain of horrible memories, the indignity of abuse, or our own tendencies toward pride and selfishness, there is ultimately one powerful choice: will we allow God to be our great Deliverer?"

—DAWN WILSON, founder
and author of t

"Excellent! Kathi has done it again. In *The Deliverer* she shines light on the darkness of human trafficking through real-to-life characters who make you want to cry and to cheer them on. She offers serious encouragement to believe God is in control and good while evil lurks. Kathi's words brings hope. A fresh look at a modern issue."

—LUCY ANN MOLL, biblical counselor, speaker, and author; lucyannmoll.com

# The Deliverer

Kathi Macias

NEW HOPE
PUBLISHERS
Gospel-Centered. Missions-Driven.

# Other Titles by
# Kathi Macias

∽∞∾

**"FREEDOM" SERIES**
*Deliver Me from Evil*
*Special Delivery*
*The Deliverer*

**"EXTREME DEVOTION" SERIES**
*More than Conquerors*
*No Greater Love*
*People of the Book*
*Red Ink*

New Hope® Publishers
P. O. Box 12065
Birmingham, AL 35202-2065
NewHopeDigital.com
New Hope Publishers is a division of WMU®.

Library of Congress Cataloging-in-Publication Data
Macias, Kathi, 1948-
  The deliverer / Kathi Macias.
     p. cm.
  ISBN 978-1-59669-308-1 (sc)
  1.  Human trafficking victims--Fiction. 2.  Human trafficking--Fiction. 3.
Uncles--Fiction.  I. Title.
  PS3563.I42319D45 2012
  813'.54--dc23
                                    2012019982

ISBN-10: 1-59669-308-8
ISBN-13: 978-1-59669-308-1

N114142 • 0812 • 5M1

# Dedication

This book and series is humbly and heartbreakingly
dedicated to all who are held in modern-day slavery.
We stand together with you with the united cry of
"Abolition!" And we look to the One who died
to set us all free.

On a more personal level, I dedicate this book and series
to my partner and best friend, Al, who daily supports
and encourages me as God calls me to
"write the vision . . . and make it plain"
(Habakkuk 2:2).

# Prologue

The sun set early in late November and, though a pleasant warm spell had kept San Diego's daytime temperatures in the lower 80s for the past week or so, the air cooled quickly as darkness approached.

Mara didn't mind. She loved watching the sun go down over the Pacific at any time of year and in any sort of weather. Just being able to sit on the seawall and watch the colorful streaks in the broad expanse of sky, seeming to frame the dark and restless ocean, reminded her of how precious her freedom was and how much she'd endured before obtaining it.

She zipped her windbreaker against the encroaching dampness and then gazed down at the envelope in her hand, postmarked Juarez, Mexico. She'd nearly memorized the words in the one-page letter, handwritten by the fifteen-year-old girl Mara had helped to rescue just months earlier. Mara had been working at her waitressing job when she spotted Francesca with her owner and immediately recognized the signs of a girl caught up in human trafficking. The situation had dredged up many of her own dark memories, but Mara was glad she'd been in the right place at the right time to assist in the girl's release and eventual return to her family.

*I'm just glad she had a family and a home to go back to*, Mara thought, resisting the tears that bit her eyes as she compared

Francesca's situation to her own. At least Francesca had been kidnapped, not sold into slavery by her own parents.

Mara shook her head. She had to stop this constant slipping back into self-pity about her past and just enjoy the present. She was free now, working and hoping to start classes at the local college after the first of the year. It was more than she had ever dreamed of during her ten years of captivity.

She pulled the letter from the envelope and squinted to reread portions of it in the fading light. *The baby will come soon . . . not sure yet about adoption . . . praying for the right answer.* Mara too had become pregnant during the years she lived as a sex slave—several times, actually—but she'd never even had the chance to choose to carry her babies to term. Always there was a forced abortion . . . and always she had to suppress her grief and go right back to the life she despised.

*Never again,* she told herself. *And never again for Francesca. But what about all the others?*

The tears won over at that point, dripping onto her cheeks as she thought of Jasmine and others who had died at the hands of their abusers. She thought too of what she'd heard about a young Thai girl named Lawan, rescued from a brothel in the Golden Triangle and even now winging her way across the ocean to join her adoptive family right here in the San Diego area.

*One more set free . . . so many left behind.* No matter how hard she tried, Mara could not banish that truth from her thoughts. She'd often talked about that very thing to her friend Barbara Whiting, the lady involved with an outreach to human trafficking victims, and Barbara too had lamented the many who never escaped. "But that doesn't mean we quit trying to help them," she'd said. "We may save only a small percentage of them, but each life we save is precious and makes our efforts worthwhile."

*Each life? Even mine?* Mara wasn't so sure, though she wanted desperately to believe it. The reminder that she had also discussed this topic with Jonathan, the handsome Bible college student who had helped rescue her more than two years earlier, brought a rush of heat to her cheeks, and she was glad for the near darkness that hid her emotions. She had tried to deny her feelings for Jonathan and to hide them from him, but he'd faithfully kept in touch with her through letters since going back to school this past fall. One of the things he said to her over and over again was that her life was precious to God and that He loved her and had a purpose for her. At times she dared to believe it, but most of the time . . .

A taunting male voice from a passing car interrupted her thoughts as he called out a suggestive comment to her and then laughed as the vehicle sped away. Mara recoiled at the sound and shoved the letter back into the envelope. She stood up from the seawall, brushed the sand off the back of her jeans and turned toward home. She had to work the breakfast shift in the morning, so she'd better get to bed early. Tomorrow was Saturday, and Mariner's would be busy. She just hoped that meant some good tips because she could sure use the money.

# Chapter 1

Lawan had a window seat but was too frightened after her first glance downward after takeoff to look outside again. The closest the not quite eleven-year-old had come to an airplane prior to boarding more than a dozen hours earlier was occasionally seeing one pass by overhead. Even that hadn't happened often once she'd been kidnapped and thrown into the brothel when she was scarcely eight years old.

Waking or sleeping, Lawan had clung to the hand of the lady named Joan Stockton, who had accompanied her on every portion of the long trip. Glancing up at the tall woman with the long brown hair, streaked with gray and clasped at the nape of her neck, Lawan felt her eyes fill with tears. Would she ever see this woman again? Once this terrifying plane got back onto the ground and Lawan's new family claimed her, would Joan turn around and fly back to the orphanage and forget all about her?

With her free hand she swiped at the tears that trickled down her cheeks. Less than three years earlier Lawan had lived in a small village with parents who could scarcely keep food on the table. *But we were together*, she thought, *and that was all that mattered. Now I know they're not even alive anymore. I will never see them again until I go to heaven.* She sighed. At least she knew they were now with their oldest daughter, Chanthra, Lawan's older sister who had died right beside her in the brothel. That left no one in Lawan's family still alive on this earth . . . except her five-year-old sister, Mali.

*Anna*, she corrected herself. *She is now called Anna. Will Anna's new parents give me a new name as well?*

Lawan did not think she would like that very much. She liked her name. Lawan meant beautiful—and besides, her true parents had given her that name. She did not wish to change it, nor did she wish to call someone else *Maae or Phor*. Only her birth parents deserved to hold the revered titles of Mother and Father.

A man's voice boomed in Lawan's ears then, and the conversational English she had learned at the orphanage told her just enough to understand that they had nearly reached their destination.

Joan opened her eyes and sat forward, craning her neck to look out the window. "Look, Lawan," she said in English, following through on her promise to help Lawan learn the language of her new country and reverting to Thai only when Lawan could not understand. "Look out the window. There's San Diego—your new home!"

Fear and curiosity wrestled in the girl's stomach, but at last she turned her eyes toward the window. The multitude and expanse of the lights below took her breath away. It looked like the entire land was on fire! How would she ever fit in to such a place?

But it was not the language or the lights that most frightened Lawan. Though she'd been through more in her short life than any human being should ever have to endure, she was terrified of what was to come when she finally turned loose of Joan's hand and went to live with her new family. True, Mali would be there to welcome her, but Lawan and her younger sister had not seen one another in more than three years. Surely they would be strangers.

Joan released Lawan's hand and pulled her into an embrace. "It's going to be all right," she whispered. "You're going to be just fine. I promise."

Lawan knew Joan had never lied to her, but this was one time she struggled to believe the kind woman's words. How could she be just fine when everyone in her family had died—except one little girl who would not remember her? And though Joan had assured her that her American parents would not think badly of her because of her past, Lawan could not imagine how anyone could do otherwise.

Joan had kept a close eye on her young charge as they crossed the ocean, as well as several time zones, on their way from Thailand to the States. How confusing and frightening all of this must be to the child who had already been through so much heartache, only to be delivered from captivity and then swept into a completely unknown way of life! Even the fact that they had left her homeland on a Friday night and flown for hours, only to find it was still Friday night because of the time difference, would make the poor girl's head swirl. Would she be able to adjust to all this change? Had Joan made a mistake in helping to push the adoption through? Might Lawan have been happier staying on at the orphanage?

Joan sighed. How many times had she asked herself these very questions and come up with no clear answers? And each time she had simply had to place the situation in the nail-scarred hands of the One who loved Lawan unconditionally, the One who promised that His plans for her were for good, and that He would give her a future and a hope as she walked with Him, one step at a time.

Joan saw the girl's eyes widen at the sound of the landing gear dropping into place, signaling their imminent arrival in San Diego. As the aircraft touched down, Lawan inhaled sharply and clutched at Joan's arm.

"What is happening?" she asked, reverting to her native Thai.

Joan smiled reassuringly. "We are back on the ground," she explained, pulling the girl back to English. "We have landed safely, and soon you will meet your new family."

Lawan's dark eyes filled with tears, and she shook her head. "I do not want to meet them," she whispered. "I have changed my mind. Can I please go home with you, back to Thailand and to my friends at the orphanage?"

Joan's heart squeezed and she fought her own tears as she leaned over to gather the child into an embrace. "Everything will be all right, Lawan," she said, praying her words would prove true. "You are going to love your new home and family—especially Anna. Won't it be wonderful to be with your little sister again?"

She sensed an almost imperceptible nod from the girl, but the child's shoulders shook at the same time, and Joan knew Lawan was anything but convinced of Joan's promises.

"Is she here yet?" Anna asked, tugging on Nyesha's hand. "Is my sister here?"

Nyesha glanced at Kyle, who gave her a nervous wink, as the three of them stood in front of the carousel that listed Lawan's flight number and where they had agreed to meet their new daughter and her escort once they had cleared customs.

"Her plane is here," Nyesha explained, kneeling down to look into Anna's dark eyes. "It's been here for a while now, but we have to be patient while Lawan and Mrs. Stockton get through customs. I'm sure they'll be here any minute now."

Anna's brows drew together. "What's a customs?"

Nyesha smiled. "It's just a place here in the airport where people have to go when they fly in from another country. As soon as they talk to some people there, they can leave and come right here to us."

The girl's smile replaced her frown, and her eyes nearly danced as she spoke. "And then we can take my sister home?"

Nyesha chuckled, and she heard Kyle do the same. "Yes, sweetheart. Then we can take your sister home."

Anna clapped her hands together and bounced with obvious excitement. "In one minute," she said. "In one minute my sister's coming!"

"I said 'any minute,' honey," Nyesha cautioned. "That means soon, but maybe more than one minute."

Her words didn't seem to dampen Anna's enthusiasm as the girl continued to bounce in place and peer toward the doorway where her father had explained that Lawan would appear. Nyesha sighed and stood up, hoping for Anna's sake that it wouldn't be much longer.

"There she is! There's my sister!"

The excited cry startled Nyesha, and she jerked her glance toward the doorway. Sure enough, there stood a lovely but frail girl, her eyes wide as she clung to the hand of a tall white woman beside her. The girl's dark hair and eyes, her dainty features were so much like Anna's that Nyesha knew in that moment that Anna had been right. Her sister had indeed arrived, and the challenges of their expanding "rainbow family" were about to become a reality.

# Chapter 2

Leah was too excited to sleep. Most of her friends, including her roommate, were out enjoying their Friday night somewhere, but she had stayed in her dorm room to catch up on some homework.

*And to pray,* she reminded herself.

She hadn't been able to accomplish much on the home-work front because her mind kept wandering to what she knew was going on at the San Diego airport right about now. She had been praying all week, ever since she found out from her mom that Anna's sister was arriving from Thailand tonight. Leah had a close relationship with the entire Johnson family, especially Anna, since Leah had been the child's primary baby-sitter almost from the day Nyesha and Kyle adopted the ador-able little girl. And now, when Leah returned to San Diego next Wednesday night for the four-day Thanksgiving weekend, she would meet the newest member of the Johnson clan.

*Lawan,* she thought. *Nyesha told me it means beautiful. How could Lawan be any more beautiful than Anna? Nyesha says there's a strong resemblance, at least from what she can tell in the picture she got from the agency. But will they have anything else in common? After all Lawan has been through, will she even be able to relate to her little sister — or to any of us? She must be terrified right now.*

The memory of all she'd learned about human trafficking victims since she and her family became involved in a ministry to help rescue them, as well as to assist them in adjusting to life apart from captivity, told her that Lawan was undoubtedly also feeling ashamed. *She probably thinks we won't accept her because of it*, Leah thought, remembering that Jonathan had also told her Mara wrestled with the same issues. *I just wish I could be there with the Johnsons right now when they meet Lawan for the first time.*

*I am there with them.*

The silent promise resonated in her heart, and she rejoiced at its truth. Yes, the One who had rescued Lawan from the brothel now stood ready to rescue her from her shame and fears. Leah knew it would be a long road, but she would pray for the hurting child—and for her new family—each step of the way.

Lawan thought her knees would buckle and she would collapse on the floor, right in front of the people who had come to pick her up. For surely that was who they were, this tall white man with the yellow hair and blue eyes, standing beside the black woman with the shiny brown eyes and a smile that seemed almost as nervous as Lawan felt. But it was the little girl standing between them that shot sparks of lightning up Lawan's spine. Lawan had not been able to recall Mali's face in a very long time, though she tried desperately to do so. Now it was as if they'd never been apart. The unmoving little girl with the sweet face and wide eyes, her hand to her mouth as she sucked on two fingers exactly as she had done since she was a baby, may have aged a bit, but Lawan would know her anywhere.

*My baby sister*, she thought, her heart roiling with emotion. *The last member of my family . . .*

A slight nudge from Joan urged Lawan forward, but she just clung more tightly to the woman's hand. It was her last tie to her past, though much of that past had been painful and heart-rending. Still, it was familiar. Everything here—with the exception of the child who still stood with her fingers in her mouth, staring at her—was not only unfamiliar to Lawan, but terrifying as well.

She sensed Joan bending down to whisper in her ear. "Let's go meet your new family," she said. "They're waiting for you."

Lawan forced herself to nod. Hadn't she been through much worse in her short life, much more frightening and painful situations than this one? Yes, she had. And hadn't Joan promised her that she was going to be very happy here in her new home with her new family? Again, yes. And yet . . .

Tears threatened to erupt from her eyes onto her cheeks, but Lawan blinked them back. How could she tell Joan that she didn't want a new home or a new family? All she wanted was her real family back—all of them, including Chanthra—even if it meant living in a one-room shack without enough food?

She shut her eyes to block out her thoughts, as she had taught herself to do in order to survive in the brothel. Surely her new life couldn't be any worse than the one she'd left behind after she was kidnapped from her village. She would get through this, even as she had the horrible times during her two years in captivity. She would cling to *phra yaeh suu*, the Lord Jesus Christ, as her beloved parents had taught her to do, and as always, He would be faithful.

And besides, she had Mali now, and that would make all the difference.

———◦❦◦———

Kyle couldn't help but wonder at Anna's quick change of mood after seeing her sister. Her immediate reaction was her usual exuberance and excitement. But since the girls' eyes met, Anna hadn't moved. Her hand had gone to her mouth, and she'd inserted two fingers the way she'd done so often when she'd first come to live with them. Kyle knew the look and the action well; it meant she was feeling shy, uncertain, even frightened.

*A natural reaction*, he told himself. *After all, the sisters haven't seen each other since Anna was eighteen months. Does she even remember her—or any part of her former life, for that matter?*

The more he watched his daughter, the more he was certain that she did. And though he'd prayed that the girls would rebond quickly, he couldn't deny that an unreasonable jealousy tugged at his heart. *Ridiculous,* he chided silently. *Just because she has some vague memories of another home and other parents doesn't mean she isn't completely your daughter now.* His brain agreed, but his heart still rebelled ever so slightly.

And then the woman they had come to know through written correspondence—Joan Stockton—stood in front of them, the girl who looked like a slightly older version of Anna clutching her hand, her eyes downcast. And Kyle's heart melted inside him.

"Hello, Lawan," he said, bending down and using his finger to gently lift her chin. "Welcome to San Diego . . . and to our family."

Slowly the girl's eyelids lifted, and the two tear-filled pools fixed on his. The terror he saw there forced a gasp from his chest. He had expected her to be apprehensive, but it was more than that.

*Of course*, he thought, the thought flashing into his mind of what she'd been through between being kidnapped and then finally rescued and taken to the orphanage. *She must be absolutely terrified of men in general. I will have to remember that and move very slowly.*

He removed his finger from her chin and stood straight, though he kept his eyes and smile fixed on her lovely face. At that moment his insightful wife stepped in and held out her hands to the girl.

"Lawan," she said, taking the child's hands in her own, "we are so glad you're here safe and sound. We've been looking forward to this day." Then she stepped back and freed one hand from Lawan's, using it to nudge Anna forward.

At last the younger girl removed her fingers from her mouth. "Lawan?" she said. "My sister?"

The tears that had gathered in Lawan's eyes spilled over onto her face, as the question hung in the air between them. Kyle found himself praying for the Lord to help the girls find their way back together.

Within seconds, their arms were around each other and they were weeping. Kyle slipped his arm around Nyesha, whose sniffling told him she, too, was crying.

"Thank You, Lord," he whispered. "Thank You, Father."

"Amen."

Kyle raised his eyes to the woman named Joan who had just spoken her affirmation to his vocal gratitude. She appeared every bit as tentative as he felt, and he realized they all had a long way to go on a journey that had only just begun.

# Chapter 3

Jefe had never been angrier, or more concerned. It was bad enough that his own niece had ruined his life, testifying against him in court and sealing his fate behind bars, after all he'd done for her. Then circumstances had worked against him again when his plan to exact revenge from the ungrateful girl backfired and she escaped. But at least he'd had his little kingdom here in prison. Wherever Jefe went, he exerted the power and influence that had earned him the name *Jefe* — Boss — and prison was no exception.

Until now. Suddenly he found he was being challenged, and he didn't like it one bit. Not only was this new guy — a huge Hispanic gang leader and warlord from the El Paso/Juarez area, who went by the name of *El Gato*, the Cat — trying to take over Jefe's position as head honcho on the yard and in their mutual cell block, but he was threatening Jefe's very existence. That could not be tolerated.

Jefe pondered the situation as he leaned against the chain link fence that surrounded the portion of the yard where he and his posse liked to hang out. The morning sun was thin this Saturday before Thanksgiving, but it warmed him nonetheless. He glanced around at his most faithful followers, at least half a dozen strong men who would defend him to the death. Bodyguards to be feared, he reminded himself. Loyal and ruthless. El Gato might need every one of his nine lives to get past them and take on Jefe.

But El Gato had bodyguards, too, and the line in the sand had been drawn. Though Jefe wouldn't admit it, he was disturbed by the number of inmates who had crossed the line into El Gato's territory. There was always room for more than one boss in any prison, but when one of them began to purposely encroach on another's territory, that was reason for alarm. It was also reason for war, and Jefe was more than willing to declare it.

Unlike most of his friends who took every possible opportunity to catch a few extra z's, especially on a Saturday morning, Jonathan had been up since sunrise. Settled into a booth at his favorite campus coffee shop, he logged in to check his emails, deleted most of them, answered the important ones, and ignored the rest. He had a term paper to work on, and he disciplined himself to ignore the social aspect of the Internet until his assignments were done.

It was tough to concentrate, though, knowing he and Leah would be driving home Wednesday evening for the long Thanksgiving weekend. He was looking forward to seeing parents and friends, feasting on decent noncafeteria food, and watching some serious football. But most of all he hoped to connect with Mara while he was there.

Even now her gorgeous hazel eyes swam in his vision, and he wondered if she thought of him even half as often as he did of her. Those first two years after he'd helped rescue her from human trafficking, he'd tried to forget about her, but when he'd run into her again this past summer, he'd finally admitted that blocking her out of his mind just wasn't going to work. He'd argued with himself to the point of exhaustion, enumerating the reasons he should not pursue a relationship with the girl.

The primary reason, beyond the fact that she had no doubt been so damaged throughout her ordeal that she'd never be able to have a normal relationship, was the fact that she wasn't a Christian. The Bible was clear about Christians not purposely getting involved in dating relationships with non-Christians, and the last thing he wanted was to be disobedient to God. And yet . . . wasn't it possible that God had placed Mara in his life so he could influence her by his faith and lead her to Christ?

Jonathan wanted desperately to believe that, but he also knew a lot of believers had walked that road ahead of him and gotten off-track in the process. He sure didn't want to be one of them. Why couldn't he have fallen for Sarah, the cute blonde friend of his sister Leah? The girl obviously had a major crush on him and, though she might not be as devout as Jonathan, they at least shared the same faith.

He sighed. Who was he kidding? Sarah was a nice girl—attractive too. But she wasn't Mara. And Mara was the one whose memory followed him everywhere he went. They had even written a few letters back and forth since he returned to school in the summer, though they'd both been careful to avoid any personal discussions. Jonathan had tried to drop a few comments here and there about God, but so far Mara had not responded. She kept her brief notes to mentions of work or the weather. Not very encouraging.

Still, Jonathan was nearly certain that Mara was as attracted to him as he was to her, and all he could do now was pray that God would somehow bring Mara to a point of personal commitment to Christ, whether her future included Jonathan or not. With that perspective, he opened the file marked "term paper in progress" and scanned his existing words before adding new ones.

27

~∞~

"So how do you think the Johnsons are doing on their first morning as a four-member family?"

The question caught Michael Flannery off-guard, interrupting the thoughts that made him smile as he watched his wife of twenty-two years preparing him a late breakfast. They had a few more chances to sleep in these days, now that both their children were off at college. But Michael knew Rosanna was as excited as he was that Jonathan and Leah were coming home soon. Rosanna would happily give up a few extra hours of sleep to get up early and fix a big breakfast for her entire family. There was nothing she liked better—and few items ahead of that on his favorites list either.

Wait. What had she asked? Oh yeah. The Johnsons.

"Must be a lot of mixed emotions flying around over there right now," he said, keeping his eyes locked on Rosanna as she put the finishing touches on their omelets and scooped them onto the plates. She had worn her thick, shoulder-length auburn hair in the same style since he first met her, and he couldn't imagine it any other way. He knew that some women lost their looks as they aged, but not Rosanna. She just got more beautiful with each passing year.

"That's for sure," she agreed, turning toward him with a loaded plate in each hand. "Nyesha and Kyle have talked and planned for this day for months, but now that it's finally here, I can't help but wonder how it's going."

Michael chuckled, even as his eyes widened at the generous offering his wife placed before him. She always added a serving of fresh fruit to every meal, hoping he'd follow up and eat it. Once in a while, he did.

"You can be sure of one thing," he said, picking up his fork. "Whatever they're doing right now, they aren't having a bigger or better breakfast than we are."

Rosanna laughed and sat down across from him at the maple dinette set in the corner of their comfortable kitchen. With both children gone, Rosanna and Michael almost never used the large dining room table except on special occasions when they had company. This Thanksgiving weekend would certainly qualify.

Michael took his wife's hand and offered a quick prayer of thanks before diving into his Denver omelet, bypassing the melon chunks and strawberry slices. Maybe later, for dessert, he told himself.

"I'm sure that it's an exciting time," Rosanna said, stabbing a ripe piece of pineapple. "Anna is thrilled right now. She's chattered for months about her big sister coming. Something tells me the two of them are going to hit it off just fine."

"I hope you're right," Michael commented, washing down his eggs with a swig of orange juice. "But Lawan has been through some really bad stuff. She no doubt has a lot of healing to do, not to mention the fact that she's left behind everything familiar to her. Anna may be her sister, but apart from that, everything is completely foreign to the poor girl. We really need to remember to pray for her adjustment to her new life. It won't be easy."

"True," Rosanna agreed. "But I know God intervened to bring that child here and to place her in that loving family. I don't know how, but He's going to restore the years that have been stolen from her, just like the Bible promises."

Michael couldn't argue with that. Rosanna was right, and God's Word was true. But that didn't mean there wouldn't be some tough trials along the way. He shot up a silent prayer for the situation before continuing with his delicious meal.

# Chapter 4

It was shaping up to be a usual busy Saturday at Mariner's, and Mara couldn't be more pleased. For one thing, lots of customers usually meant a better haul in tips, though there were always a couple of people who either left nothing or maybe plopped a shiny quarter down on the table after she waited on them for more than an hour. But overall she found people to be generous and grateful for good service, so that's what she delivered. If she kept living frugally and saving money, she'd be able to start school the next semester.

*Am I crazy to even consider it? she thought, wiping down a messy booth so a family of four waiting by the door could sit down for a late breakfast or early lunch. I have almost no real education and had to teach myself most of what I know. But I did manage to get my GED, so maybe I'll make it through some college classes too. She winced and corrected herself. OK, junior college. That's all I can afford, but it's more than I ever thought I'd be able to do. She swallowed a smirk. Who am I kidding? Working as a waitress is more than I ever dreamed of when I belonged to Tio.*

She motioned the family over to the now clean table and placed their menus in front of them. "Welcome to Mariner's," she said, smiling at the two teenagers who skulked in with their parents as if they wished they could become invisible. Mara wanted to tell them to be glad they had a mother and father who cared for them and hadn't sold them into slavery for a few extra bucks, but she resisted the temptation and announced the day's specials instead. A couple of spoiled teens were not her problem; she had enough on her own plate to keep her busy.

*Like Jonathan coming home Wednesday night,* she thought, hating the heat that rose up from her neck and no doubt colored her cheeks. Why couldn't she stop thinking about him? After all, she'd had enough of the male population during her growing-up years to last her a lifetime. She could easily do without them now . . . couldn't she?

Well, most of them anyway. All of them, actually, except Jonathan Flannery. The tall Bible college student with the auburn hair and warm brown eyes had won her heart from the first time she saw him. That he turned out to be the one to rescue her from a life she thought she'd never escape just sealed the deal for her. She was crazy about Jonathan, and she might as well just accept it. She also might just as well accept the impossibility of ever being with him, though. After all, a Bible college student, the son of a preacher, from a respected family . . . Where did she fit into a scenario like that? She didn't, and that was the end of it.

Heading for the counter to retrieve her newest customers' drink orders, she once again fought to block out the image of the man who made her heart race and her skin tingle. Why couldn't she forget about him? She was just setting herself up for a broken heart, and hadn't she had enough pain in her lifetime already?

But with every admonishment to forget about him and not even try to see him while he was home, her anticipation of a hoped-for call when he arrived grew, and she knew if he asked to see her, she'd have a hard time turning him down.

～✦～

Joan fought the hot tears that seemed a perpetual threat since saying good-bye to Lawan and leaving her with her new family. The Johnsons had graciously asked her to stay with them at least for a night or two before returning to Thailand, but Joan had made up her mind before coming that it would be a quick turnaround trip. The only thing that would help her get Lawan out of her thoughts was digging back into the never-ending stream of work at the orphanage.

Why had Lawan touched her so much more than many of the others? Not a child who passed through the doors of the orphanage had come from an easy life. Each had suffered before finding refuge within the orphanage walls. But soon the children moved past their pain and memories and bonded with each other, forming a family among themselves where Joan and her husband, Mort, felt privileged to serve as a set of surrogate parents. The other workers, both Thai and foreign, felt much the same way, and there was a closeness among the residents, both grownups and children, that soothed aching hearts.

*Including mine,* Joan thought, gazing out the window into the darkness that signaled Saturday night in Thailand where she would soon land. *God never blessed Mort and me with children of our own, but look at how many little ones He has placed in our care. I couldn't be happier.*

And yet her heart longed for the little girl she had left behind. Was it because Lawan had truly not been allowed to be a little girl, at least not from the point where she was kidnapped? True, many children, both boys and girls, experienced such tragedies; the brothels were full of them. And so few were ever rescued. But knowing Lawan's story, hearing it not only from her lips but also from the lips of Klahan, the man who had spirited her away from the brothel and eventually delivered her to the orphanage, sacrificing himself in the process, somehow made it that much more real . . . and tragic.

Klahan's face took shape in her mind, as she considered the man's last-minute decision to give up his own life in order to give Lawan a chance at finding hers. *Klahan stole Lawan away from the brothel with wrong intentions and even committed murder to have her for himself. But in the end he found Christ and did the right thing. Thank You, Lord! There truly is nothing too hard for You, is there?*

A sense of peace descended upon her, and she welcomed the warm blanket of love that she knew so well from previous moments with her Savior. She prayed that same peace would cover little Lawan and her new family, this day and always.

Lawan had lain awake for more than an hour when she first awoke that Saturday morning and found herself staring across the room at the five-year-old girl in a bed that matched her own. Her first thought was that someone had given BanChuen a grand new bed, but then she realized the sleeping child was Mali, her very own sister, and that she was now in a new home, in a new land, with a new family.

Her emotions had churned at the thought. Lawan missed BanChuen, the child who had first befriended her at the orphanage and who had indeed become like her own little sister. But Lawan had left BanChuen and the others behind to come to a strange place called America and to live with a strange family of different-colored skin and different customs and manners. Joan had assured her they all shared the same Lord and the same Christian faith, and Lawan had tried to reassure herself with that knowledge, but the strangeness had dug a cold pit into her heart that she just couldn't seem to dislodge.

But at last Mali had awakened and immediately bounded from her own bed into Lawan's. "My sister," she'd cried, over and over again. "My sister is really here!"

The girl was lovable, Lawan had to admit, and already she was growing attached to her. They had even made a deal that Mali would help Lawan perfect her English if Lawan would teach her some words in Thai. But the hardest thing for Lawan was remembering to call her little sister by her American name, Anna. Even though her new parents had assured her that they had kept Mali as Anna's middle name, Lawan didn't see why they hadn't just called her Mali instead of Anna. After all, that was her real name, given to her by her real parents.

The memory of her *maae* and *phor* brought a fresh threat of tears to her eyes as she sat with Anna and Mr. and Mrs. Johnson at a picnic table in the backyard, eating a strange lunch, which her little sister explained was something called peanut butter and jelly sandwiches—Anna's favorite, though Lawan couldn't imagine why. She liked the flavor of peanuts, something she ate often in her homeland, but she didn't care for the sticky consistency of the sandwich. She wondered how often the family served this particular dish at meals.

"What would you like to do when we finish lunch?" the woman named Nyesha Johnson asked.

Lawan knew she was to call the woman mother or mom, but she wasn't sure she would be able to say either one, knowing what they meant. She shrugged, not knowing how to answer the question.

"I know," Anna announced, a smile spreading across her face. "Let's go to the zoo!"

35

Zoo? That was a word Lawan did not know. Was it something she would like? Anna certainly seemed excited about it.

"That's a great idea, Anna," Mr. Johnson answered, a smile lighting up his blue eyes as he turned to look at Lawan. "Would you like that, Lawan?"

Lawan swallowed a sticky wad of sandwich and nodded. Why not? It couldn't be any worse than staying here and eating more of Anna's favorite lunch.

# Chapter 5

Sarah had been antsy all week, but it was getting worse as Thanksgiving approached. Jonathan would be home Wednesday night, and the thought was making her crazy.

"He's not interested in you," she declared aloud to the petite blonde with the sky-blue eyes and a sprinkling of freckles across her nose, who stared back at her from her bedroom mirror. "Not the way you want him to be anyway." She shook her head, wishing she could transfer the surety of that statement from her brain to her heart. There was no doubt in her mind of its truth, but her emotions seemed unwilling to accept it.

Why? Was it because she was too young for him? She doubted that. After all, Jonathan was only two years older. She supposed it didn't help that she and Leah had been best friends almost forever, and therefore Jonathan consider her as another little sister. But deep down she knew even that wasn't the reason.

"Mara," she said, putting her hands on her hips and glaring at the image that glared right back. "It's Mara, and you know it. Jonathan is in love with her, even if he hasn't admitted it to anyone yet. And she feels the same way. I saw it when they looked at each other."

The memory of that summer evening just a few months earlier, when Leah and Sarah had spotted Jonathan on Mara's porch, tormented her yet again. It was at that very moment that Sarah had realized she didn't have a chance with the guy she'd been crazy about since grade school. She'd always be a little sister to him, a good friend maybe, but never a romantic interest. His heart had turned in a different direction.

The girl in the mirror didn't seem convinced. Sarah squinted at her. "I know. I do have the advantage of being able to hang out at his house while he's home. I mean, Leah's coming home with him, right? And Leah's my best friend. So . . ." She took a deep breath and nodded. "OK, one last try. What have I got to lose? It's not like Mara has an open invitation to their house, so why not spend as much time there as I can?" She grinned. "And of course, it won't hurt to look extra nice when I drop in."

Blocking out the silent voice that told her the situation was hopeless, she shrugged and told her doubtful counterpart, "Hey, it just might work. You never know unless you try. It's only Saturday afternoon now, so I have four whole days to plan — and the first part of that plan is to be at their house waiting for them when they get there Wednesday night."

Lawan clung tightly to Nyesha's hand, wishing it were Joan's and that she was back in Thailand. Had she made a terrible mistake by coming here just so she could be with her little sister? When she'd first heard that her parents were dead, and knowing that her older sister, Chanthra, was as well, Lawan had yearned to be with the last remaining member of her family. And though she had already begun to bond with Mali — Anna, she reminded herself — since arriving the night before, they really had little in common except their past. Anna seemed to fit in so well in this new country with her new family. But Lawan? Would she ever be able to make such an adjustment? The bigger question that danced through her mind was . . . did she even want to?

Lawan had to admit that the Johnsons had tried very hard to give her an enjoyable day. Anna had been delighted by all the animal exhibits, but Lawan had just been reminded of the elephants and monkeys that lived uncaged in many parts of her homeland.

Still clinging to Nyesha's hand as they headed toward the zoo's exit and the autumn sun retreated from the cloudless sky, Lawan kept her eyes fixed on the man Anna called Daddy. He walked just ahead of her, carrying an exhausted Anna whose head lay comfortably on his shoulder. Her eyes had been closed nearly from the moment he lifted her to that position. Strangely, though Klahan was not her father, it was his face that came to mind as she watched Kyle Johnson carry the weary but trusting child in his arms. It hadn't been that many months ago that Klahan had carried Lawan in much the same way, as they made their escape from a past that had caused Lawan more pain than she could allow herself to remember.

Where was he now, this man who had rescued her from such a terrible life, even killing two people in the process? Lawan had repeatedly asked Joan about Klahan's fate, but the woman had explained that it was best not to dwell on the details. She had assured Lawan, however, that Klahan was safe in God's hands where he had placed himself when he asked for forgiveness and became a follower of *phra yaeh suu*. That knowledge had comforted Lawan, and so she had finally stopped asking about the man whose name meant brave.

And now she was here, in a place called the United States where nearly everyone had at least one car, usually two, a large house, and plenty of food. She only hoped she would eventually grow to like some of that food better than Anna's peanut butter and jelly sandwiches.

Mara's feet were beginning to ache a bit when she looked up and saw Barbara Whiting walk in the front door. Their eyes met, and reciprocal smiles lit up their faces. Barbara was at least old enough to be Mara's mother, but they had become fast friends since Mara's escape from her tio's brothel more than two years earlier and especially since their renewed relationship a few months ago when Mara herself had been involved in helping another girl escape a similar situation.

*Francesca,* Mara thought, as the girl's lovely young face flitted through her mind. *Her baby will be born soon. I wonder what she'll decide about the adoption. I'll have to remember to tell Barbara about my most recent letter from her.*

Stepping up to the attractive middle-aged woman with the short dark curls, streaked with gray, and the blue eyes that mirrored the emotions in her heart, Mara welcomed Barbara and asked her if she'd like to be seated at the counter and have a cup of coffee.

"I just have a couple more things to do before I can leave," she explained, glancing at her watch. "Ten minutes, tops."

"Perfect," Barbara said, helping herself to an empty stool and setting her purse on the counter in front of her. "I was just thinking a cup of coffee would keep me going for a few more hours." She grinned. "Been a long day, and a busy one, but I imagine it has for you too."

Mara nodded. "Very. But I'm looking forward to our girls' night out."

Barbara laughed, and Mara found herself wondering why she couldn't remember the sound of her own mother's laughter. Was it simply because she hadn't been a happy woman, or had Mara just blotted out the memories that were too painful to contemplate?

Mara shook her head. What did it matter? That was then, and this was now. Barbara had become her friend and confidante, and sometimes even served as a surrogate mother as well. What else did she need? When Barbara called that morning and invited her to dinner—"somewhere other than Mariner's," she'd insisted—Mara had jumped at the opportunity. She liked Mariner's, and she knew Barbara did too, but it was nice to go somewhere different now and then, especially with company she so enjoyed.

She poured Barbara's coffee and cleared up her final business before removing her apron and hanging it on the hook beside the back door in the kitchen.

"Taking off for the night?"

Stephen's familiar voice interrupted her exit from the kitchen, and she turned to look at the middle-aged man whose cheeks were perpetually pink from standing over the grill.

She smiled. "Sure am. Going out to dinner with my friend Barbara."

The cook's feigned offense was obvious. "You mean, you aren't going to eat here? What's the matter? You don't trust my cooking?"

Mara laughed. "I love your cooking, Stephen, and I recommend it to everyone who asks. But tonight I want a change of scenery."

Stephen laughed and nodded. "Good for you! Go. And have a good time. A nice young girl like you should get out once in a while. Life isn't all about work, work, work, you know."

Mara nodded her agreement and waved as she turned and headed for the counter to pick up her dinner partner. Stephen was right, of course, and she was glad to be getting out for a change. But right now work had to remain her focus. If she was going to get started at the junior college this next semester, she needed to save all the money she could between now and then. She liked her job at Mariner's, but it wasn't what she wanted to do all her life. Becoming a social worker was an idea she was at least toying with, and she planned to discuss that very possibility over dinner with Barbara. If anyone would understand, she would. But would she think it was an impossible dream for someone like Mara? And even if she did, would she be truthful and say so?

Mara hoped so. After having such a large portion of her life stolen from her in the past, she certainly didn't want to waste any of the future that still lay ahead of her.

# Chapter 6

The November sun had already set by the time the two women exited the eatery and headed for Barbara's car in the lot. Even when Southern California enjoyed its relatively warm winter days, the nights nearly always turned chilly, and this was no exception.

Mara shivered as she tugged her light sweater closed and fumbled with the buttons, wishing she'd thought to wear something warmer. It had already been nice when she'd left for work that morning, and she hadn't planned ahead to her evening date with Barbara. But she shrugged it off as she eased into the passenger side of the comfy and only slightly used sedan. They'd be eating inside somewhere, and Barbara would give her a ride home, so what did it matter about the weather?

By the time they'd pulled into a little Italian place and settled into a corner booth where they munched on breadsticks while waiting for their pizza and salad, Mara had forgotten all about the chill in the air. Getting to know Barbara had been one of the few positives in her life, and she was more than grateful for the woman's time and attention.

*Is this what it would have been like to have a mother?*

The thought niggled its way into her consciousness as she and Barbara discussed Francesca's latest letter and whether or not the young girl and her family would opt to keep the baby or adopt it out. Mara had been so happy for Francesca when her parents rushed to pick her up the moment they knew she was alive and well. Unlike Mara's parents, who had sold her to her *tio* and into a life of degradation and servitude, Francesca's family had welcomed her home after anguishing over her disappearance and praying for her safe return. How different might Mara's life have been if she, too, had been blessed with loving, caring parents!

*But I wasn't,* she reminded herself. *And as bad as my* tio *was, my parents were worse. They let him take me for a few* pesos. *Enough for what? A week's worth of drugs or booze? Even if it was for food for my* hermanitos, *were my little brothers truly worth that much more that our parents would sell me for a sack of* frijoles *and a few dozen* tortillas?

She shook her head, trying to dislodge the negative thoughts. She was with Barbara now, a fine and respectable woman who cared enough to spend time with her and treat her as an equal. Mara still couldn't understand why such an amazing lady would do such a thing, but she was glad she did.

Will she feel the same when I tell her of my dream to do something meaningful with my life, maybe even become a social worker like her?

She eyed her friend, sitting across the table from her, laughing and chatting with her as if Mara were just like anyone else, not spoiled or ruined the way she so clearly imagined herself. How do I ever stop thinking of myself that way? More than ten years of being abused by more men than I can count, seeing people beaten and killed . . . It's a miracle I'm alive today. But I am, and I want what's left of my life to count for something.

Taking a deep breath, Mara nodded at Barbara's last comment and then plunged ahead, determined to tell Barbara

44

of her plans and hopeful the woman she now considered a mother would give her some wise advice for her future.

It was good to be back in Thailand. The business of running an orphanage with hundreds of displaced and abandoned children kept Joan's mind and body occupied, and she was more than ready to throw herself back into it.

Mort had met her at the airport and driven her home in a rattletrap jeep that Joan always expected would fall apart each time it hit one of the many potholes or obstructions in the road. But somehow they'd made it safe and sound and now, as the morning sun rose over the valley, outlining the tops of the bamboo forest even as the sounds of birds and monkeys and elephants greeted the new day, she smiled. Though she'd only been on the ground in the States long enough to deliver her precious cargo and reboard for the long flight home, it had been enough to remind her that Thailand now seemed more home to her than America.

She remembered when God first called her to leave her comfortable existence and go to what she then considered a primitive land. Oh, how she had argued and resisted! But Mort, too, had heard the call, and his enthusiasm, coupled with God's wooing, finally won her over. Her prayer then had been that if God truly wanted her in another country, He would transplant her heart. Quite obviously He had answered that prayer.

"Now," she whispered, "will you please transplant Lawan's heart to her new home and family as well? I know she needs time and lots of love and healing, Lord, but I believe You've placed her exactly where she needs to be to receive it. Thank You, Father. And thank You for allowing me to be a part of it."

"*Maae* Joan?"

The tiny voice cut into her thoughts just as she spoke her amen. Joan turned from her perch where she sat in front of the open window, watching the sunrise. Beside her stood the child called BanChuen, the little girl about Anna's age who slept on the pallet next to Lawan's and first befriended the frightened girl when she arrived.

Joan smiled and dipped her head in a slight bow, extending her hands as she spoke. "Good morning, BanChuen. How are you this morning? Did you sleep well?"

The child didn't answer or step into Joan's embrace, but her dark eyes pooled with tears. "Lawan? Did she come back with you?"

The pain of a hot poker stabbed Joan's heart as she pulled the little girl into her arms. "No, sweetheart, Lawan did not come back with me," she whispered, stroking the child's dark, silky hair. "She stayed in America with her new family."

BanChuen's shoulders shook with sobs. "But we are her family," she whimpered. "Did she not love us anymore?"

Tears bit Joan's eyes as she fought to answer. "She will always love us," she said, praying her voice would not break. "But she needed to be with her new family right now . . . and her sister, Mali. Remember, we explained that to you before she left."

Slowly, the girl nodded, though the hiccupping sobs continued. "But I did not want her to go. I wanted her to stay here with us."

Joan pulled the girl closer. "I know, baby. I know you did. We all did. But we must do what God knows is best, even if we do not always understand it at the time."

She sighed and closed her eyes, continuing to stroke BanChuen's hair. These children had already lost so much by the time they came to this place; the last thing Joan wanted to do was to take something more from them. She could only pray that God would work it all out for the best, for each one of them, and that somehow He would give her the wisdom and grace to help make that happen.

Hours later, as Sunday came to a close at the orphanage in Thailand, a new day was underway not only in the United States but also in a remote, poverty-stricken village in Mexico. Cecelia Jimenez pounded the tattered rug that hung over the clothesline, ignoring the clouds of dust that billowed around her. Everything was dusty in their dry, desolate neighborhood. Rain was scarce, and food even more so. That they still had a roof over their heads made them more fortunate than many in their little village. But Cecelia had long since ceased to consider herself fortunate. When she saw a homeless woman begging for food, her children clutching at her skirt and crying for nourishment, she longed to trade places with the desperate mother.

47

*At least she did not sell her own child to ease her family's suffering. She may be homeless, but she has not shamed herself as a mother. Her children are with her, and that's all that matters. Why did I not stand up to mi esposo when he insisted we sell our own child? Si, the man who bought her was her tio, but he was still an evil man — and I knew it. Rudolfo would not tell me what his brother did to earn all his dinero, but I knew even then it was a bad thing. How could we have trusted our little hijita to such a man? What did he do to her? Is she even alive after all these years? She would be such a beautiful young woman by now.*

For just a moment Cecelia neglected her task to wipe away the tears that had gathered in her eyes. How many times had she dreamed that she might one day see her little Maria again? Yet she knew that even if the girl was still alive, she would never forgive the parents who sold her to fill their own bellies and those of their sons.

"We chose our sons over you, *mijita*," Cecelia whispered. "I am so very sorry. If only I could beg your forgiveness, would you give it to me . . . after all these years? Would you somehow understand that I had so little choice?"

The silent answer echoed in the dust mites that settled in the woman's hair and on her shoulders. Ignoring the tears that still dripped down her face, she returned to her work, beating the rug as if it were her own filthy soul.

# Chapter 7

You ready to go, Sis?"

Jonathan poked his head through Leah's open dorm room doorway and glanced around. Where was everybody? He'd told Leah he'd pick her up at three so they could get going before the traffic got too bad.

*Like it isn't already awful,* he thought. *Tomorrow's Thanksgiving, and half the population of California is probably on the road already.*

One look at Leah's twin bed against the far wall told him she was packed. The red suitcase bulged at the seams, and Jonathan chuckled when he thought of the handful of items he'd thrown into his overnight bag. *How much stuff can one person use for a weekend?* He shook his head. Girls. He'd never understand them, but then he doubted very many other men did either.

*So where is she? Even her roommate's not here. What's going on?*

"Hey, Bro!"

The greeting came from behind, along with the sound of footsteps charging up the stairs at double-time. "Sorry about the wait," Leah said as she came into view, her long red curls looking as if they'd exploded from her head. Jonathan had a sudden vision of his little sister at age three or four, trying to do summersaults on the living room floor and refusing to give up until she got it right.

"I like your hair," he smirked.

She stopped in front of him, catching her breath as her cheeks flushed a shade pinker. A chuckle erupted from her throat as she reached up and tried in vain to tame her locks. "Yeah, I'll bet," she laughed. "Actually, I've been running."

Jonathan raised his eyebrows. "No kidding! I would never have guessed."

Leah frowned, though her smile remained as she punched him in the arm, a gesture he'd long since grown accustomed to ignoring. "Very funny. I had to return a book to the library by the end of the day today or be fined. But I made it, and now I'm ready to go." She charged into the room and straight to her bed, where she picked up the overstuffed bag and slung it over her shoulder. "So what's the hold-up?" she demanded, crossing the room to stand in front of him. "Are we going home or not?"

Jonathan shook his head and laughed. "Some things never change, do they?"

She grinned. "Not a bit."

He glanced at the cargo weighing her down and gave her a quizzical look. "You going to carry that all the way to the car, or are you going to use the built-in wheels like any normal person?"

She wrinkled her nose in disgust. "Very funny. The wheels don't work for some reason."

"You probably broke them with all the extra weight you've got in there." He reached out and wrested the case from her grip before throwing it over his own shoulder. "Come on, let's go. Mom and Dad are waiting, and I for one can't wait to get home to Mom's cooking. I plan to eat my way right through this entire weekend—while watching football, of course."

"Of course. What a surprise! Isn't that what you and Dad do every Thanksgiving?"

She pushed past him and out the door, as a smiling Jonathan

50

followed along behind, toting a suitcase that he imagined weighed more than an army of elephants.

The Johnson family had eaten an early supper and then attended a special Thanksgiving communion service at church, held in lieu of the normal Wednesday night meeting. By the time they piled back in the house through the kitchen door from the garage, Lawan thought she was more tired than she'd been since she'd been forced to work the long nights at the brothel.

*Joan warned me about something called jet lag,* she mused, yawning as she headed toward the hallway to make her way to the bedroom she shared with Anna. *Maybe that's what's wrong with me. I just want to sleep and sleep.*

She'd nearly arrived at the bedroom door and reached out to turn the knob when her sister's voice stopped her from behind.

"Wait, Lawan," she called, running up behind her. "Mom's going to make us some hot chocolate before we go to bed. It's a *dishun* on the night before Thanksgiving."

Lawan frowned. There were a lot of English words she hadn't heard or learned yet, and obviously *dishun* was one of them. She sighed and nodded at the bright-eyed girl who looked up at her expectantly.

"OK," she said. At least she was familiar with hot chocolate and knew that was something she liked, though she would have much preferred to curl up in her bed and close her eyes. Sometimes when she did that she drifted right off to sleep; other times her mind raced for hours, as she tried to block out the memories of her former life and convince herself that this new one was better.

"Come on," Anna said, reaching out to take Lawan's hand. "We'll all sit in the kitchen and drink our chocolate."

Lawan allowed herself to be led by the hand back to the kitchen, where the woman Anna called Mom stirred something in a pot on the stove. The man of the household waited at the table. When Anna spotted him, she immediately dropped Lawan's hand and ran to climb up on his lap.

"Tell my sister about our *dishun*," she said, looking up at her father.

He grinned down at her before diverting his attention to Lawan. "She means tradition," he explained, indicating a spot next to them at the table.

Lawan slid onto the empty seat and forced a smile. "*Kop koon*," she said, then quickly switched to English. "Thank you."

The man named Kyle broadened his smile and nodded. "You are very welcome, Lawan," he said. "And we are so thankful that you are here with us on this Thanksgiving Eve." He paused then, his blue eyes radiating what appeared to be concern, though Lawan had not seen the emotion often enough to be certain.

"Our family always goes to the special communion service at church the night before Thanksgiving, and then we come home and have hot chocolate together and talk about the things we're thankful for." He glanced up at his wife as she brought two steaming mugs to the table and set them down before returning for the other two. When each place at the small table contained its own full cup, she sat down to join them. Lawan didn't miss the smile that passed between them. A vague memory of her parents' interactions tugged at her heart, but she shoved down the bittersweet pain that accompanied it.

"We are thankful for so many things," Kyle continued, his hand reaching toward Lawan as if he were about to cover hers. Without thinking she snatched it away and placed it safely in her lap. Kyle pulled back and used both hands to move Anna from his lap to the one empty chair beside him. "You are truly one of those things we are most grateful for," he said, and a tinge of guilt twisted Lawan's heart as she wondered if she had hurt him by pulling away. But she just wasn't ready to let him touch her yet.

The woman named Nyesha spoke up then, her voice soft and warm, like the honey they occasionally used at the orphanage to sweeten their tea. "Are you familiar at all with Thanksgiving Day?" she asked.

Lawan turned her face toward the woman, fighting the urge to climb onto her lap as Anna had done with her father. She blinked back tears and shook her head. "No," she whispered, feeling somehow ashamed that she did not understand what it was they were celebrating, or why.

Nyesha smiled. "It's a holiday we celebrate here in our country," she said, "a time when we remember our many blessings and thank God for giving them to us. Would you like to hear the story of how the celebration of Thanksgiving started?"

Lawan nodded. She wasn't sure if she wanted to hear it or not, but she liked the sound of the woman's voice as it soothed the broken, frozen places in her heart. Though she was certain Nyesha would never take her real *maae's* place, she was beginning to think that maybe she could at least trust this woman—and that would be enough.

Sarah's eyelids were heavy, but she was determined to stay awake until Leah and Jonathan arrived. She was grateful to their parents for allowing her to wait in Leah's room, though she couldn't imagine what was taking the returning college students so long.

"Where are you?" she whispered, sprawled out on Leah's double bed as she'd done so many times during sleepovers throughout the years. "It doesn't take that long to drive a couple hundred miles, does it?"

Mr. Flannery had reminded her when she arrived after church service that the Wednesday evening before Thanksgiving traffic was always extremely heavy and she might have a long wait, but she had been so sure they'd be here before this. *I want to look fresh when they show up, with my makeup in place and my hair just right—*

The familiar sound of the VW's beater engine penetrated her thoughts, and she jerked to attention, sitting upright on the bed, her ears straining. Then she heard it. The engine shut off and two cars doors creaked open before slamming shut, followed by excited chatter from her best friend and her brother, the one who had long ago won her heart. Should she continue to wait here in Leah's room or race down the stairs and greet them as they walked inside?

*I should wait at least for a little while, she told herself. Let them say hello to their parents before I interrupt their family time . . . shouldn't I?*

She sized herself up in Leah's mirror. Her hair was perfect, her cheeks pink but not obviously so, her new jeans and sweater fitting just right. No, she wasn't about to wait up here for Leah and chance missing Jonathan if he went straight to his room. It had been a long time since she'd waved him off when he and Leah left for school months ago, and she wasn't going to waste one more moment playing hard to get.

"As if you ever have when it comes to Jonathan," she whispered, still staring in the mirror. "He already knows how you feel, so quit pretending and just go downstairs already."

Determined to at least hug Leah before turning to Jonathan, she nearly launched herself out Leah's bedroom door and toward the stairs, restraining herself only enough so she didn't give in to the impulse to slide down the banister and catapult herself into Jonathan's arms. She had no idea how this four-day Thanksgiving weekend would turn out, but she was going to make the best of every minute of it.

# Chapter 8

Thanksgiving morning dawned much like any other morning in prison. Loud, raucous catcalls reverberated from all corners of the cellblock as inmates waited to be let out of their cages and escorted to the dining area for breakfast. Though prison authorities did what they could to ensure that everything was kept clean, the odors of sweat and urine hung in the air like permanent fixtures.

Jefe knew not to expect anything special for breakfast on the day when the meal focus would be on the so-called holiday fare that would be served up several hours later. Though the prison's version of a turkey feast didn't line up with what most people outside prison walls were accustomed to, it was at least a cut above the usual slop.

His door slid open with a screech and clank, and he stepped outside his miniscule home ahead of his cellmate, who followed close behind. They situated themselves in their assigned places and waited for the command to move forward in what would become a chow line, closely watched by correctional officers who intervened at the slightest deviation from approved behavior.

Jefe didn't question the need for such monitoring. The two most dangerous times in any prison were the times when inmates were outside in the yard or at meal times. With the looming threat of El Gato and his followers trying to infringe on Jefe's territory, the older man was no longer taking his privileged position for granted. Even now, as the line began to move toward the stairs that would take them from their cells toward the chow hall, his eyes scanned in front of him, as well as side to side. His biggest threat came from behind, where he couldn't see, but he counted on his cellie to have his back. If the man known as Feo, meaning ugly, ever betrayed him, Jefe knew he could be in trouble. But he counted on Feo's loyalty not to let that happen.

The aroma of stale, burnt coffee assailed Jefe's nostrils, and he resigned himself to another dull, tasteless breakfast, as memories of omelet bars and delicate quiches made his mouth water. Would he ever taste such delectable food again? Short of a miracle, he didn't see how. But a guy could dream, couldn't he? So long as he didn't let those dreams dull his edge and lull him into complacency. No one knew better than he how deadly such distractions could be.

Lawan opened her eyes on Thanksgiving morning to find her sister standing next to her bed, staring down at her. The moment Lawan blinked up at her, an expectant grin spread across Anna's face.

"It's Thanksgiving," she announced, bringing to Lawan's mind the discussion at the kitchen table the night before, as she'd learned the history of the holiday and a little bit about what to expect today.

"Mom's already starting the pies," Anna continued. "Let's go help her."

Lawan stifled a groan but let her yawn escape. Not only was she still tired and not excited about getting up, but she certainly didn't want to race downstairs and start helping with something she'd never done before. Still, she did enjoy being around the woman Nyesha, whom Anna called Mom. Lawan wasn't sure she'd ever be able to call the kind woman with the honey voice anything but Nyesha or Mrs. Johnson, but she had to admit that she at least felt safe with her. She wasn't nearly as sure about the man Anna considered her father.

She sighed. As much as she would prefer to roll over in her soft bed and snuggle down deeper in her covers, she knew Anna wasn't about to go away quietly, and she certainly didn't want to hurt her little sister's feelings. "OK," she said, pushing the covers off and sitting up on the side of the bed. "I come with you."

Anna clapped her hands in obvious glee, as Lawan slid her feet into her slippers and made her way to the bathroom the two girls shared. She couldn't help but remember the room she'd shared at the brothel, first with her older sister, Chanthra, and then with the girl named Kulap. Was Kulap still there in that horrible, dark room, working for the boss man and his assistant, Adung? Probably—unless, of course, she was dead like Chanthra.

Lawan pushed the thought away, along with the comparison of the room she'd lived in for two years after she was kidnapped with the room she now lived in with Mali. *Anna,* she reminded herself. *You have to remember to call her Anna.* The plush rug under her slippers, the soft mattress and warm blankets, the bathroom used just by the two of them—and all of it was clean. That was the starkest contrast, the one that epitomized the incredible changes Lawan had experienced in the past few months. True, the orphanage had been cleaner than the brothel, but it didn't begin to line up with the home she lived in now. Still, Lawan missed Joan and BanChuen and the others at the orphanage nearly as much as she missed her parents, though she hadn't seen them since before she was kidnapped and would not see them now until she joined them in heaven.

She flipped on the light and shuffled into the bathroom, ready to throw some water on her face and get ready for a day that she had been told would include not only roast turkey and pie but also something called football. She couldn't imagine what football might be, but she hoped it wasn't anything like the peanut butter and jelly sandwiches Anna seemed so fond of eating.

Lawan peered in the mirror at her droopy eyes, puffy face, and dark tousled hair. It was a strange land she had come to, this America, but it was where her only living relative was, so she'd had no choice. She supposed she'd just have to learn to adapt to their ways and make the best of it.

Jonathan dreaded heading downstairs. He'd been awake for nearly an hour, lying in bed and staring at the ceiling, listening for Sarah's voice. Did he dare hope she had gone home by now? He had been more than slightly surprised to find her there when he and Leah arrived the previous evening, but Sarah was Leah's best friend and it wasn't really unusual that she would want to be there to greet her when she came home from college for the Thanksgiving holiday. Still, Jonathan couldn't shake the feeling that she was there more to see him than Leah.

*How into yourself are you?* He grinned. *Yeah, more than a little conceited there, buddy. But how sharp do you have to be to notice her batting those baby-blues at you nonstop?*

Jonathan sighed. It's not like the girl was ugly — not by a long shot. In fact, she was really cute, and nice too. He'd even tried to convince himself at one time that he could be interested in her and consider her more than just another kid sister, but it hadn't worked. He'd tried just as hard to convince himself that his heart wasn't caught up with the beautiful hazel-eyed Mara that he'd helped rescue from human trafficking a couple of years earlier, but that hadn't worked either.

Her face swam in his thoughts now, and he wondered if he'd have a chance to see her while he was home. They'd had a little written communication while he was gone, but she'd kept the letters impersonal, never giving him any reason to hope for more. And yet he did. And he was determined to get past Sarah and over to the boarding house where Mara lived before the weekend was over — the sooner, the better, as a matter of fact.

*I wonder what she's doing for Thanksgiving,* he mused. He'd dropped her a note a couple of weeks earlier, asking her that very question, but she hadn't answered. He sure wished she did email, but she said she didn't have a computer and he couldn't text her because she hadn't offered her cell phone number, so the only way to connect with her was to drive over to her place and hope to catch her at home.

Hoisting himself from bed, he grabbed some clean clothes and headed for the door. Might as well make a dash for the shower and then see about sneaking out without running into Sarah. Maybe by the time he got back she'd already have gone home.

# Chapter 9

Mariner's was closed for Thanksgiving Day, so Mara had planned to pamper herself with a nice long sleep-in with no alarm clock. Trouble is, she still woke up early and tossed and turned for a couple of hours, trying to get back to sleep. What was the point of getting up when she didn't have anything to do until afternoon when she was supposed to go over to Barbara's place for dinner?

The sun was already shining through her window, easily penetrating the flimsy curtain that did little to block it out. She rolled to her side and pulled the covers up under her chin. Maybe she could ignore the light and drift back off if she kept her eyes closed long enough. She had been so pleased when Barbara invited her for dinner that she hadn't even though to ask if she could come early to help with something.

*Sure, like I could be of any help fixing a Thanksgiving dinner. I might work in a café, but all I do is take orders and serve meals. My cooking is limited to what I can warm up in the microwave here in my room.* She sighed. The only real Thanksgiving dinner she'd ever had was the last couple of years when she managed to find a place open that was serving turkey and all the trimmings. But this year would be different; this year she'd be eating with a real family — Barbara's family. She only hoped they liked her and she didn't do anything to embarrass herself.

*Or Barbara. She's taking a big chance inviting somebody like me to have dinner with her family. I wonder what they'll think of me. Surely Barbara hasn't told them. . . .*

She sighed again and opened her eyes, giving up as she threw the covers back and decided to grab a shower and then head down to the beach for a walk and a cup of coffee. Maybe she'd even find a bagel or something. After all, it was a long time until dinner, and it was obvious she wasn't going to get any more sleep.

Rosanna had been up for hours. There was nothing she liked better than cooking a huge Thanksgiving meal, especially when she had both her children home.

*And one extra,* she thought, smiling at Sarah's feeble attempt to pretend she had come over strictly to welcome Leah home when it was obvious she was there as much or more to see Jonathan.

Rosanna donned her oven mitt and checked the pies. Soon they'd be cooling on the antique sideboard, and she'd have to keep an eye on her two grown children to keep them from trying to sneak a piece before dinner. *And on Michael too,* she reminded herself. *He's always been the worst one about snatching bites of dessert before they've even cooled.*

A squeaking stairstep caught her attention. "Is that you, Michael?" she called out, wondering if her husband had torn himself away from the pregame show long enough to head upstairs for something.

"It's me, Mom."

Jonathan's voice seemed subdued, and she turned from her work to see him standing in the kitchen doorway. Was it just her imagination, or had he actually grown taller during the three months he'd been away at college? He was already six-foot-two when he left, so maybe it was just that he looked a bit more mature now.

She raised her eyebrows, noticing the car keys in his hand. "Going somewhere?"

His voice still a notch below normal, he said, "Just making a quick run to . . . see a friend." He smiled, but the nonchalance seemed forced.

"Anyone I know?" she asked, wiping her hands on her apron as she approached him.

He shrugged. "Probably," he said, his brown eyes darting away from hers as he jingled his keys. "Listen, I gotta go." He leaned down and planted a kiss on top of her head. "I'll be back in plenty of time for dinner."

"Well, I certainly hope so," she said, watching his back as he hurried toward the entryway and out the door. Where was he going in such a hurry?

Voices and clattering footsteps drew her attention back to the stairs as she turned to see Leah and Sarah hurrying down toward her.

"Was that Jonathan?" Leah asked, frowning. "Where was he going?"

Rosanna shrugged. "To see a friend," she said. "That's all I know. Said he'd be back for dinner."

The disappointment on Sarah's face was undeniable, but Rosanna turned back to the kitchen. She had work to do and couldn't second guess her children's romantic issues. Still, she couldn't help but think the feelings between Sarah and Jonathan were more than slightly one-sided.

"I hope that's not your Thanksgiving dinner."

The statement came from behind Mara, where she sat on the seawall, looking out at the waves and munching on a cheese bagel. She managed to restrain herself from a visible, physical reaction as the familiar voice pulled her back from her daydreams.

She turned her head slowly, aware of the sun's warmth on her hair and face as she blinked into its brightness. "Jonathan," she said, as if it were the most natural thing in the world to find him standing behind her. Her racing heart decried her nonchalance, but she was determined to maintain her uninterested façade.

"What a surprise," she commented, allowing herself a slight smile.

Even in the brightness of the midday sunshine, she could see Jonathan's eyebrows raise. "Really? I wrote and told you I'd be home for the weekend."

Mara shrugged. "Sure. But I didn't expect to find you hovering over me a block from home."

Jonathan's grin was sheepish, and Mara had to fight the urge to throw her arms around him in welcome. "Yeah, well . . . if I had your phone number I'd have called before coming over to look for you. But since I don't . . ."

He hesitated, but Mara ignored the wordless invitation. She might decide to give him her number before he went back to school on Sunday, but she wasn't sure yet.

"Since I don't," he continued, his eyes dropping momentarily as if he were interested in the sandy sidewalk he was scuffing with the toe of his worn tennis shoe, "I stopped by your place, and when I didn't find you, I thought you might be . . . well, here." He looked back up, and his smile widened. "And here you are."

She nodded, wondering how much longer she could hold out before allowing her joy at seeing him to spill over into her words and actions. "Here I am. And here you are, as well." She smiled, keeping her expression and tone polite. "So what are your plans for the day? I imagine your family is having a big Thanksgiving feast."

Jonathan nodded. "I can't wait," he said. "College food is . . . well, college food, as you know." His cheeks flamed suddenly, as if he'd realized his gaffe.

No, Mara did not know about college food, though she certainly hoped to find out soon. To date, however, her life had not leant itself to the type of normal events that most people experienced. Past Thanksgivings, for the most part, hadn't been any different from any other day, with the exception that a few more men found the opportunity to steal away and stop by Tio's compound for a quick visit with one of his slaves before returning to home and family.

"Anyway," Jonathan continued, "I'm looking forward to my mom's cooking." He paused before squinting his eyes slightly, as if he were concentrating. "I just . . . wondered about you. I mean, do you have plans for the day? Because if you don't . . . well, I just thought it might be nice if you joined us for dinner." His cheeks flushed again. "If you're not already busy, that is."

Mara smiled, more warmly this time. "Actually, I am," she said, sincere regret tingeing her voice despite the fact that she tried to hide it. "Barbara Whiting invited me to join her and her family for dinner this afternoon. I'll be heading over there in a few hours."

Jonathan's shoulders slumped, and he nodded. "Sure," he said. "I should have realized she'd invite you." He smiled. "You two have become good friends, haven't you?"

"We have," Mara said. "She's probably the closest thing I've ever had to a mother."

Jonathan's brow drew together slightly. "But . . . you have a mother . . . somewhere. Don't you? In Mexico, or . . . ?"

Mara's smile faded away, as did her warm feelings. "My mother is dead to me," she said. "My father, too. They're the ones who sold me to my *tio* and made my life an absolute hell for so many years. If they showed up on this sidewalk today, right now, and tried to talk to me, I'd walk away and never look back. So in answer to your question, no, I do not have a mother. Just Barbara."

She noticed Jonathan's Adam's apple slide up and then down again, as he swallowed before responding. "Sorry," he said. "I shouldn't have brought it up."

"No problem," Mara responded, wishing her statement were true. She was no psychiatrist, but she knew enough to understand that what her parents did to her really was a problem or it wouldn't still bother her so much. Regardless, she wasn't about to talk about it to Jonathan . . . or anyone else.

She stuffed what was left of her bagel into the sack, along with her empty Styrofoam coffee cup, and slid off the seawall to stand facing Jonathan. "I'd better get back," she said. "I need to shower and change before I go to Barbara's."

"I'll walk with you."

"What about your car?"

"I left it in front of your place." He grinned. "I was hoping to find you close by."

Mara nodded. "Then I guess we're heading in the same direction anyway. We may as well walk together."

Turning toward home, she found herself wondering what it would be like to hold hands with Jonathan while they walked, but she quickly shoved her hand closest to him in her pocket and the thought from her mind.

# Chapter 10

Cecelia Jimenez knew nothing of an American holiday called Thanksgiving. She knew only that her stomach rumbled with hunger and her heart ached with regret. But those feelings were an everyday occurrence in her dreary life, and she did her best to ignore them as she stirred the pot of beans that bubbled over an open fire in the yard. The gas to their home was shut off, as it often was when her *esposo*, Rudolfo, used what little money they had to buy alcohol rather than pay the bills. Their sons were grown and gone now, and Cecelia seldom saw them or their families. Her husband spent most of his time drinking whatever alcohol he could get hold of and the rest of the time sleeping off its effects. Though she much preferred her life when Rudolfo was asleep, it still left her with far too much time to think . . . and remember.

*America, she thought. The United States. That's where my brother-in-law said he was taking my little girl, to give her a better life. Did he do that? Did he take good care of her and find her a good home? I have seen him only a few times since he took my Maria from me, and he never answers my questions—only says she is fine and happy. Is that true? He is not a nice man. Why should I believe anything he tells me? Does Maria ever think of me or the home she shared with us when she was a little girl?*

Hot tears burned her eyes at the thought that Maria might have forgotten her by now—worse yet, that she might remember but hate her. If only there were some way to let her know that Cecelia only agreed to let Maria's *tio* take her away because she thought it was best for her! But of course, there was not. Though she had prayed for years for a chance to see her daughter or speak to her one more time, *El Señor* had not answered. Soon it would be too late. Life was hard here, and Cecelia's cough so much worse than even a few months ago. She struggled to breathe and sensed that her time on earth would end before she lived long enough to be consider a true *vieja,* an old woman. Did she dare hope that she could be forgiven for what she had done and that she would one day see Maria in heaven?

Cecelia gave the beans another stir and then laid the wooden spoon aside. She would spend more time on her knees this day, as Rudolfo slept. Perhaps *El Señor* would even yet give her a miracle.

⤙✧⤚

Jonathan wrestled with his desire to tell Mara how he felt and to ask her to please change her plans and come to his house for dinner instead of Barbara's. Not only would that be rude, he told himself, but Mara might reject him entirely and stop writing to him altogether. Though he wanted so much more in a relationship with this beautiful young woman, he was ever mindful of the fact that she did not share his faith. He knew, too, that even if she did, she was nowhere near ready to get involved with anyone romantically.

*Will she ever be,* he wondered, as he matched his pace to hers, wishing they weren't so close to where she lived. He would gladly give up his Thanksgiving dinner just to spend the day walking with her. But of course, that wasn't an option.

"Are you thankful for your life, Jonathan?"

The question jarred him from his daydreaming, and he glanced over at Mara. She still walked with her eyes straight ahead, but he knew he hadn't imagined her question.

"Sure," he said, wondering even as he spoke where she was going with this thought. He caught himself before he repeated the question back to her, relatively certain that she would not respond positively.

"I am too," she said. "Now, anyway. The past is over, and I plan to leave it there. But even now, with all the opportunities in front of me that I never thought I'd have, I'm confused. People like you know exactly who to be thankful to—God, right? But me? I'm not even sure there is a God, and if there is, do I thank Him for finally getting me out of the living hell I endured for so long? If He's as good as people like you say He is, why did He allow me to be there in the first place? And what about the others who are still there now? Or the ones who died there?"

She stopped in the middle of the sidewalk, and he stopped with her, waiting as she turned her hazel eyes up at him and flashed them as she spoke, cutting his heart with her words. "What kind of God does something like that? Wouldn't it be easier to believe there is no God than to think He doesn't care enough to stop this sort of thing?"

Scriptures and logic flooded Jonathan's mind, and it took all the self-control he had not to open his mouth and let them fly. But He knew God was telling him not to, and so instead he took a chance and laid his hand on Mara's shoulder. He felt her flinch, but she stood her ground.

"Only God Himself can answer those questions for you, Mara," he said, blinking back the prick of tears. "I can tell you God is good because I know it to be true, but I can't transfer that knowledge from my heart to yours . . . though I would if I could." He swallowed before continuing. "I will promise you this, though. I will pray that God will show you, as only He can, that He'll answer your questions and your doubts. I know He will."

Their eyes locked as they stood facing one another, silently, for a moment until at last Mara dropped her gaze. "Fine," she said, turning to resume her walk toward home. "But you'd better pray hard because right now, I'm not expecting Him to answer."

Jonathan continued wordlessly beside her, reminding himself that if God didn't answer and reveal His love to Mara, then Jonathan's pursuit of the mysterious girl was pointless. How could he even consider a relationship with someone who didn't share his faith or dreams of lifelong ministry? He couldn't, and that's all there was to it.

The realization added to his determination to pray for the girl who had won his heart the first time he looked into her captivating but terrified eyes. Only God could break through the barrier that Mara had understandably erected around her heart. Jonathan would just have to continue to pray, as he'd said he would do . . . and then wait to see how God answered.

Joan had become so accustomed to the night sounds of the jungle that she scarcely noticed the occasional monkeys' calls or insects' buzz. Instead she lay on her pallet beneath the mosquito netting, beside her sleeping husband, and listened to his even breathing and occasional snort, as she allowed her mind to drift to the home she'd once known and loved in the US. How had she come so far that her heart now fully belonged to this overcrowded orphanage full of children with stories so sad she could scarcely allow herself to think about them?

*Lawan*, she thought. *Yours was one of the saddest, and yet it has the potential to be one of the happiest. This is your first*

*Thanksgiving with your new family. How are you adjusting? It's still fairly early in the day there, so you probably haven't dug into your meal yet. But maybe you're helping your new mother prepare the turkey and pies. Or perhaps you're sitting in front of the television watching the parade. What must you think of all that? And will you have a chance to watch your first football game?*

She smiled at the memories her thoughts evoked. Thanksgiving had always been her favorite holiday, even more so than Christmas or her birthday. Everyone from both sides of their family had gathered at her parents' home, bringing piles and stacks of food to add to the already existing abundance that Joan was certain they would never be able to consume. But oh, how her mouth had watered at the smell of turkey roasting all day, mingled with the aroma of pies cooling on the window-sill as she and her cousins were shooed outside to play until dinnertime, only to sneak back in and soon be spotted and exiled again.

Yes, the memories of America and Thanksgiving and family tugged at her heart on occasion, but nothing strong enough to pull her from this place full of little ones who had been beaten, abused, abandoned, and rejected. She was needed here, and though she and Mort had acknowledged Thanksgiving in united prayer before their otherwise modest meal, the day had passed as any other. Now she would pray for Lawan as she experienced her first such holiday in her new home. Oh, how Joan hoped the girl would transition to her new life with as little difficulty as possible!

# Chapter 11

Lawan had to admit that the house smelled wonderful. Though she and Anna had shared a breakfast of cereal and bananas, Lawan had kept her eyes focused on Nyesha, as the woman hummed and bustled around the cozy, colorful kitchen. Three pies decorated the counters, a turkey the size of a horse filled the oven, and Lawan thought Nyesha was peeling enough potatoes to feed everyone for miles around.

Now, her stomach content but her mouth still watering at the delicious aromas that filled the house, Lawan sat on the couch in the family room with Anna, watching something called the Macy's Day Parade on a huge flat-screen television. Anna had asked Lawan if she'd ever seen the parade on TV before, and Lawan had tried to explain to her little sister that she'd never watched anything on TV until her plane ride from Thailand. And then she had been too terrified to pay attention.

She watched closely now, though, fascinated with what Anna explained were floats and giant balloons. How wealthy these Americans must be! So much more so than Lawan had even begun to expect, for how else could they afford or justify such extravagance?

Lawan thought of the children at the orphanage, eating their rice and vegetables and glad to have them. She knew only too well the pangs of a hungry stomach, but Lawan had experienced pain much worse than that. She squeezed her eyes shut, willing the memories to go away. That Kulap and others were still there at the boss-man's brothel, suffering at the hands of evil men day after day, with little or no hope of ever escaping, was more weight than the girl could carry. But the guilt that she had escaped while they had not continued to assail her.

*Oh,* phrae yaeh suu, *I do not mean to be ungrateful,* she prayed silently, *but I so wish You would have delivered me while Chanthra was still alive. If we had to lose our parents, it would have at least been bearable if we three sisters were still together.* A pang of guilt tweaked her heart as she continued. *Forgive me,* phrae yaeh suu. *I am indeed grateful that you have reunited me with Mali — Anna — but I so miss Chanthra! And our parents too.*

She brushed away the tears before Anna could notice and returned her thoughts to the colorful display on the screen in front of her. Would she ever be able to put the pain of her past life behind her and enjoy the life she now had — without feeling guilty? She desperately wanted to believe she could, but even with God's help it seemed an impossible mountain to climb.

Jonathan had folded himself into his VW after saying good-bye to Mara on the front porch, then drove around the block and parked. He grasped the steering wheel and leaned his head on it, frustrated at his lack of progress with Mara. But what had he expected would happen? As God had so gently reminded him, Mara was not only deeply wounded and in need of healing before she could even consider a serious relationship, she was also not a believer—and therefore off limits. As much as Jonathan cared for her, he could not allow himself to become emotionally entangled with someone who did not share his faith.

With that thought echoing in his heart, he raised his head and focused on the road in front of him, tapping his accelerator before gunning it down the street toward home. He had a family and Thanksgiving dinner waiting for him, and it wasn't right to keep them waiting.

When he pulled into the driveway, he immediately wondered if Sarah was still there. He didn't see her mother's car, which she often drove, but it hadn't been there the night before either. Apparently she had gotten a ride over, so very possibly she was there right now, waiting for him to return. It seemed the only way to find out was to go inside.

The unmistakable smells of turkey and sage, cinnamon and cloves assailed his nostrils the minute he opened the door. The sounds of the pregame show reached his ears, and he knew exactly where he would find his dad. Turning toward the family room, he stepped inside to see Michael Flannery precisely where Jonathan had expected he would be — leaned back in the recliner, dozing while he waited for the game to start.

"Hey, Dad," he called out, stepping past the recliner and sprawling on the adjoining couch. "Catching a few z's before the kickoff?"

Michael's eyes fluttered open and he turned his head toward Jonathan. "You're back," he said, a smile spreading across his face. "I didn't hear you come in."

"No kidding," Jonathan answered, grinning as he kicked off his shoes. "I wonder why."

Michael laughed. "I just closed my eyes for a minute. I don't know how I could have dozed off so fast — especially with all this wonderful cooking going on around here."

"Ain't that the truth," Jonathan said. "It smells fantastic in here. I guess Mom and Leah must be in the kitchen, slicing and peeling and all that stuff."

Michael nodded. "And Sarah too. With three cooks already at work, I decided it was safer to stay out here."

Jonathan raised his eyebrows. "Sarah's still here? I would've thought she'd gone home to be with her own family by now."

"I guess they're visiting relatives for the weekend," Michael explained. "Sarah didn't want to go along, so she's staying here until they come back on Sunday."

"Mmm." Jonathan wasn't quite sure how to respond to his dad's announcement. True, he'd just told himself he needed to put thoughts of a relationship with Mara on long-term hold, and true, Sarah was a believer who quite obviously had a crush on him. But no matter how he tried, Jonathan just wasn't interested. Sarah was nice, she was cute, and she was available . . . but she wasn't Mara. And that was the bottom line.

He leaned his head back against the couch cushions and settled in for what looked like it could be a very long weekend. But at least the food and the football would be great.

Mara had stood at her window, looking out onto the street where Jonathan's car had been parked, long after he pulled away from the curb and chugged down the street. Her heart yearned for him to turn around and come back and ask her just one more time to change her plans and spend the day with him instead of Barbara. But even as she longed for that to happen, she knew it wouldn't. It couldn't. Even if Jonathan asked her a hundred times, she'd have to say no. Not only had she already promised Barbara, who was her only real friend in the whole world, but she had no business giving false hope to Jonathan. He was too good for her. Couldn't he see that? They had nothing in common, and that was the end of it.

Sighing, she'd at last pulled herself away from the window and browsed through her small closet, trying to decide what to wear. How was she supposed to dress for a holiday dinner with a friend and the friend's family? Mara felt comfortable with Barbara, but she'd never been around Barbara's relatives. What would they think of her?

There was little doubt they knew how Barbara had met Mara. The very thought nearly caused her to dial Barbara's number and cancel. She could always say she didn't feel well, but . . .

No. She had too much respect for Barbara to lie to her. She'd just have to pick something nice and then check the bus schedule to see how soon she'd have to be at the bus stop to catch a ride to Barbara's house in time for dinner. She'd gone there by bus before, but never on a holiday.

Picking through the half dozen or so outfits that seemed at least somewhat acceptable, Mara finally decided on a pair of gray slacks and a long-sleeved pink blouse. The colors went well together, and the look was safe. She'd add a strand of department-store pearls, and she'd be ready to go.

By the time she'd showered and dressed, applied a touch of makeup and run a comb through her stylish short hair, she decided she'd better get going so she wouldn't miss the bus, which she'd discovered from the schedule only ran once an hour that day. She'd also noticed they stopped running at eight that evening, so she'd have a perfect excuse to leave soon after dinner.

Snatching up her purse and grabbing a light sweater in case the temperature dropped later in the afternoon, she had just turned toward the door when someone knocked. Frowning, her heart raced at the thought that it might be Jonathan. Taking a deep breath, she put on her most casual expression and opened the door.

"Hey," Barbara announced, her face flushed as she stood facing her. "Looks like you're all ready to go."

Mara blinked. "Well, yes, but . . . I was about to catch the bus. Did I miss something?"

Barbara laughed. "Don't you ever check phone messages? I called a little while ago and told you I was on my way."

"I must have been in the shower." She smiled. "And you're right. I really need to start checking my phone messages."

"So, are you ready? Got everything?"

When Mara nodded, Barbara slipped her arm through hers and proceeded to escort her out the door, stopping only long enough for Mara to close and lock it behind them. And then they were off.

# Chapter 12

Lawan sat at the large, rectangular dining room table between Anna, who was perched on a pillow so she could see everyone and reach her food, and Kyle's mother, who sat on Lawan's right with her husband on the other side. Despite the fact that Lawan had been aware of the ongoing meal preparation throughout the day and had even helped with some of it, she was stunned at the amount of food that now sat atop the lace tablecloth. How could they even begin to eat it all?

True, in addition to Kyle's parents, Nyesha's widowed mother was with them, but otherwise it was just Anna, her parents—and Lawan, who was used to surviving on very little. Once again she thought of the children at the orphanage in Thailand, who subsisted for the most part on rice and vegetables, with occasional fish or chicken and fruit as a special treat. How many of them could fill their stomachs for days on the food arrayed in front of her right now!

As Kyle called them to prayer and they joined hands around the table, stretching their arms to complete the circle, Lawan ventured a peek at the others. All of them sat with heads bowed, as Kyle gave thanks for their abundant blessings. Lawan did not doubt that God loved all people equally, but she did find herself wondering why some seemed to have so much more than others.

Nyesha's mother, whom Lawan had been instructed to call Grandma Stewart, sat directly across from Lawan. With Grandma Stewart's head bowed, Lawan could see how much of the woman's dark hair was interspersed with gray. Lawan knew the woman's husband had died years earlier and that she now resided in an independent living facility for seniors in a nearby city, though she had no idea what such a facility was like. Nyesha had told her they would go visit Grandma Stewart there one day soon so Lawan could see the place called Peaceful Acres. Anna had told her there wasn't much to do there, so they'd better bring books and games.

A glance to her right showed Kyle's mother, Grandma Johnson, in profile. Her nose was a bit pointed, like Kyle's, and her hair was blonde, but otherwise Lawan thought she and Kyle looked nothing alike. She had decided the moment she met Grandpa Johnson that Kyle definitely favored his father. With the exception of his nearly bald head, this new grandfather of hers looked exactly like an older version of the man Anna called Daddy.

Grandma Johnson opened her eyes and turned her head then, catching Lawan's glance before she had a chance to avert it. The girl felt her cheeks flush despite the woman's warm smile. She quickly turned away and closed her eyes, determined to pay attention to the words being spoken.

"And thank You too, Father," Kyle was saying, "for the family you have blessed us with—especially the newest member, Lawan. We are so grateful that she has joined us, and we ask You to bless her and help her feel comfortable with us, and to know that she is welcome and loved."

His voice turned to a faint buzz, as Lawan felt herself drifting away once again. Welcome and loved? Oh, how she wanted to believe it! But how could it be so? They all knew of her past, of what had happened to her during those two years after she was kidnapped from her village, before Klahan rescued her. . . .

Klahan. Her heart squeezed at the memory of the man who had lived up to the meaning of his name and risked his very life to spirit her away from the brothel. Joan had tried to explain to her that the man had selfish intentions, but that hadn't changed the gratitude Lawan felt toward him. She prayed daily that he would find favor, even in prison, for hadn't he given his heart and life to *phrae yaeh suu,* even as she had? Though it seemed so far away, Lawan took comfort in knowing she would one day see Klahan again, even if not until they all arrived in heaven.

"Amen."

The word echoed around the table, and Lawan realized Kyle was through praying. She lifted her head and fixed her eyes once again on the huge golden bird in the middle of the table, surrounded by bowls and plates full of potatoes and gravy, stuffing and cranberries, salads and vegetables. Her stomach hurt just to think about trying to consume some of everything, but she didn't want to offend the Johnsons. Still, how much could any one person eat?

She darted a glance toward Anna and found her grinning back at her. Lawan would follow her little sister's lead and eat only as much as Anna. Strange, she realized, even as the plates began to circulate around the table, that she was already looking forward to crawling into bed tonight, when this meal was finally over and their company had gone home, and going right to sleep.

Mara felt completely out of place, and yet she desperately yearned to belong. These people gathered around the table, with their cheery voices and laughter and comfortable camaraderie, were what family was all about—everything she'd never experienced with her own parents and siblings. Even before they'd sold her to her *tio*, Mara—known then as Maria—realized she was not the favored child. She was the only girl, and her brothers were the honored offspring.

*Maybe that's why I believed my* tio *meant the things he said, she thought. About how beautiful I was and how he loved me, how he took the time to help me learn English and reading . . . But all along he was just tricking me into thinking he cared so he could use me to make money for him and those disgusting men who helped him.*

She shook her head, forcing her attention to the overloaded plate in front of her. This was no time to dwell on Jefe or his henchmen, or on the terrible betrayal or suffering she had experienced. She was free, no longer a slave without rights or privileges. She could make her own choices from now on—choices about where and how to work, what classes to take in school, what friendships to pursue . . . or not.

Mara toyed with her food, pushing her fork around her plate as she tried to banish Jonathan's face. How she had wanted to speak at least one word of encouragement to him when he came to see her that morning, but she knew the futility of it. There was no sense in pursuing a relationship that could never be.

"So, Mara," came a voice from across the table, "I hear you work at Mariner's. I love that place."

Mara jerked her head up, feeling her eyes widen as she realized someone had spoken to her. The words had come from the young woman named Leila, with eyes so blue they appeared violet and dark hair that hung nearly to her waist. Mara imagined they were close to the same age, but beyond that she was certain they had nothing in common.

"I'm . . . sorry," she mumbled, feeling the heat rise to her face and wishing she could recall the girl's specific comment. "What did you say?"

Leila smiled. "I said, I heard you worked at Mariner's. I don't get there nearly as often as I'd like, but I love their clam chowder."

Mara nodded, relieved that her response could be a simple one. "I do too. It's one of their specialties."

As others chimed in about the good food at Mariner's, comparing it to other places that also serviced chowder and fish and chips, Mara did her best to enter in and become one of the group. But as nice as Barbara's family was, including her niece Leila, Mara knew it was all a façade. She would never fit in with these nice, normal people. They weren't spoiled or ruined, like her. They hadn't experienced the darkest side of life, where hope and joy have long ceased to exist and survival is an all-consuming job. Mara had not only experienced it, but she sometimes felt she had become it, and she despaired of ever breaking free of that darkness.

Still, she smiled and participated in the conversation, even as she dabbled at the delicious offerings of turkey and ham, plus so many side dishes Mara couldn't count. She felt at the moment that she'd never be hungry again . . . and yet she felt as if she were starving at the very same time.

*I don't understand,* she thought, her words a silent prayer to a God she wasn't sure existed or listened. *What is wrong with me? Am I too broken to ever be like normal people? If I am, then why am I trying to do anything with my life? What's the point? Can You hear me? Are You even there?*

Tears threatened and she willed them away, hardening her heart as she had taught herself to do throughout her many years of captivity. She would get through this, as she had gotten through much worse in the past. But she would make a point to limit her relationship with Barbara to the two of them only. Being around Barbara's family just reminded her of what she had missed in her own life, bringing with that reminder a pain that was more than she was willing to risk repeating. The only thing that hurt more was when she thought of Jonathan . . . and realized she could never tell him how she felt or how much she wanted to be with him.

By the time Rosanna insisted Michael and Jonathan turn off the game and come to the table for dinner, Sarah had popped into the family room at least a half-dozen times to see if they needed anything — cold drinks, snacks, a smile.

86

Jonathan knew why she was there, and his father no doubt knew the same, but they played along, not wanting to embarrass her. Sarah looked especially cute today, her cheeks flushed from helping in the kitchen, her hair freshly washed and fluffed out the way Jonathan had once mentioned he liked it, and her makeup just right — not too much but just enough to bring out the blue in her eyes.

Still, Jonathan's mind drifted every few minutes to the frightened hazel eyes he had first seen when he met Mara more than two years earlier. He had been drawn to her then, and he was drawn to her now. But it seemed he couldn't find a way to break through the wall she had built around herself — understandably so, he reminded himself — and besides, she did not share his faith, and that pretty much ruled out a relationship between them.

With that reminder again hovering at the front of his thoughts, he pulled himself from the couch and followed his dad into the dining room, nearly gasping at the sight of all the food piled on the table. The turkey was just the right golden color, and he couldn't wait to claim one of those huge, juicy drumsticks. His father would surely grab the other one, while the women aimed for the breast, slicing the white meat thin and covering it with gravy.

Wait a minute. He knew his mother and Leah liked the breast meat, but what about Sarah? Would she want a drumstick too? He knew the chivalrous thing to do would be to offer it to her just in case, but he wasn't sure just how chivalrous he was feeling now that his mouth was already watering.

"Let's pray and offer thanks," Michael said, pulling Jonathan's thoughts back to the proper priorities. As they reached out their hands to join them together, Jonathan was surprised to see that Sarah had squeezed her way between him and Leah. She took his hand and smiled up at him before closing her eyes and bowing her head. Jonathan hoped his dad would keep the offering short.

"You do the honors, son," Michael said when he'd finished praying. He nodded toward the turkey and the carving knife that sat beside it. Then he sat down and waited, as everyone but Jonathan followed his lead and took their seats.

Jonathan retrieved the knife and shot up a quick prayer for wisdom. He was now in the position of offering their guest first choice from the carved bird, so it appeared he might be forced into chivalry in spite of himself.

"Drumstick?" he said, looking at Sarah as he held the knife at the ready.

She shook her head. "No, thanks," she answered. "I prefer white meat."

Jonathan smiled. This Thanksgiving dinner just might have a chance to be redeemed after all.

Laying a couple of perfectly carved slices of breast meat on Sarah's plate, he ignored the smile she sent his way and proceeded to carve additional slices for his mother and sister. At last he was able to place a drumstick on his father's plate and one on his own. As the family passed around the steaming dishes of potatoes and vegetables, he sighed with relief. They were going to get through dinner just fine, and then he and his dad could escape back to the football game—though he imagined he should at least make an offer of helping with the dishes before his mom shooed him off and told him she already had plenty of help.

There was something to be said for traditional holidays, he thought, biting into his drumstick with gusto. He was already looking forward to the pumpkin pie he and his dad would devour during the second half of the Cowboys game.

# Chapter 13

The dishes were steaming in the dishwasher and the last bowl of leftovers had been covered and squeezed into the overcrowded refrigerator. Grandpa and Grandma Johnson had given hugs and kisses all around before leaving to drive home, and Kyle had offered to drive Grandma Stewart back to her place. Anna had jumped at the chance to ride with them, but Lawan had declined the invitation to join them. The day had exhausted her, and she was more anxious than ever to retreat to the comfort of her bed.

She lay there now, the early evening darkness of winter enveloping the room, with the exception of a nightlight that Anna insisted be kept on at all times. Lawan wondered if Anna would flip the overhead light on when she came home. Not that it mattered, she decided. She was so tired she doubted anything could wake her once she'd fallen asleep.

Rolling to her side, she bent her knees and drew them up slightly. It was her favorite sleeping position, as it made her feel safe somehow. She pushed the thought from her mind that it hadn't helped one bit when she was in the brothel. There she had fallen asleep in any position, too tired even to roll over or pull up the covers after her last customer had left for the night. The memories of those two years were almost more than Lawan could handle, and she squeezed her eyes shut as tightly as she could, refocusing her mind on the day that had just passed.

*Thanksgiving,* she thought. *So that's what the holiday is about—getting together with family, eating a lot, watching football and parades on television, remembering what you're grateful for, and thanking God for it all.*

She sighed, as the hint of hot tears pricked her eyelids. Refusing to let them flow for fear they would never stop, she took a deep breath and went over the many things she had to be thankful for this night. At the top of her list, of course, was her escape from the brothel. If it hadn't been for Klahan, she would still be there at this very moment, hungry and weary and miserable. But she wasn't, and that was enough to make her grateful to God forever.

Still, why couldn't she have gotten away from there before her parents died? Better yet, why did she have to be kidnapped in the first place?

The tears burst forth then, along with a sob, as the thought that had tortured her for so long came back to torment her once again. *It was my fault. Mine! I'm the one who wandered too far from the village. My* maae *and* phor *warned me so many times, but I didn't listen. If I had obeyed them, I wouldn't have been caught, and maybe my parents wouldn't have died. I might still be with them, there in their little hut instead of here in this great big house with strangers. . . .*

Anna's face swam into view then, and she tried to gain control of her emotions, telling herself that not everyone in the Johnson family was a stranger to her. Reason told Lawan that if she had never been captured and forced into the brothel, she would never again have seen her little sister—or her older one, for that matter. For it was in the brothel that she was reunited with her older sister, Chanthra . . . only to see her die and pass into the arms of phrae yaeh suu.

*They are together now, aren't they?* Lawan prayed silently.

*With You,* phrae yaeh suu. *And now You have reunited the last of our family — Mali and me. Forgive me for calling her Mali and not Anna, but she will always be Mali in my heart.*

A soft sound behind her told her the door to the room had opened, and she was surprised that her sister had returned so quickly. She did her best to stifle her sobs, wiping her tears with the sheet. But when she felt the weight on the side of her bed, she knew it was not Anna who had come to her. It had to be Nyesha, coming in response to her cries.

She wondered briefly if the woman might go away if she lay very still and refused to cry anymore. But then she felt a hand on her head, brushing her hair back from her face. Surely Nyesha had felt the dampness on her skin; there was no longer any hope of pretending she was asleep.

Turning slowly toward Nyesha, Lawan told herself she would insist she was fine and convince the woman to leave her. But when Nyesha leaned down and pulled her into her arms, Lawan's determination evaporated.

"Go ahead and cry, baby girl," Nyesha crooned. "It's all right, sweetheart. You just cry as much as you need to. I'll be right here for you whenever you need me."

And then she began to rock Lawan, slowly and gently, Nyesha's body trembling slightly with sobs of her own. When the woman's tears landed on Lawan's head, the girl threw her arms around Nyesha's waist and wailed. It was as if God Himself had come down to hold her in His arms and cry with her, and Lawan wondered if the tears would ever stop.

With the exception of a slightly better meal at the end of the day, Thanksgiving had passed like any other dull yet dangerous day behind the bars of a maximum security prison. Jefe's anger simmered at the thought of his ungrateful niece, wandering free and easy on the outside, without gratitude or consideration for anything he had ever done for her. That she had turned on him in such a way that now forced him into confinement for life was sometimes more than he could bear. And yet he knew he could not allow his thirst for revenge to dull his edge or make him forget about the immediate threat to the little kingdom he had built for himself, even within the limits of his own cell.

He approached that cell now, keeping up with the man in front of him and leading the way for the one behind, even as a pair of armed correctional officers kept close watch on the line of inmates getting ready to be locked in for the night. How he despised the men—worse yet, the handful of women—who watched over his every move! It was bad enough to be controlled by male officers, but *women*? Jefe had to restrain himself from spitting in their eyes each time a female guard dared to tell him what to do.

*Before Mara sold me out,* he thought, stopping in front of his cell and waiting for the command to enter, *I would have taught those pitiful excuses for women their place in life. They would have served me, just like the others did, or I would have made them beg for another chance before they died.*

Once again he fought for control of his thoughts. He reminded himself that if it weren't for Mara, he wouldn't have to put up with the female officers in this dump. It was his niece who was to blame for this whole mess, including El Gato, the ignorant slimeball who dared to try to encroach on his territory. He might have to concentrate on taking him out first, but when he was done, he would once again find a way to get to Mara and make her pay for her treachery. And this time he would not fail.

❦

Mara was greatly relieved to see the evening end as Barbara's guests began to gather their things and head for the door.

"How about a ride?" Leila asked, stopping in front of Mara who still sat on the couch in the family room where they'd all gathered after dinner. "Aunt Barbara brought you over in her car, right?"

Mara looked up, surprised. She had been glad that Barbara picked her up earlier and had assured her of a ride home at the end of the day, but she had just assumed that Barbara would be the one to provide it. What was she to do with this offer?

"I . . ." She paused and darted a glance toward Barbara, who was rising from her recliner to begin her good-bye hugs. *Should I tell her I'm already getting a ride with Barbara? But what if I'm not? Barbara didn't actually say she'd take me, just that I'd have a ride. . . .*

Leila turned to follow Mara's gaze. "Aunt Barbara," she said, "do you mind if I give Mara a ride home? It's on my way, and it would save you having to go out again."

Barbara's face lit up. "That's a lovely idea!" She smiled at Mara. "You don't mind, do you?"

Heat rushed into Mara's face, but she tried to cover it by keeping her answer nonchalant. "Of course not," she said, shrugging as if she didn't mind one way or the other. "Why would I? I mean, if she's heading that direction anyway."

Leila turned back and locked her nearly violet eyes on Mara's, her smile warm. "Wonderful! It will give us a great chance to get to know each other better."

Mara cringed, though she forced a smile in return, rising from the couch and grabbing her purse from the floor beside her. "That'll be nice," she said, the turkey and pumpkin pie in her stomach doing somersaults at the thought. What in the world would she say to someone like Leila, a single woman who had only recently graduated from some sort of computer college and was now working somewhere or other? Oh, why hadn't she paid more attention when Leila was telling the others about her new job? And what could she possibly say in return about her own life? They'd already covered the menu at Mariner's during their discussion at dinner, so if Leila didn't already know about Mara's past, she would no doubt ask about it. And there was no way Mara was going to let the conversation go there.

Fifteen minutes, twenty tops. That's what she figured it would take to get home from Barbara's. And each of those minutes was going to be painfully long and awkward. As Mara joined in the good-byes that were going around the room and then followed Leila to the door, she reminded herself never again to accept an invitation from anyone that included a family gathering. She would have stuck to a bologna sandwich in her room if she'd known the day was going to end up like this.

# Chapter 14

Jonathan couldn't sleep. He'd tossed and turned for nearly an hour and finally given up. Often, when he had trouble falling asleep, he simply went down to the kitchen for a snack and then returned to bed and was out in minutes. This time he suspected part of the reason he couldn't sleep was too much food in the first place, so a snack would only compound the problem.

Tossing on jeans and a T-shirt, he grabbed a light jacket and made a beeline for the back door, relieved that he didn't encounter anyone along the way. The house was quiet and dark except for a few strategically placed nightlights, but the moment he stepped out into the backyard he was greeted by a nearly full moon.

*Perfect,* he thought. *Just right for a little late-night fresh air.*

He settled into the porch swing, careful not to let it move too quickly and start squeaking. Lifting his legs onto the cushions, he sat still, trying to focus on the clear night sky to see if he could recognize the familiar stars.

A smile touched his lips as he thought of the many times he and his dad had sat out in the yard at night, staring up at the sky together. Jonathan had been in awe at his father's knowledge about the celestial bodies scattered across the heavens. But even as Michael Flannery had pointed out the individual stars and called many of them by name, Jonathan waited, knowing that his father would soon move on to tell him of the heavens beyond the ones we could see, the vast universe created and controlled by the One who spoke them into being. He always scooted closer to his dad as he listened, feeling tiny and insignificant at the thought of a God so immense and mighty that He could create an entire galaxy with a word.

"I didn't know You personally then," Jonathan whispered, "though I knew about You. Dad made sure of that. But I never really understood what he was trying to tell me about the need to have a relationship with You until a couple of years ago." He shook his head. "How could I have been so dense, when the truth was right there in front of me all the time? I sure am glad You're patient."

A faint squeak caught his attention, and he turned from the sky to look at the back door. Sarah's short blonde hair seemed illuminated by a lunar outline, and he sighed. How had she found him? He was sure he hadn't made a sound when he left his room and came downstairs. Now she stood there, wrapped in a robe and looking at him in a way that somehow frightened him.

*What do I do about Sarah, Lord?* he prayed silently. *I can't deny her crush on me anymore. And maybe if it weren't for Mara, I'd welcome the attention. But it just isn't fair to her . . . is it?*

She was smiling and moving toward him now, and he sighed in resignation. It seemed his only choice was either to speak up and tell her point blank that he wasn't interested . . . or sit here and have a conversation with her, hoping she wouldn't paint him into a corner and force the issue.

"Hey, Sarah," he said, deciding not to move his legs and give her the opportunity to sit down beside him. If she was determined to join him, she'd have to find another place to sit down.

"Hi, Jonathan," she said, her eyes moving from the swing to a nearby lounge chair. When he remained in the same position, she quickly retrieved the chair and moved it in front of the swing. She sat down, still smiling, as if she were exactly where she'd wanted to be all along.

"I thought I heard someone get up," she said. "I couldn't sleep either, so I decided to come down and see if I could join you."

Jonathan wondered if it was normal to feel flattered by her obvious pursuit, even while wishing she'd end it and move on to someone else. He supposed it was a male ego thing, and with Mara's continued lack of interest, a natural source of encouragement.

"I think I just ate too much," he said, returning her smile. "I always do on Thanksgiving."

Sarah laughed, and Jonathan suppressed a shiver. If Mara didn't already hold an unshakeable place in his heart, he realized he would probably respond to Sarah's charms—which were more plentiful than he'd ever realized.

"Who doesn't?" she asked. "That's part of the Thanksgiving tradition, isn't it? If I wasn't staying over here with your family, I'd be home with my own, moaning and groaning about eating too much there." She shrugged. "It just goes with the territory, don't you think?"

Jonathan nodded. "I suppose so. At least in our country and culture. It sure is a reminder, though, of how blessed we are in comparison to so many who live in very different circumstances."

A flicker of what appeared to be confusion passed over Sarah's face, and it occurred to Jonathan that though Sarah was a Christian, she wasn't truly devoted to ministry or caring for others. Her world, Christian or otherwise, revolved around the life of relative comfort and ease she'd always known.

*And why shouldn't it? My life was exactly the same until I ran into Mara and Jasmine at the motel that night . . .* The thought of the young girl who had died at the hands of human traffickers squeezed Jonathan's heart, and he found himself swinging his legs to the ground and standing up. "Excuse me, will you?" He forced himself to smile as he spoke, hoping to ease the effects of his hasty exit. "I think I'm feeling tired after all. I'm going to head back up to bed. I'll catch you in the morning."

The hurt was as obvious in her eyes as the surprise that accompanied it, but he couldn't help himself. He needed to be alone with God and with his thoughts. Sarah just wouldn't understand.

Mara lay in bed, staring at an unseen ceiling. Barbara and her family had gone out of their way to make her feel welcome, and the food had been delicious. They'd even sent her home with enough leftovers to last her for a week. And Leila had been warm and gracious as she drove her home, never once implying that she considered herself better than Mara in any way.

*But she is,* Mara thought. *She's good and pure and . . . and everything I'm not. She said she wanted to get to know me better, to spend time with me and become friends. Is it possible Barbara hasn't told her family about my past? Even if she hasn't, what are the odds they won't eventually find out? That would end any friendships between them and me, that's for sure.*

*Not that I care,* she reminded herself. *I mean, it's not like I went there looking for friends. Barbara is my friend, the closest thing I have to a mother, and that's enough. I don't need anyone else . . . not even Jonathan.*

She hated the way her heart and mind always returned to the tall young man with the kind brown eyes who had helped her escape from her tio's clutches. After ten years of torture and humiliation, she had nearly given up any hope of getting out alive, but thanks to Jonathan, she had. How could she not think of him? Wasn't it normal to have feelings for him—and even to misinterpret those feelings and make them more personal than they were?

Possibly. But even now, lying in her bed in the quiet of her room, she knew exactly what she felt for Jonathan Flannery. With all her heart she wished she didn't, but she did. And there didn't seem to be a thing she could do to change it.

Cecelia Jimenez had rolled from side to side more times than she could count, even as her husband snored contentedly beside her. Their tiny one-bedroom home seemed so empty now that their two sons were grown and gone, but never did it feel emptier than when Cecelia allowed her thoughts to drift to her little girl.

"Maria," she whispered, careful not to disturb Rudolfo; he could get mean when awakened from a deep sleep. "My beautiful baby." Tears slipped from her eyes as she lay on her back now, picturing the female child that had brought her such joy until Rudolfo began to treat her as an inconvenience. He had made it clear, even in Maria's presence, that she was nothing more than an extra mouth to feed, and he resented her very existence. The child's slightest misbehavior brought extensive punishment, until Maria cowered each time her father walked into the room.

*No wonder she attached herself to her* tio, *Cecelia reasoned. He treated her with love and kindness, telling her she was beautiful and special. He even taught her to speak English and read books to her. Oh, I pray I didn't do the wrong thing when I agreed to let her go with him to the United States!*

Hot tears coursed down her cheeks now, dripping into her hair and ears. Cecelia hadn't realized that the day her brother-in-law loaded her little girl into his fancy car and drove away that she would never see the child again.

*So many years and not a word.* She stifled a sob, even as she turned her head to look at her sleeping husband, who continued to snore, his mouth open and his breath sour from a mixture of cheap alcohol and rotten teeth. *You know, don't you?* she accused silently. *You know but have refused to tell me where your brother took her, what he did with her, where she is now. Why? Why would you take my daughter from me and not even reassure me that she is all right?*

It was hard not to hate this man, though she had shared her life with him for nearly a quarter of a century. How much longer? How much longer would they continue in this sad and meaningless existence? How much longer until God took pity on them and allowed them to fade away into the darkness? It would be a kindness, one that she anticipated except for one small thing: she still held out hope that she would one day see Maria again. For that reason alone, she continued to inhale and exhale, to live and wait and wonder . . . and even dare to pray.

Tonight was no exception. Perhaps *El Señor* would at long last listen and grant her request.

# Chapter 15

Lawan awakened before Anna, one of only a couple times since the older girl arrived in her new home. She slipped from her bed and padded to the bathroom she shared with her little sister, careful not to wake her. She adored Anna and appreciated being near the only living relative she had on this earth, but sometimes the little girl's enthusiasm made her tired. She was sure this morning would be one of those times.

As she stood at the sink and splashed warm water on her face, she once again marveled at the many conveniences and luxuries available to her in this new home of hers. And yet she knew she'd trade them all in a moment for a chance to be back in the tiny hut she'd once shared with her real family in Thailand.

Maae, she thought. *Will I ever stop missing you? I still see your face and hear your voice, but sometimes they grow faint, and that scares me.*

She brushed away tears and grabbed a soft towel to pat her face dry. A growl in her stomach surprised her, particularly after all they had eaten the day before, but she found herself thinking about a bowl of cereal, one of the few foods she had taken to immediately—unlike Anna's peanut butter sandwiches.

Lawan wrinkled her nose at the thought and exited the bathroom, heading straight for the bedroom door and then down the hall and into the kitchen. She heard voices coming from that direction and assumed Kyle and Nyesha were already there, having breakfast.

Her heart sank at the realization that Kyle had not yet left for work. She had hoped to have Nyesha to herself for a little while, especially after the time they'd spent together the night before. It was the first time Lawan had dared to hope that she might at least develop a friendship with the woman Anna called Mom, though Lawan knew Nyesha would never occupy the place of Mother in her heart.

She stepped shyly into the kitchen, just in time to hear Nyesha say, "I don't think Lawan is ready for public school yet. Her English is passable, but her emotional state is just too fragile. I think it would be better if I homeschooled her for a while, at least through this school year. We can think about putting her into public school next fall, after she's had time to settle in and adjust—to feel more like part of our family."

Lawan didn't move. She was unaccustomed to hearing people talk about her, and she felt uncomfortable about coming in unannounced. Should she back out and return to her room?

"Lawan." Kyle's voice expressed surprise, though it was mixed with a welcome. "You're up early. I thought you girls would sleep in this morning. Yesterday was quite a busy day for all of us."

What should she say? Lawan understood that she should respond, but the words just didn't form in her mind. She nodded instead.

Nyesha had turned to look at her by then, and her warm smile drew Lawan in. Hesitantly she stepped forward, moving toward Nyesha's outstretched arms.

"Good morning, sweetheart," she said, wrapping the trembling girl in a hug. "Are you cold?"

Lawan shook her head. She was hungry but wasn't sure it was all right to say so.

Kyle pulled back the chair that sat between him and Nyesha. "Have a seat," he said. "I'm off today and serving as cook for a change—giving the real cook a much-needed break." A smile that came more from their eyes than their lips passed between the two adults before Kyle continued. "How about some hot chocolate and a nice stack of pancakes?"

Lawan knew about hot chocolate and had a vague understanding of pancakes, though she still wanted cereal. But she certainly didn't want to appear ungrateful. She nodded. "Yes, please," she said, remembering how Anna had responded when asked if she would like something.

Kyle smiled down at her, and Nyesha patted her shoulder reassuringly. "Hot chocolate and pancakes, coming up," he said, standing to his feet and heading for the refrigerator just as Anna appeared in the doorway.

"I want hot chocolate too," she said, shuffling her fuzzy-slippered feet to the table and climbing up into the chair that had been Kyle's just a moment earlier.

"And pancakes?" Kyle asked.

Anna shook her head. "No pancakes," she said, yawning before adding, "just cereal."

Nyesha looked surprised. "You'd rather have cereal than pancakes?"

Anna nodded. "Yes, please."

"All right," Kyle said, continuing to pull ingredients from the refrigerator and cupboards. "Pancakes for Lawan and cereal for Anna—and hot chocolate all the way around. Coming up!"

Lawan pressed her lips together, resisting the urge to join Anna in her request for cereal. Maybe after she'd been here longer she'd be able to voice her thoughts without fear, but she wasn't there yet and doubted she would be for quite a while.

Joan had fallen into bed in absolute exhaustion. Her husband seemed to have fallen asleep before he was in a prone position. Two of their assistants had been out of commission today, neither of them feeling well, leaving the others to take up the slack. They had, but not without paying a price.

"I'm getting too old for these twenty-hour days," Joan mumbled, not expecting any answer from Mort and not receiving one. She sighed. Neither of the workers seemed seriously ill, but she had agreed that they should steer clear of the children just in case one or the other of them had something contagious. If all went well, they would be back to a full staff by morning, though she wouldn't be surprised if it was at least another day or so.

She reached up and pulled the mosquito netting down over the sides of the bed, grateful that all seemed quiet in the compound—other than the usual night noises of the jungle, particularly the insects. At least the children had all appeared to be sleeping soundly when she'd finally turned in for the night.

It had taken a little while to get BanChuen settled down. She had been a bit lethargic much of the day, and Joan had wondered if she might be coming down with something, too, causing her to think that perhaps the ill workers were contagious after all. But it had turned out to be a lingering sadness, a sort of "Lawan-sickness," as she missed the girl who had become like an older sister to her during the girl's brief time at the orphanage.

Joan sighed. She too still missed Lawan, and she had promised BanChuen to help her write a letter to Lawan the following day. With that assurance, BanChuen had finally closed her eyes and drifted off to sleep—unlike Joan, who had thought she would fall asleep as quickly as Mort.

*Afraid not,* she mused. *Why is it the more tired I get, the harder it is for me to get to sleep? Way too much on my mind, I suppose.*

And then she remembered what she told the children when they had trouble sleeping at night. "When you can't get to sleep and someone is on your mind, perhaps God wants you to pray for that person."

Hmm . . . Perhaps indeed.

She closed her eyes and focused on the beautiful girl who had been forced to grow up in the most violent and depraved ways imaginable, and began to pray that God would bring healing to her heart and help her adjust to her new life. Joan knew it wouldn't happen quickly or easily, but she knew God's love could heal anything or anyone—and that's what she was counting on, even as she imagined that Lawan was at that very moment celebrating the morning after her first Thanksgiving holiday. What was she doing? Having breakfast with her new family, no doubt. And that, Joan decided, was surely a good beginning.

Mara was so glad that Mariner's was open again and that she had volunteered to work the rest of the weekend. Other employees wanted the days following Thanksgiving off, but someone had to be on duty to feed the weekend visitors—and the San Diego area would be inundated with them over the four-day holiday.

She was up early and walking to the café long before she needed to do so, anxious to get some cool morning air to clear her head and get her blood moving. She'd happily work a double shift if they'd let her. After all, she could use the money, especially the tips, and she sure didn't want to spend any more hours than necessary stuck in her room, reminiscing about the previous day.

*Would it have been better if I'd somehow ended up spending the day with Jonathan and his family?* The thought rolled around in her head as she crossed the quiet side street that led to the shoreline. Since she had plenty of time she might as well take the long way to work and enjoy the scenery. Besides, she had time for a quick cup of coffee and a bagel, and there was nowhere she'd rather consume them than on the seawall, watching the breakers roll in and the early-morning surfers showing off their skills.

By the time she'd retrieved her breakfast and perched atop the wall, relishing in the winter sun that warmed her face as she tilted her head upward, she'd decided the day would most certainly not have been better with Jonathan. Who was she kidding? No matter how interested he seemed, he couldn't possibly have serious intentions toward her. A future between a Bible college student from a preacher's family and a girl who had been forced into sexual slavery for the majority of her life? Ha! What were the chances?

*Zero and none*, she told herself, taking a swig of hot coffee. *And that's just where I'm going to leave it. Why set myself up for any more heartache? Haven't I had enough for one lifetime? How crazy would I have to be to sign up for more?*

She shook her head. No. No more daydreams about her knight in shining armor. He'd shown up once and rescued her. Wonderful. He would always be her hero. But that was it. She would not allow herself to imagine him as anything more. She had her freedom now, and her future was in her hands—no one else's. Not Jonathan's, not her *tio's*—and certainly not God's. She was the master of her own fate at last, and nothing, or no one, was going to steer her off course.

# Chapter 16

Nyesha helped Kyle clear the breakfast dishes from the table as she listened to the sounds of her two daughters trooping down the hallway toward their room.

"Two daughters," she said aloud, opening the dishwasher door. "We have two daughters now."

Kyle frowned. "Is that supposed to be a news flash?" He grinned as he rinsed dishes before placing them in the racks. "Is this the first time you took a head count?"

Nyesha swished a dishtowel at him playfully. "Very funny, Einstein. I just meant that I'm still getting used to it. We went from an empty nest a few years ago to one daughter, and now we have two. That those two daughters really are sisters is no small coincidence."

"No 'co-inkidinks' with God, remember?"

Nyesha nodded. "Absolutely not. I know God purposed for those two girls to be reunited, and I couldn't be happier that He chose us to raise them. But . . . " She sighed and shook her head. "I think we have a lot more baggage with Lawan than we did with Anna."

Kyle shut the water off and gave her his full attention. "You're not surprised by that, are you? We did talk about that before she came."

Nyesha nodded again. "I know. And how could the poor child not have baggage after the horrible things she's been through?"

She swiped at the tears that had sprung to her eyes. "When I think about what those people did to her . . ."

Kyle reached out and pulled her against his chest. "I know," he whispered. "I think about it myself, but I try not to dwell on it. It I do, it'll make me crazy. I want to choke somebody—or at least smash them in the face."

"How is it possible that adults can convince themselves that treating children that way is OK?" She sobbed into her husband's chest, glad for the strength of his arms around her. "It's not OK," she cried. "It is absolutely not OK!"

Kyle patted her shoulder and stroked her hair. "I know, baby. I know."

After a moment she said, "Remember how we talked about naming her Alisha? How we'd have two daughters, two sisters named Anna Mali and Alisha Lawan?" She shook her head. "We can't do that to her, you know. At least not for a long time. It's not like it was with Anna. Lawan isn't a toddler. She's a not-quite-eleven-year-old girl who has been raped and abused for two years of her life and then told her parents are dead. She watched her older sister die in the room they shared at a brothel. How can we ever hope for her to have a normal life?"

"Shh," Kyle whispered. "We can love her and be patient. That's all we can do. And pray. Only God can heal her, you know. We just provide a place for Him to work. There's nothing too hard for Him, remember?"

Nyesha sighed and nodded. "I know that's true," she whispered. "But all I could do last night was hold her and cry with her."

"I imagine that's all God wanted you to do," Kyle said. "I believe that's exactly what that brokenhearted little girl needed. And God used you to give it to her."

Gratitude flooded Nyesha's heart, as she thought for perhaps the millionth time how God had given her just the husband she needed to be her partner in this life. "Thank You," she said, not minding that Kyle would attribute her gratitude to himself. "I love you," she added, this time speaking directly to him.

"I love you, too, beautiful lady," he said. "And don't you ever doubt that God knew exactly what He was doing when He placed that wounded child here in our home. It wasn't just to reunite those two sisters; it was also because He knew you would be the perfect mother for both of them. I'm just glad I'm your husband so I can be a part of this miracle myself."

Jonathan couldn't help but notice how withdrawn Sarah had been all morning. Even though she'd joined Leah and Rosanna in the kitchen to make a big breakfast of waffles and bacon for everyone, she barely touched her food after they all sat down to eat.

*It's my fault,* Jonathan thought, irritated with himself for handling things so poorly the night before. True, he'd been surprised and even uncomfortable when she'd come out to join him in the backyard, but the way he'd retreated without so much as a gracious exit or even the slightest attempt at an explanation had no doubt left the poor girl feeling rejected and embarrassed. Should he try to make it up to her, or would any effort on his part just compound the problem?

Realizing that he, too, was toying with his food, he popped a piece of syrup-dripping bacon in his mouth and dared a glance at the dejected blonde across the table. He couldn't remember when he'd seen her so quiet, despite the fact that Leah was chattering at her usual ninety-mile-an-hour pace, with Rosanna responding on occasion and even Michael Flannery grunting now and then between bites.

He forced a smile and waited for a chance to jump in. "So," he said, a forkful of waffles hovering between his plate and mouth, "anyone up for a ride to the beach today?"

Leah blinked as a frown puckered her forehead. Obviously she hadn't seen that one coming. His parents both raised their eyebrows in surprise, but it was Sarah who reacted most visibly. Her blue eyes widened as color rose to her cheeks, and it appeared for a moment that she would choke on the orange juice she'd just sipped from her glass. But she swallowed and recovered quickly. "I am," she said, and then her color deepened as she cut her eyes to Leah. "That is, if you are. Unless . . . you have something else you'd rather do."

Her words ended in more of a question than a statement, and it was obvious that Leah had caught on to her friend's unspoken request nearly as quickly as Jonathan did. Uh oh. He had meant his invitation to come out as being for the entire family, or at least for both the girls, but something told him he'd just landed himself in a twosome for the day.

"You two go ahead," Leah said. "I'm beat from yesterday. I think I'll just stay home and kick back today."

A glance between Jonathan's parents told him they, too, suspected that their son and Sarah wanted a chance for some time alone together, so they weren't going to be any help.

"I have things to do too," Rosanna said. "Lots of things to catch up on. I think I'll pass."

Michael nodded. "Me too. The beach will be crowded today. I'd rather just stay here with your mother." He smiled, his green eyes sparkling as if he'd just discovered a wonderful secret. "You two go ahead. Pack some turkey sandwiches and make a day of it."

Jonathan's heart sank. How had things gone so wrong so fast? He just wanted to make up to Sarah for hurting her; now he was in danger of causing everyone in the room to think he had a romantic interest in her.

When was he going to learn to keep his big mouth shut? He sighed. It was too late now. Leah and Sarah were already jumping up from the table, yammering about making sandwiches and filling the thermos with iced tea. He might as well just keep smiling and make the best of it.

Business had been slow all morning, and Mara was more than ready for a lunch break, even though she wasn't very hungry. She grabbed a fish sandwich and stuffed it in a bag to carry with her. All she really wanted to do was get some air and some midday sunshine, and she didn't know anywhere better to do that than the boardwalk.

The occasional call of a seagull circling overhead blended with the sounds of holiday traffic and children squealing as they darted in and out of the frigid Pacific waters. But Mara scarcely noticed. She walked at a leisurely pace and let the sun warm her face, her sandwich still waiting for her to find the perfect spot for a short rest. An empty bench under a very tall palm tree seemed to have her name on it, so she plunked down with her back to the traffic, facing the ocean.

She smiled at the thought of the conversation she'd had with the cook that morning. Stephen was from New York and said his favorite thing about living in California was wintertime. He loved being able to go outside on the day after Thanksgiving without a jacket while all his relatives back east were shoveling snow and drinking hot cider.

As a light bead of sweat trickled between her eyes, she knew Stephen was right. There she sat, watching a middle-aged couple stroll along the wet sand, carrying their shoes in their hands, and it was almost December. Of course, Mara had never lived in a climate that had cold winters, but listening to Stephen decry the many inconveniences of doing so, she was sure she never wanted to try it.

The somewhat familiar sound of what she imagined to be an older car pulled up behind her, but she resisted the temptation to turn and look. There were lots of cars that made that sort of noise. Besides, the last person in the world she expected or even hoped to see at that moment was Jonathan Flannery.

She opened her bag and pulled out her sandwich, taking her time as she unwrapped it, stopping to push a stray lock of hair from her eyes. The ocean breeze pushed it right back, and this time she ignored it, pausing instead to listen to snippets of a conversation behind her.

"Looks like a good spot."

"Yeah. Not too crowded."

A girl's giggle blocked out the next words, but Mara would know the sound of the male voice anywhere.

*Jonathan. It's him! What's he doing here?*

Once again resisting the urge to turn around, she stared straight ahead as the voices drew nearer.

"I'm starved, aren't you?"

She thought her heart would explode from her chest when Jonathan answered. "That's because you didn't eat your breakfast. I had two waffles plus a boatload of bacon, remember? Still, I have to admit, those turkey sandwiches are calling my name."

Tears bit Mara's eyes, and she hated herself for it. Oh, how she hoped they would walk by without spotting her. Maybe if she sat very still . . .

In seconds the two passed by her, apparently oblivious to her presence. So why didn't she feel relieved? *I'm invisible,* she thought. *It's what I wanted, but you'd think he would at least have noticed.*

When she was sure they had moved far enough that they wouldn't turn and see her, she shoved the sandwich back in her bag and hurried from the bench back to the boardwalk. If she'd ever had any doubts that she was doing the right thing by avoiding Jonathan Flannery, they were gone now. What a fool she'd been to think he was interested in her in the first place! Quite obviously he already had a girlfriend — one much more suited to him and his lifestyle. One he didn't have to be ashamed of.

Still blinking back tears, she made it back to Mariner's in record time.

# Chapter 17

In spite of his misgivings, Jonathan was pleasantly surprised to discover that he was actually enjoying his picnic at the beach with Sarah—though he couldn't deny that he would have liked it better if Mara was with him.

*But she's not,* he reminded himself. *She's just not interested in you, so get over it.*

He bit into the turkey sandwich that Sarah had unwrapped and handed to him minutes earlier, his eyes focused on a couple of preteen boys slipping and sliding on boogie boards at the surf's edge. *Admit it, dude. Mara blows you off every time you see her. I mean, it's not like she even tries to be subtle or anything. She's just flat not into you. Is that really all that hard to figure out?*

"Iced tea?"

Sarah's voice cut into his thoughts, and he blinked and turned his gaze toward the blonde sitting across the blanket from him. The midday sun shone on her hair, turning it to gold, and her smile was warm. The plastic tumbler she held out to him trembled only slightly in her hand.

"Thanks," he said, taking the drink but being careful not to touch her in the process. He smiled his gratitude and quickly turned his attention back to the action on the beach.

"We have chips too," Sarah said, "and cookies."

Jonathan nodded, still watching the boys. "Maybe later," he said, determined not to show more interest than the situation warranted. He was just out with his sister's friend, that's it. In fact, he wouldn't be here at all if he hadn't been trapped into it at the breakfast table. It wouldn't be fair to her to give her false hope that there was anything else involved in his gesture.

They munched their sandwiches in silence for a few moments, the distant sound of surf and seagulls and children at play blending with the warmth of the sun to dull Jonathan's senses. When he found his eyes growing heavy, he decided it was time to get up and get his blood moving before the gulls mistook him for a sand sculpture.

"I'm going for a walk," he announced, standing to his feet. "I won't be long."

Sarah was on her feet before he could take the first step. "I'll go with you."

The smile on her face and the light in her eyes was more than Jonathan could withstand. "Sure," he said, shrugging. "Why not? But we should put this food away first. I'll help you."

When everything was safely stowed back in the picnic basket, they set out for the packed, wet sand of the shoreline where walking was easier. It wasn't until Sarah slipped her hand into his that Jonathan realized just how big a mistake he'd made when he let himself get hijacked into this day at the beach.

~∞~

With Jonathan and Sarah gone and Michael at the church catching up on a few odds and ends before the weekend, Rosanna had decided to serve lunch outside on the patio. She set the redwood picnic table for two and brought out an identical lunch to the one she had helped pack for Sarah and Jonathan earlier.

"Got everything?" Leah asked as she followed her mother outside with the pitcher of iced tea and glasses.

"Looks that way," Rosanna said, seating herself on one side of the table while Leah straddled the bench opposite her. "Hungry?"

Leah grinned, her red hair aflame in the sunlight. "I didn't think I would be after all that breakfast I ate, but there's something about leftover turkey sandwiches."

Rosanna returned her daughter's smile. "So true," she agreed, reaching across the table. "Would you like to pray before we eat?"

Leah took her hand, and Rosanna couldn't help but notice how young and smooth the girl's skin felt. Had it really been more than twenty years since she had that youthful feel about her—before endless dishes and midnight feedings and toilet scrubbing took their toll?

She continued to smile as Leah prayed, knowing she wouldn't have it any other way. Even as she offered an "amen" to her daughter's brief prayer, she silently added a thank You to the Lord for the many blessings He had bestowed upon her and her family over the years. Dishpan hands were a small price to pay for the many joys they had shared.

"What do you think Jonathan and Sarah are doing right now?" Leah asked, reaching for a half sandwich from the platter in the middle of the table.

Rosanna raised her eyebrows. She had wondered the same thing more than once since the two of them had set out in Jonathan's old blue Beetle. "Who knows? I imagine they're devouring that lunch we packed for them." She chuckled. "I think we overdid it, don't you? I know Jonathan has a good appetite, but even he can only eat so much."

Leah laughed. "We made enough for an army, didn't we?" She took another bite and waited until she'd swallowed to speak again. Her smile was gone now, and her eyes had taken on a more serious expression.

"Do you think anything will ever happen between those two? I mean, I know Sarah has a serious crush on Jonathan, but he's always insisted he doesn't feel that way about her."

Rosanna studied her daughter. She appeared genuinely concerned, and she imagined it was about her friend's feelings. "I don't know," Rosanna answered honestly. "I wish I did. And I must admit, Sarah is a lovely girl. I've always considered her part of the family anyway, so I wouldn't really have any objections if the two of them did end up getting together at some point. But . . ."

Leah's eyebrows shot up. "But?"

Rosanna sighed. "But I'm not sure Sarah is nearly serious enough about her walk with the Lord to be a good partner for Jonathan. That could change, of course, and I hope it does, whether anything further comes of their friendship or not. But right now . . ."

Leah nodded. "I've been thinking the same thing. And I sure don't want either one of them to get hurt over this."

"Nor do I." Rosanna set her uneaten sandwich down on her paper plate. "But all we can do is pray about it and leave it in God's hands. Only He knows."

Leah's smile was tight as she nodded again. "I've been doing that—praying about it, I mean. You have too, right?"

"Right." Rosanna reached across the table. "Maybe it's time we joined forces. You know what the Scriptures say about two or more agreeing together in prayer in Jesus' name."

Once again Leah took her mother's hands, and they began to pray about a situation involving two people they both loved very much.

Jonathan kept the walk as short as he could without risking yet another insult or hurt feelings for Sarah. He was still beating himself up over the way he'd handled that scenario the night before, and he certainly didn't want a repeat. As a result he allowed Sarah's hand to remain in his until they got to a place that would serve as a natural turnaround spot. To continue on would have required climbing over sand dunes and a rocky jetty, so instead he turned a full 180 degrees as casually as possible, dropping Sarah's hand in the process.

"Ready to go back?" he asked.

She shrugged, her smile tentative. "Sure. I guess so."

He took a step and she did the same. As they strolled back past the people and landmarks they had passed just moments earlier, Jonathan found himself praying for wisdom. *How do I discourage her interest in me without hurting her feelings?* he asked, somehow hoping for an immediate and audible answer.

None came. He sighed and continued on in silence, being careful to keep his arms close to his side and maintaining enough distance between them that she couldn't easily reach over and grab his hand again.

"It's beautiful here, isn't it?"

Sarah's question pulled his attention from the immediate problem, and he nodded, his eyes still straight ahead. "It is," he agreed. "I've always liked this beach. Not quite as crowded as some a little further north."

"I'm glad you brought me here." She paused, as if waiting for Jonathan to respond, but he couldn't think of anything safe to say.

"I . . . never thought you'd want to have a picnic with me," Sarah said. "But I'm glad you did."

Another statement requiring a response, but again Jonathan opted for silence, even as he scolded himself for being a coward.

Wouldn't it be kinder to just jump in and let her know there was no chance — none — for a future for the two of them? For Pete's sake, it's not like there was . . . was there?

He dared a quick glance at the girl who walked beside him and had to admit that she was fast becoming more of a woman than a girl. Did he wrestle with seeing her as a woman just because he'd known her for so long and always considered her just another little sister?

Quickly averting his eyes before she caught him looking at her, he decided their past relationship certainly did have a lot to do with the way he viewed her now. But he knew it also had a lot to do with a certain young woman with hazel eyes and golden brown skin who called to his heart despite the fact that she refused to have anything to do with him. When was he going to learn? Why couldn't he enjoy a casual relationship with a nice girl like Sarah, and if it turned into something, fine. If not . . .

If not, what? Sarah would be hurt even more than if he ended it right now, nipped it in the bud, as the saying went, before it had time to bloom. Was that the right thing to do? Was he jumping to conclusions, assuming that God's will was for him to dismiss even the possibility of a relationship with Sarah? What if God's plan and purpose for his life included Sarah? She might not be a strong believer, but at least she was a Christian . . . unlike Mara.

He sighed. *It sure would be easier if You'd just give me a clear-cut yes or no, Father,* he prayed silently. *But I guess You're not going to do that, are You?*

Jonathan had barely finished the thought when Sarah somehow found a way to breach the divide between them and once again slip her hand into his. Her skin was soft and warm, and he was surprised that his own palm immediately began to sweat. Was it just from the sun overhead . . . or could it be at least some level of interest in the girl who so obviously wanted to explore a future with him?

Maybe there was only one way to find out after all. Jonathan wasn't ready to make a commitment to pursue that possible relationship, but he decided he was at least willing to consider it—and to continue praying about it.

# Chapter 18

B y the time Mara got off work the sun was just edging toward the horizon, ready to disappear for the night, despite the fact that it was only five o'clock. Mara appreciated the mild temperatures so prominent throughout all the seasons in the San Diego area, but she did miss the longer daylight hours of summer, particularly when she had to walk home alone.

*Another good reason to opt for the early shift at work,* she reminded herself, though she'd never been much of an early bird. Sadly, most of her so-called work throughout her growing-up years was done late in the day and during the night hours, often not coming to an end until nearly sunup. No wonder she wasn't an early riser!

But she had a real job now, she reminded herself, one where she actually had input regarding the hours she worked. Though her boss had the final say, he always asked his employees what shifts they preferred. In the beginning Mara had chosen the dinner crowd because they usually tipped better and she was able to sleep in each morning. But after the episode she'd had a few months earlier when her *tio's* hired goon, known as Alleycat, had kidnapped and nearly killed her one dark night as she was leaving work alone, she tended to opt for the early shift whenever she could get it.

A cool breeze caught her off-guard as she rounded the corner, headed for home. She pulled her jacket tighter and picked up her pace. Only a couple more blocks and she'd be safe and warm in her room, and right now that sounded really good.

She'd gone only a few more steps when she heard the familiar car motor once again, and this time she didn't try to convince herself that it was someone other than Jonathan. Had he been at the beach with that girl all day? The thought nipped at the edges of her heart, but she pushed it from her mind.

*What do I care? It's not like he means anything to me. Sure, he helped save my life, but that's it. End of story. So what if he has a cute little blonde girlfriend? Why wouldn't he, anyway? He probably has a ton of other ones back at school. Just because he wrote to me a few times while he was gone . . .*

She turned her head just in time to see the familiar blue VW chug by on the street behind her, right where she'd been walking a moment earlier. Thank goodness she'd already turned the corner and they didn't see her! The last thing she wanted was to be forced into a polite conversation with Jonathan while he was with his girlfriend.

The tears that had plagued her earlier when she saw the couple at the beach now threatened her once again, but she steeled her heart as she had learned to do over the years and forged ahead. This was no time to give in to sentimentality. She had to stay focused on her future, and there was no way Jonathan Flannery would be involved in it — even if he wanted to be. And quite obviously he did not.

There were days when Francesca wondered if she would explode if her stomach stretched any tighter. This cool November evening was no exception, as she sat on the rickety porch of her parents' small but comfortable home in the poor, rural community where she'd grown up, and listened to the crickets and frogs that were just starting their nighttime symphony. How she had missed these familiar sounds during the months of her captivity! And how grateful she was to God for rescuing her from that horrible life and restoring her to her family. Her parents were completely supportive and accepting of her situation, understanding that she'd had nothing to say about the condition she now found herself in and allowing her to make the final decision.

The fifteen-year-old had adjusted to the idea that she was carrying a child whose father would probably never be known to her, but she still hadn't been able to decide for certain whether to keep the baby and try to raise it with her parents' help—or give it up for adoption. How could she ever make such a decision?

*Giving my baby up would be the most unselfish thing to do,* she reasoned for what seemed the millionth time. *There are wealthy people who can't have children and who would give my little one such a better life than I could ever dream of doing. But . . .*

The thought of never holding her baby in her arms, not watching him or her start school or attend church or play with friends was nearly more than she could bear, but she also realized those were selfish reasons and therefore not the sort of reasons to justify her decision.

*I must decide soon,* she reminded herself. *The baby could be born any day, though the doctor thinks not for a couple of weeks or so.* She rubbed her swollen stomach and wondered how she could possibly get any bigger. But she could not depend on those extra weeks; she must decide now, tonight if possible. The choice must be made before the pains her mama had told her about began, or she knew it would be too late. But all she could think about at the moment was how empty their *casita* would be if her little one lived somewhere else.

*Mara,* she thought. *How I wish she lived closer so we could talk! Maybe I could write her a letter, tell her how I feel and what I'm thinking. Even if she didn't answer me in time, it might help to write it all down.*

Hoisting herself from the wooden chair that creaked at her effort, she slid her swollen feet into her *huaraches* and shuffled into the house to find a pen and some paper.

Jonathan had been more than slightly surprised when he realized he and Sarah had sat on their blanket, talking and eating until the sun was nearly down. It was the cool ocean breeze, ruffling their napkins and nearly sending their paper plates flying that finally got his attention.

"Hey, it's getting kind of late," he'd said, quickly gathering up the remnants of their second picnic meal of the day. "We'd better get back."

Sarah's face glowed, her cheeks pink and her short blonde hair tossing in the wind. "I'm not in any hurry," she said. "And besides, we have jackets in the car, remember? Your mom insisted that we bring them."

Jonathan chuckled. "Yeah, why am I not surprised that Mom would do that? But we've been here long enough, don't you think?" He glanced around. "We're practically the only ones still here."

She smiled and laid a hand on his arm. "Is that so bad?"

Jonathan felt the blood rush to his cheeks and tried to shrug it off. "Not at all," he answered, ignoring her hand and continuing to fill the picnic basket. "I just think we should go, that's all."

"OK," Sarah said, joining him in his packing-up pursuit. "But does that mean we have to go straight home? Couldn't we . . . go somewhere else?"

Jonathan stopped stuffing the basket and looked up at her. "What do you have in mind?"

Even in the fading light, he knew it was her turn to blush, and he had to admit that it looked good on her.

"Nothing really," she said. "Just . . . anywhere." Her lips spread in a smile that was both sweet and inviting. "As long as we're together."

Jonathan swallowed. Though he'd told himself he would at least consider the possibility of exploring a relationship with Sarah, he wasn't ready to move quite this fast. He'd better set some parameters . . . fast.

"How about that place that has the great sundaes?"

Her smile widened. "That would be perfect! I'd love it."

He nodded and resumed his task, keeping his eyes turned from hers. "Good. It's a date then. Let's get out of here and go pig out on hot fudge."

She'd giggled as they carried their blanket and food basket back to the car and loaded up. He really wasn't hungry for ice cream—or anything, for that matter—but it was a safe way to end their day.

He started the car, tapped the accelerator, and then gunned it as they jerked forward from their parking space and out into the road. He just wished the nearest route didn't take them within a couple blocks of Mara's place. True, he could take the longer way, but part of him wanted to drive as close as possible to where he imagined Mara to be at this moment—either working at Mariner's or at home, or possibly even somewhere in between.

As they passed the corner where he would have had to turn if he were heading to Mara's place, he'd looked down the street just long enough to see a young woman glance in his direction. Could it be?

Nah. He was imagining things. What were the chances that he'd be thinking of her walking down that very street and then look up and see her? Astronomical. Surely it was someone else who resembled her.

He sighed and turned his eyes back to the road in front of him. One thing was certain. If Sarah hadn't been with him, he would have turned down that road and found out for sure whether or not the woman he'd seen was Mara. And if it had been? As much as he hated to admit it and even knowing that she would no doubt have rejected him one more time, he would have stopped and done his best to convince her to go for a ride with him. Sarah was a nice girl, a cute and sweet young woman who was crazy about him, but he would much rather be on his way to share an ice cream sundae with Mara.

But of course he wasn't. And so he flashed a smile at Sarah and continued on his way.

# Chapter 19

Leah had been in bed — though not even close to sleeping — for nearly an hour when she finally heard the front door open, ushering in hushed voices and muffled laughter. She glanced at the digital clock beside her bed. Nearly eleven! It seemed her big brother and best friend had enjoyed a very long day together.

Resisting the urge to rush downstairs and confront them, she remained where she was, straining to listen but not able to discern any specific words. The tone, however, came through loud and clear. The two people downstairs were interacting much more like a couple than two platonic friends, and Leah wasn't at all sure how she felt about that.

At last she heard the sound of two pairs of feet climbing the stairs. Even then there were muffled giggles and loud shushes, as the pair no doubt tried to sneak in without waking anyone.

*Fat chance of that,* she fumed, crossing her arms over her chest as she lay under the covers. *A picnic is one thing, but twelve hours? Puh-leeze!*

The bedroom door pushed open, slowly and almost silently, until Leah could make out her friend's silhouette. She watched Sarah tiptoe inside and close the door behind her, but before the girl could turn and make an attempt to creep into bed unnoticed, Leah reached up and flipped on the bedside lamp.

"Oh!" Sarah jerked her head up, her eyes wide and her cheeks flaming. "I didn't realize you were awake."

"No kidding," Leah answered, raising herself up and fluffing the pillows behind her as she settled in for some late-night girl talk. "Well, I am, and you're not going to sleep until I hear all about your day with my brother." She patted the side of the bed. "So sit . . . and talk."

Sarah's smile was hesitant as she nodded and complied, crossing the room to lower herself gently onto the side of the bed beside Leah. "OK," she said, her flushed cheeks and glistening eyes tinged only slightly by a hint of guilt. "What do you want to know?"

"Everything," Leah said, her heart softening a bit as she began to absorb some of her friend's excitement. "Absolutely everything. And don't you dare leave out one single detail."

Sarah's smile broadened. "All right, you asked for it. But it might take a while."

Leah returned the smile. "I've got all night, and I'm all ears."

～∞～

Jonathan had no sooner said goodnight to Sarah and secluded himself in his room than the guilt returned. What had he been thinking? He'd allowed himself to fall into "couple behavior" with Sarah, laughing and joking and talking nonstop about everything and nothing, while they shared a mountain-sized hot fudge sundae. Anyone watching them would have assumed they were an item, so how could he be surprised if Sarah came away with the same impression?

He flopped down onto his bed and sighed. If he'd never met Mara, never looked into those hazel pools and seen the grief and fear, as well as the hope and longing, maybe he could just pursue this thing with Sarah with abandon. If something came of it, fine. If not . . . well, it wouldn't be the first time in the history of the world.

But he had met Mara. He had looked into her eyes. And he had connected with her at a place so deep and intimate that he doubted he could ever really be free of her. At the same time, she had made it obvious, time and again, that she did not return his feelings or interest, so at some point he had to walk away . . . didn't he?

He reached up and turned off the bedside lamp, still lying fully clothed on top of the navy blue comforter. He crossed his legs at the ankles, reached up and put his hands under his head, interlacing his fingers, and whispered aloud to the One he knew lived inside him and yet, at the moment, seemed galaxies away.

131

"What should I do, Father? I'm so confused. You know me better than I do. You know the deepest things in my heart that I haven't even identified yet. Please show me, Lord. Please direct me and guide me to do the right thing. I don't want to hurt Sarah, but when I'm with her I'm able to forget Mara—at least, a little. And I really do have fun with Sarah. She's a great girl, and it's obvious she's crazy about me. Why, I can't imagine, but she is." Guilt caved in on him again, and he sighed. "But that's the very reason I don't want to encourage her if this thing isn't going to go anywhere. Is it, Lord? Can you just give me some sort of red light/green light sign or something? I mean, at least Sarah is a Christian, and maybe our relationship will draw her closer to You. Then again . . . what if I end up disappointing her and she goes in the opposite direction?"

He closed his eyes. Life was easier without girls, period. Lonelier? Sure. But definitely easier. And it would have been easier still if he just hadn't collided with Mara along the way.

*But if I hadn't, she might still be under her uncle's control in that awful place.* He frowned at the thought and opened his eyes to stare into the darkness. *Is that the only reason You brought me into her life, Father? Because if it is, that's enough. Really, it is. But could You please just help me to accept that and to get past these feelings I have for her? It would sure be a whole lot easier to have a relationship with Sarah—or anyone else—if I didn't already feel tied to Mara.*

He sighed again and kicked off his shoes, shoving them off the edge of the bed. It had been a long day, and things might seem a whole lot clearer after a good night's sleep.

Sarah couldn't stop grinning. She felt like an idiot, but she couldn't help it. Jonathan had spent nearly the entire day with her, and he'd even let her hold his hand! She'd dreamed of a day like this for years, and it had finally happened. And now Leah wanted to hear all about it. How much should she tell her? She was her best friend, after all, and Sarah was bursting to tell someone. Who better than the girl she'd known nearly her entire life?

"It was incredible," she said. "Absolutely amazing! From the time we left until we got home, it couldn't have been better. Jonathan was so sweet. He found the perfect spot at the beach, and after we ate lunch we went for a walk, and . . ." She ducked her head and felt the heat rise to her cheeks. But she raised her head again and looked straight into Leah's green eyes. "He held my hand."

Leah's eyebrows shot up. "He did? He actually took your hand and held it while you were walking?"

Sarah felt her blush deepen. "Well . . ." She swallowed. As much as she liked the way it sounded to say that Jonathan initiated the hand-holding, she knew it wasn't true, and she didn't want to lie to her best friend. "Not really," she admitted. "It was actually me that started it. But he didn't pull away or anything. He just kept walking like it was perfectly normal for us to be holding hands." She leaned forward and lowered her voice slightly. "His hand even started sweating a little after I grabbed it. Do you think that meant his heart was racing? Because mine sure was. I was so happy I thought I'd explode."

Leah's eyebrows lowered a notch. "I think you still might," she said, a smile teasing her lips. "I haven't seen you this excited since your dad got you that new puppy for Christmas."

Sarah laughed. "I was seven then. This is different. I've waited for this for so long, and now it's finally happening." She sighed deeply, relishing the memory of Jonathan's hand wrapped around hers. "And that's not all," she said. "We stayed at the beach almost until sunset, and then we went out for a seriously huge hot fudge sundae . . . which we shared, by the way."

133

Sarah paused, letting the impact of her statement sink in. Surely Leah understood that casual friends didn't take hand-holding walks and eat ice cream out of the same bowl. Her grin grew as she waited for Leah's response.

"Wow," her friend said at last. "Sounds like things might be heading in a serious direction with you two."

Sarah nodded. "I'm sure of it. I thought for a while that Jonathan was giving me the brush-off because of that other girl—you know, Mara—but now I think he was just trying to keep things from moving too fast. Today he just . . . let go, I guess. Let his feelings take over or something." She shrugged, still smiling. "Whatever the reason, it was wonderful." She took Leah's hands in hers and whispered, "He likes me, Leah. He really does. And not just as your friend or another little sister. I mean, he really likes me—like a girlfriend. Don't you think?"

Leah pressed her lips together and raised her eyebrows again before answering. At last she nodded. "I think it's possible. But . . . just don't move too fast, you know? I mean, Jonathan and I have to head back to school on Sunday, and I don't want you left behind with any false hopes or wrong impressions. You're my best friend, and I don't want you to be hurt."

Sarah frowned, the air in her balloon leaking only slightly. "What are you trying to tell me? Jonathan doesn't have a girlfriend back at school, does he?"

Leah shook her head. "No. Not that I know of anyway. But . . ." She shrugged. "I don't know. I just want both of you to take it slow, to be sure. . . ."

Sarah laughed. "Sure? Leah, I've never been more sure of anything in my life. I've been in love with Jonathan for years, but I kept it a secret because I didn't think there was any chance for me. But now . . ."

"But now," Leah interrupted, "now there is. OK, maybe so. Maybe there's a chance. But a chance and a sure thing aren't the same. You know that, right?"

Sarah nodded and nearly laughed again. "Of course I know it. But I also know this is going to work out between us. I've been praying about it for years, and I think God has finally answered my prayers."

The flicker of doubt in Leah's eyes pricked Sarah's heart for a split second, but she dismissed it as quickly as it came. She wasn't about to let anything or anyone — not even her best friend — steal her happiness about what was happening between her and Jonathan. At last Jonathan was going to realize how much she loved him and how perfect they would be together . . . and then he would love her back. That was really all Sarah wanted out of life, and it looked like it was just about to come true.

# Chapter 20

Saturday dawned bright and warm, another perfect Southern California winter morning. But Mara didn't even notice. When the alarm on her cell phone sounded, blasting her latest downloaded song, she punched it off and nearly rolled over and went back to sleep. Her eyes felt like she'd dipped them in maple syrup and they were determined to stay shut. Her head pounded and her heart was raw. But the worst part was her self-loathing. Why in the world had she given in to the tears when she hit the bed last night? What man in the entire world was worth crying over? Not one, she reminded herself—not even Jonathan Flannery.

But no matter how many times she had tried to convince herself of that fact as she lay in the dark, hugging her pillow, the tears had continued to pour out of her. Sobs wracked her body for what seemed hours, and now even her diaphragm was sore. Had she really cried so hard and so long just because she'd seen Jonathan with another girl? Or was it possible the event had just triggered all the tears she'd been holding in for so many years?

Knowing the latter was probably the case didn't make her feel any better, and a part of her considered calling in sick. But then she reconsidered. The idea of being alone with her pain all day was not a pleasant option. She immediately dragged herself from bed and headed for the shower. A busy day at Mariner's, even if she had to risk questions about her stuffy nose and red eyes, was better than staying here and risking yet more tears.

*I thought I was stronger than that,* she mused, reaching into the shower to turn on the faucet and adjust the temperature. *I survived things that would have killed some people — and did, as a matter of fact.* She banished the image of Jasmine that had popped into her mind and stepped into the shower, sighing at the sensation of the warm water pouring over her aching body. Lifting her head to the nozzle, she closed her eyes and allowed the stinging spray to punish her face.

From now one, she resolved, she would be more careful not to give in to that first teardrop. For after that, there seemed to be no stopping them.

Anna opened her eyes and blinked at the sunlight that already shone through the window. Before Lawan came to live with them, Anna kept her curtains closed so the sun wouldn't interrupt her sleep in the morning, but Lawan said she liked as much light in the room as possible. So as usual, their mother insisted they do whatever they could to make Lawan feel welcome.

Anna glanced across the room to Lawan's bed. The covers were thrown back, and it was empty. Anna sighed. When she woke up first, she always went straight to Lawan's bed and waited for a chance to say good morning. For some reason, Lawan didn't do the same for her. Sometimes Anna wondered if her sister just didn't like her, but then she thought it was probably because she missed the orphanage in Thailand and wasn't used to her new home and family yet.

Thailand. The name seemed so strange and far away. And yet Anna knew she had once lived there. Her parents had told her many times of how they had flown there to get her and bring her home to be their little girl, and she knew it was true. But she didn't remember the day it happened.

What she did remember—or at least, she thought she did—was a tiny room with a low ceiling. She was lying on her back on a pallet on the floor, with a sister sleeping on each side. One was slightly older than her, the other quite a bit older.

*Lawan and Chanthra,* she thought, wishing she could remember Chanthra's face. But the face she did remember was the one that belonged to the dark-haired woman who stood over their pallets, gazing down at them. Though the features were fuzzy, the expression of love was clear. Anna might be only five years old, and she knew that her parents told her she couldn't possibly remember anything from when she was so young, but she knew better. She knew the face that showed her so much love was her real mom—her *maae,* as Lawan called her.

Anna immediately felt guilty at the thought. She knew the woman who now raised her was her mother, and she was glad of it. Her American parents took good care of her, and she loved them very much. But she also knew she once had other parents, and one day she planned to ask Lawan to tell her all about them.

Lawan. Anna untangled herself from her covers and jumped from her bed, determined to find her sister and tell her good morning. What would they do today? And then Anna remembered that her daddy was off for two more days. The whole family would be together, and that meant they would probably do something special.

Racing to the bedroom door, she yanked it open and rushed down the hallway to the kitchen, where the sound of voices greeted her before she even arrived.

❧

Lawan sat quietly at the kitchen table, between the two people who were considered her new parents. She awoke early and followed the rumblings of her stomach to the kitchen, pleased that Anna was still asleep. That meant her parents would ask her what she'd like for breakfast and then give her whatever she desired, rather than going with Anna's wishes. As a result, Lawan was contentedly munching a bowl of cereal, entering into the conversation only when absolutely necessary. And then Anna blew in through the doorway, her dark hair tousled and her eyes bright.

"There you are," she said, racing straight toward Lawan. "I woke up and you were gone."

Lawan held her spoon full of milk-dripping cereal halfway between the bowl and her mouth. How was she supposed to respond to such a greeting? It was almost as if Anna were accusing her of doing something wrong, of leaving their room without permission. Lawan realized that probably wasn't what Anna meant, but it pricked her irritation level nonetheless.

"I woke up early," she said, and then crammed the full spoon into her mouth as if she had said enough to satisfy her little sister. Apparently not.

"Why didn't you wake me up?" Anna demanded, standing beside her now and raising her beautiful dark eyes toward Lawan. "I always wake you up."

Lawan knew that was true and had wished sometimes it weren't. She offered a tight smile, even as she continued to chew, and shrugged. When Anna continued to stare at her and it was obvious she wanted an explanation, Lawan swallowed.

"I thought you wanted to sleep," she said, wondering why they were even having such a conversation.

Anna shook her head. "Not when you're awake." She grinned and turned to her mother first, and then her father, before looking back at Lawan. "But now we're all up," she announced, clapping her hands. "And we're all here. What are we going to do today?"

Both adults broke into laughter, and even Lawan had to resist the urge to join them. How could she stay annoyed with her little sister, her only remaining relative, particularly when she was so cute and spontaneous?

"I guess we'll have to think of something really special," the man named Kyle said as he reached down to pull Anna onto his lap. "Any ideas?"

"The zoo!"

Kyle laughed again and shook his head. "Don't you think we should take your sister somewhere else? She's only been here a few days, and already she's seen all the animals at the zoo. I know that's your favorite place, but there are a lot of other things to see and do around here. How about the park?"

Anna squealed and clapped her hands again. "Yay! The park! I love the park!"

As plans progressed for the day, Lawan continued to eat her cereal, nodding or speaking only if necessary. It didn't really matter where they went today, the park or otherwise. But she did find it surprising that Americans seemed to need to go somewhere or do something all the time. Most days in Thailand were spent working, hoping for enough food and adequate shelter by nightfall.

Unless, of course, you were kidnapped and thrown into a brothel. Then being hungry and sleeping on the street didn't really sound all that bad. In fact, there had been many nights when Lawan dreamed of living on the street, begging for food, if only she didn't have to entertain one more customer.

# Chapter 21

nother warm winter day in California. Jefe almost found himself wishing for a storm just to break the monotony. Then again, on the few days when the weather was bad, they didn't get to go out in the yard. Spending all day in a tiny room with bars on the windows and doors and no one but your cellie for company was not a good way to spend the endless hours of prison life.

*Especially when your cellie is named Feo*, Jefe smirked silently, glancing across the basketball court that separated him from the heavyset but muscular man with the scarred face and bald head, aptly named for his looks—Feo or Ugly. Jefe had to admit that most of the gang or street names bestowed upon the people he knew—himself included—were appropriate either for their looks or personality.

*And I'm no exception. I didn't get the name Jefe for nothing. I worked hard, and I earned it. I was the boss on the outside, and I'm the boss in here. And nobody better forget it.*

His gaze shifted from Feo to El Gato, hanging out with his homies on the opposite side of the yard. Gangs and races usually stuck to themselves in prison, establishing their territory early on and not violating those boundaries without expecting a fight. Jefe knew there would be a fight—a bloody one—if El Gato crossed the boundaries and tried to encroach on his territory. Jefe also knew that El Gato knew this, so if the interloper ever made a move, it was because he not only expected but was prepared for battle.

*I'll never go down without taking someone with me,* Jefe vowed silently, watching the wiry man who had a reputation for moving swiftly and acting cunningly, just like the animal he was named for. *El Gato better be ready because the minute he even looks like he's going to violate my space, he's done.*

As if reading Jefe's thoughts, El Gato raised his head and locked his eyes on the older man looking in his direction. Neither flinched or dropped his gaze until the horn blasted through the loud speakers, signaling the end of yard time. With one last silent threat, the two men sent messages across the dividing line of their respective turf, and then turned to follow the others back inside.

"More football?"

Rosanna stood in the doorway to the family room, her hands on her hips as she confronted the two men in her family. She'd known long before the weekend arrived that whatever time wasn't spent eating would be devoted to football, but she liked to tease them about it anyway.

Michael's face registered surprise and innocence as he gazed up at her from the recliner, though Rosanna knew both were feigned. "Did you have something else you wanted to do today?" he asked. "Because Jonathan and I can shut the TV off anytime you want and take you girls somewhere. You name it; we're at your disposal."

Rosanna chuckled. "Laying it on a little thick, aren't you?" She approached the recliner and eased down onto the arm. "Do you really want me to believe that you'd give up a football game without a fight?"

Michael grinned. "It's a college game," he said, his expression morphing to sheepish. "We have two kids in college. Shouldn't we support them?"

Rosanna laughed out loud. "Their college isn't even playing!"

Jonathan's laugh joined hers. "She's right, Dad. I really think you're going to have to do better than that."

Michael turned toward his son. "A lot of help you are," he said. "You're supposed to jump in when you hear me going down for the count like that. Now we might be doomed."

"Doomed to what?"

The question from the doorway drew the attention of all three of them toward Sarah and Leah, who stood watching them. The words had come from Leah, whose eyes cut from one to the other of them, while Sarah's gazed only at Jonathan.

"To leave our football game and go do something else," Michael explained.

"Oh, no way," Sarah gushed, hurrying from the doorway to the couch and plopping down in the center, right next to Jonathan. "I love to watch football. Who's playing?"

Jonathan's grin spread slowly but genuinely as he apparently processed Sarah's comment. "You like football? I didn't know that."

Sarah's smile was reserved only for him as she looked into his eyes and said, "There are all sorts of things you don't know about me . . . yet. But you'll learn."

Rosanna felt her cheeks grow warm, as if she'd been eavesdropping on a private conversation. Clearing her throat, she jumped up from the arm of Michael's chair and announced, "Well, since it appears we're all going to be watching football, I may as well get some chips and drinks to tide us over until dinner."

"I'll help you," Leah answered.

Rosanna exited the room with her daughter following. She couldn't help but notice that Sarah hadn't offered to help, instead remaining like a star-struck fan beside her hero. She sighed. There seemed to be a romance brewing in their house, whether they liked it or not. And right now, she wasn't quite sure which way she felt about it.

What Mariner's had lacked in business on Friday, they more than made up for Saturday. The stream of customers had appeared never-ending, and before she knew it Mara had worked right through her lunch break. When things finally slowed down midafternoon, the cook called to her as she headed toward the restroom.

"Looks like a break in the crowd out there," Stephen said. "Why don't you take advantage of it and grab something to eat while you've got the chance?"

Mara glanced at her watch. He was right. She still had three hours until she got off, but she'd skipped breakfast that morning and her stomach was rumbling. She nodded. "Think I'll take you up on that," she said.

"Take this," Stephen offered, wrapping a ham sandwich in cellophane and handing it to her. "I thought you might be sick of turkey by now."

Mara smiled. He was right. Barbara had sent enough turkey home with her to last a lifetime, and she was more than ready for something else. She thanked him and took the sandwich, grateful that no one had pointed out to her how terrible she looked when she came in that morning. Maybe she'd make it through the day after all.

Once outside in the early afternoon sunshine, she squinted until she'd retrieved her sunglasses from her purse and put them on. Should she take a chance and head toward the beach, as she usually did? Surely Jonathan wouldn't be in the same place two days in a row. Still, there was no sense taking chances. Besides, she wasn't up for the emotional reminder right now.

Instead she turned in the opposite direction, where she seldom went but where she doubted there was any chance of running into Jonathan or his blonde friend. It was actually quite a bit more secluded and quiet this side of the café anyway, so why not?

She walked a few blocks and then scouted the area for a good place to sit down and eat. That's when she saw the church. She imagined she'd seen it before, as it was rather large and in plain sight, but this time it seemed to jump out at her. And the doors were open.

Without really knowing why, she approached the entrance and peered inside. It was quiet and empty and nearly dark. She knew it wouldn't be right to sit down in a pew and eat her lunch in such a place, but maybe it wouldn't hurt to just slip into a back row and think for a few minutes.

The next thing she knew she was sitting on a hard wooden bench, her sandwich forgotten beside her purse. Candles flickered in front of the church, and a plain wooden cross decorated the wall, directly in her line of sight. Though she told herself she didn't really believe in God, she did find herself wondering if it would be all right to pray.

*But what would I pray about?* she wondered.

*What's in your heart?*

The question seemed to come out of nowhere, and yet her gut contracted at the silent words, as if they had been squeezed from her very soul. How could she answer such a question when she wasn't sure of the answer?

"Show me," she whispered. "Show me what's in my heart, and then maybe I'll know how to pray."

A slight stirring in one of the front pews caught her attention, and she realized for the first time that she wasn't alone. A man rose up from where he knelt and turned toward the back of the church. Did he see her? Was it possible he had asked the question she heard?

No. The words had come from somewhere else—*Someone* else. Of that she was certain. But whoever the man was walking toward her, she wasn't willing to risk having to speak with him. Quickly and silently, she grabbed her purse and nearly ran out the door, back into the afternoon sunlight. She didn't even think about the sandwich she had left behind until she was nearly back at Mariner's and ready to check back in to work.

# Chapter 22

By the time Saturday night rolled around, Jonathan was once again feeling full from way too much food. Even football was beginning to fade to a blur as his eyes grew heavy and he leaned his head back against the couch. But though they'd all taken a break to gather at the dining room table for hot turkey and gravy, poured over mashed potatoes and dressing, they had returned to the family room afterward. Michael, as always, had reclaimed his favorite spot on the recliner, and Jonathan had settled into a corner seat on the couch. Sarah snuggled in beside him before he had time to get comfortable. This time she didn't wait for a natural moment or worry about what anyone might think. She immediately slid her arm through his and interlaced their fingers as she rested her head on his shoulder.

Jonathan caught the look that passed between his parents, but rather than make an awkward moment more so, he returned his attention to the game and kept his mouth shut. He imagined he'd hear about it from Leah in the car on the way back to school the next day, and he wasn't looking forward to it. He wasn't even sure what to expect from that conversation. Was Leah in favor of a relationship between him and Sarah? Sneaking a peek at her now, perched in the rocker beside their dad's recliner, he couldn't tell. Her face was expressionless, as she, too, watched the current play unfold on the screen.

His mother occupied the third seat on the couch, at the opposite end of Jonathan and on the other side of the recliner. They were all lined up, eyes glued to the television, but Jonathan suspected that none of them was paying much attention to the game. He wasn't too thrilled about being at the center of everyone's thoughts and speculations, but he didn't imagine there was much he could do about it at the moment. Besides, he was getting used to the feel of Sarah's hand in his, and he had to admit that it wasn't a bad sensation.

Sarah imagined her heart had never beaten faster. She just hoped it wasn't as loud as it sounded in her own ears. Her excitement was tempered a bit by the knowledge that Jonathan and Leah would be leaving right after church to head back to school and she wouldn't see them again until they came home for Christmas break. But she planned to write to Jonathan every day, not to mention making lots of special plans for his next visit at home.

*I wonder if it's too soon to tell people we're a couple,* she mused, her eyes staring at the TV but her mind not registering anything she saw. The fact that they were sitting together and holding hands right in front of his family only proved that it was true, didn't it? If they weren't, Jonathan would have said something to her about cooling it, or got up and walked away or . . . something. But he just sat right there, holding her hand like it was the most natural thing in the world.

*And it is, she told herself. I've always known it, and now he knows it too — and so does his family.* She had to gnaw at the inside of her lip to keep herself from breaking out into a silly grin. Sometimes she thought she would explode from happiness, just knowing that Jonathan felt the same way about her as she did about him. How she had dreamed of this day, and now it was finally here!

She moved her head just enough that she could raise her gaze and see his profile, but his eyes were straight ahead. A slight quiver of his jaw told her that just maybe he knew she was looking at him, and the realization stirred up an entire flock of butterflies in her stomach. Though she knew they probably wouldn't have any time alone in the morning, since the entire family was going to church together and then Jonathan and Leah would leave directly after the service, Sarah was determined to snag at least five minutes alone with Jonathan tonight. And when she did, she was going to make sure she finally got the kiss she'd been longing for since she was far too young to mention it. The memory of that kiss would just have to hold her until Jonathan came back and they had two whole weeks to spend together.

*One day we'll be together forever,* she told herself, sighing at the thought. *Mrs. Jonathan Flannery. It's going to happen; I just know it is. My dreams are finally coming true!*

Lawan was looking forward to going to church the next day, especially since they hadn't gone the previous Sunday, just a couple of days after Lawan arrived from Thailand. Apparently the Johnsons thought they were doing her a favor by letting her sleep in that morning, but she'd been disappointed when she realized they weren't going to church that day. Attending church was one of the things she'd missed most while she was locked up in the brothel. Her parents, as poor as they'd been, had always taken them to the weekly gathering that met in the little building in the next village. And during the brief time Lawan was at the orphanage, she had attended services as well. It would be interesting to see how these Americans worshipped, she decided. She'd heard their churches were enormous, a thought that intimidated her, but then most everything about her new life made her nervous. At least this outing would be something she would enjoy.

She stared up at the ceiling, listening to her sister's even breathing. It seemed Anna fell asleep in seconds, and for that Lawan was grateful. She enjoyed the quiet time at night, the solitude she found as she reviewed the day or prayed for the people whose faces floated through her mind. Tonight she considered the trip they'd taken to the park, and she had to admit that she'd actually enjoyed it. The weather had been perfect, and the woman named Nyesha had packed tuna sandwiches, something Lawan much preferred to Anna's favorite peanut butter. The entire holiday weekend so far had been much more pleasant than Lawan had expected, though her heart still ached for her homeland and all she had left behind there.

*Except for the boss-man and Adung,* she reminded herself. There was nothing about her time at the brothel that she missed except, of course, her time with Chanthra. Her eyes pooled at the thought. Why couldn't Klahan have rescued her before Chanthra died, and then they might both have escaped and come here to live with their youngest sister? But he hadn't, and there was nothing to be done about it. Her parents and older sister were dead; Mali was all she had left.

The thought sent warm, salty tears spilling from her eyes onto her cheeks, where they dripped down into her ears and hair. But she didn't even try to wipe them away. She missed her family and, though she knew she would one day see them all again when she, too, passed from this life to the next, it didn't stop the ache from burning in her heart right now.

# Chapter 23

Sarah shoved down the guilt she felt at feigning sleep so Leah wouldn't keep her up all night yakking. When the family had opted to turn in early because of church the next morning and then Jonathan and Leah's trip back to school right afterward, Sarah had despaired of getting Jonathan alone even for a brief moment. But as she trudged upstairs behind Leah, a plan had formed in her mind. She'd practically had to swallow her grin so Leah wouldn't know she was up to something.

She lay very still now, listening to her friend's even breathing. The house was quiet, and she decided it was time to put her plan into action. Slipping soundlessly into a light robe and slippers, she slid her cell phone into her pocket and tiptoed out the bedroom door and down the stairs. She didn't stop until she was safely outside in the backyard, where she took her phone from her pocket and punched the number that would awaken Jonathan.

*If he's even asleep yet,* she thought, pressing the phone to her ear and listening to it ring. *Maybe he's still awake. Maybe he's even thinking about me—*

"Hello?"

His voice sounded puzzled, even a bit sleepy, and she smiled.

"Jonathan? It's me. Sarah." *Duh.* Why did she always say such dumb things? It wasn't like he didn't have caller ID.

She took a deep breath and continued. "I . . . I wondered if we . . . could talk. Just for a minute. I mean, you're leaving tomorrow, and I know we won't have any time in the morning because of church and . . . well . . . could you come downstairs for a minute?"

After a pause, Jonathan said, "Downstairs? Why? What's going on down there?"

Sarah felt her cheeks warm as she tried to explain without sounding as dumb as she felt. "Nothing really. I mean, I just wanted to see you alone for a minute, before you have to leave to go back to school." She swallowed. "And I'm not really downstairs. Well, I am, but . . . I'm actually in the backyard. Can you come down? Please?"

Another pause while Sarah listened to her heart pounding in her ears. Would he come, or would he turn her down? And if he came, what would happen?

"Yeah, sure," he said at last. "I guess so. Hold on. I'll be right there."

Tears sprang to her eyes as she flipped the phone shut and shoved it back in her pocket. He was coming! She was right. He did care after all.

She resisted the urge to pace while she waited, going instead to the porch swing, intending to sit down and invite him to join her until she remembered that the swing squeaked. She glanced around and spotted two redwood lawn chairs, just inches apart under an old oak tree in the corner. Perfect!

She'd just sat down when the back door opened and she saw Jonathan outlined in the moonlight.

"Over here," she called in a loud whisper, waving her hand.

His head turned in her direction, and then he stepped toward her. By the time he reached her side, she was trembling but determined to push ahead with her plan.

He stood looking down at her, and she could just see his features in the near darkness. Why was he frowning?

"Sit down with me," she invited, her voice shaking only slightly. "It's a beautiful night, and it would be nice to spend a few minutes together before you go back to school tomorrow, don't you think? I mean, it'll be nearly a month before you come back for Christmas."

Jonathan hesitated before joining her, but at last he eased himself into the chair next to her, though he made no attempt to reach across the small divide between them. It looked like she'd have to take the initiative again.

"I'm going to miss you," she said, her hand snaking toward his. He flinched when she found her mark but didn't draw away. She laced her fingers in his, glad for the warmth and wishing she could hold on forever.

"A month isn't that long," he said at last, his gaze fixed on the night sky.

"It seems long to me," she said, amazed that she had the courage to finally voice the feelings she'd kept inside for so many years. "I'll be counting the days."

She waited, and after what seemed like a lifetime, Jonathan turned his gaze toward her. The corners of his mouth turned up slightly. "I'll be back before you know it," he said.

Oh, if only he would take some initiative and give her some sort of encouragement! But so far he hadn't pulled away from her advances, so at least that was something.

Boldness, mixed with desperation, pushed her onward, and she leaned toward him. "Kiss me, Jonathan," she whispered. "Please."

153

His eyes widened, and she watched the war of emotions play out on his face. She could scarcely breathe, imagining how terrible it would be if he turned her down — but how absolutely wonderful it would be if he accepted.

And then he leaned forward and placed his lips on hers, briefly but tenderly, and she thought her heart would explode right out of her chest. When he pulled away she wanted to beg him to kiss her again, but she sensed that she'd better not push him any farther. The next move would have to be up to him.

She smiled. "Thank you," she whispered. "I'll hang on to that while you're gone."

He nodded, and then gently pulled his hand away and stood up. "We'd better get inside," he said. "We've got church in the morning."

Sarah's heart sank a bit, but not entirely. He had kissed her after all, so how could she be discouraged? He just wanted to be careful, and that was a good thing. It was part of the reason she loved him . . . wasn't it?

Yes, it was. And she would honor and respect that.

She rose from the chair and looked up at him. "Sleep well," she said.

His smile was tight and his voice gruff. "You too."

Then he cleared his throat, turned, and strode purposely toward the back door, with Sarah following close behind.

～⚮～

Jonathan had made it a point to plunk down between Leah and their mother the minute they settled into a pew at church, leaving Sarah looking more than slightly bewildered as she took a seat on the other side of her friend. Jonathan wasn't trying to be mean, but he needed some space — both physically and figuratively. But then Sarah had leaned over and whispered into Leah's ear, and after only a moment's hesitation, the girls swapped seats. Jonathan suppressed a sigh and offered Sarah a brief smile before turning his attention to the front of the church.

*As if I could concentrate on anything that's being said,* he thought. But he was determined to try. This was no time to cut corners when it came to corporate worship or study of the Word. In fact, if anything, he needed it more than ever. He purposely held his Bible in his lap throughout the service, refusing to give Sarah an opportunity to once again slip her hand in his.

He sang heartily as the worship began, his eyes straight forward but his mind betraying him as it strayed to the memory of the kiss they had shared under the moonlight. How had he allowed their relationship to get to that point? How had things gone in such a different direction than what he had planned and hoped?

The memory of Sarah's kiss faded then, as an image of Mara took its place, her sad, hazel eyes wooing him even as her words and actions rejected his every attempt. How differently would he feel if he had shared that late-night kiss with Mara? Very differently, he conceded. And that was the problem.

Continuing to sing by rote, he realized that it wasn't so much that he had kissed Sarah that bothered him. After all, it isn't as if they'd pledged their undying love and committed to a future together. But no matter how cute she was or how much she seemed to care for him, Jonathan knew deep down that he didn't return her feelings, and he no doubt never would. He was simply feeding his wounded ego, and that was wrong. Sooner or later, Sarah was going to be hurt, and he had no right to take advantage of her and encourage her false hopes.

He glanced at her from the corner of his eye. She was already watching him, and her smile was immediate. Like a knife to his heart, her expectant expression was a sharp but clear point of conviction that he could not allow this façade to continue. No doubt he wouldn't have time to talk to her and straighten it out before he and Leah left for school right after church, but he'd have to make a point of writing to her the minute he got back to his dorm room. She would be hurt, and he felt like a heel for inflicting such pain and disappointment on her, but it could only get worse if he put it off.

*Forgive me, Lord,* he prayed silently. *I had no right. Please, prepare her heart . . . and give me the right words.*

"Leah!"

Lawan stopped in front of the church as the congregation continued to stream out the doors. Her little sister had spotted a young woman whom Nyesha explained was Anna's favorite babysitter, and it was obvious now that the families would have to stop and chat before moving on.

Anna threw her arms around Leah's legs, and the girl with the wild red hair scooped her up and kissed her as Anna's arms squeezed Leah's neck. Lawan was amazed at the closeness of the relationship between the two, and even a little jealous, though she told herself that was silly.

She smiled as Leah and her family greeted each of them. She had not yet met the Flannerys, though she'd heard about them. Anna had told her that Leah and her brother went to college now and that she missed them, but who was the blonde girl standing beside the one named Jonathan?

Lawan continued to smile and nod and say hello as each family member was introduced, and she soon learned that the blonde, whose name was Sarah, was Leah's friend. And yet, she noticed the way Sarah stood near Jonathan and looked up at him with shining eyes. The girl's interest in the family was obviously more than a simple friendship with Leah.

"This is my big sister, Lawan," Anna announced, interrupting the greetings that made their way around the circle. She grabbed Lawan's hand. "She came all the way from Thailand to live with us."

Lawan felt her cheeks flush, though she wasn't sure why. The Flannerys no doubt already knew she had come from Thailand and that she was Anna's sister. But there was something about hearing Anna proclaim it that made her uncomfortable, as if she were on display . . . the way she had so often been when forced to dance nearly naked in the windows of the brothel, inviting customers to come inside.

157

She squeezed her eyes shut to block out the image. No wonder she had blushed. It was a shameful thing. If these people really knew what she'd been through, would they want anything to do with her?

"Come to our place for lunch?"

Nyesha's words pulled Lawan back from a past she wished desperately to forget. What had she said? It sounded like an invitation for the Flannerys to come to their home to eat.

"I'm afraid we can't," Mrs. Flannery answered. "Jonathan and Leah have to get on the road. They've got a long drive back to campus, and we've got to drop Sarah off at home." Her glance flicked from Nyesha to Sarah and back again. "She's been at our place all weekend, and I'm sure her parents are anxious to have her back."

As the conversation continued and Kyle finally peeled Anna away from Leah's arms so everyone could continue on their way, Lawan felt a sliver of relief. She wasn't ready for a lot of people yet, no matter how nice they might be. Her first encounter with an American church had been draining for her, though she'd loved the worship and had understood most of the message. But for now she just wanted to go home and rest.

# Chapter 24

Sarah stood between Mr. and Mrs. Flannery as she watched the old blue Beetle *putt* down the road. Leah's red hair popped out the passenger side window as she leaned through the opening and looked back for one last wave. But Jonathan didn't turn around or slow down or wave . . . or anything. He had just given her one last look—which Sarah was sure was tinged with sadness—and climbed in his car, pulling the door shut behind him.

*Well, why shouldn't he be sad?* she reasoned. *After all, we just started to get close, and now we won't see each other for nearly a month. I'm sad too!* She smiled, glad to think that he was going to miss her. And though she felt badly that they would be apart until Jonathan and Leah returned a few days before Christmas, she was thrilled that the relationship she'd dreamed of for so long was at last becoming a reality.

"Well," Mr. Flannery said, placing his hand on Sarah's shoulder, "we'd better get you home. Your parents are going to forget what you look like. I just hope they didn't miss you too much at Thanksgiving dinner."

Sarah swallowed a tinge of guilt. She knew she should have accompanied her parents on their out-of-town trip to visit relatives for Thanksgiving, but she just couldn't give up her chance to see Jonathan while he was home. And she sure was glad she hadn't! Just look at the progress they'd made over the last four days. Though she had hoped and dreamed for something like this to happen, she had also thought it was more than slightly unlikely. But now she could wrap herself in the memories of the hours they'd spent together—especially that kiss the previous night—and stay warm in them until Jonathan came back for Christmas. With all that had happened between them during the past four days, she could only imagine all that could take place during the two-week break next month.

Still smiling, she nodded at Mr. Flannery and turned to walk back to the car with them. "I really appreciate you two letting me spend the weekend with you," she said. "It was so good to see Jon—." She caught herself just in time, though she kept her head down so they wouldn't see the redness creep into her face as she finished her thought. "Jonathan and Leah again. I've missed them since they went to school in September."

"I imagine you have," Mrs. Flannery commented as she stood beside the car, smiling as she waited for her husband to open her door.

Sarah ignored what she imagined was Mrs. Flannery's double meaning and climbed into the backseat. As she drew her seatbelt over her shoulder, she watched Jonathan's parents interact as they always did, with love and respect, nearly finishing one another's sentences. That was the way she wanted to be with Jonathan one day—and after this weekend, she had hope that it just might happen.

Leah leaned her head back, scooping her long hair up above her head and letting it hang over the seat. The warm air blew in the window and tossed red tendrils in her face, but she closed her eyes and settled in for the ride.

"Just let me know if you want me to drive awhile," she murmured.

Jonathan's laugh sounded more like a snort. "Yeah, right. No danger of that, Sis. I'd like to get there before dark."

She opened one eye and peered at him. "Are you trying to say that I drive slow?"

Still grinning, he raised an eyebrow, though he continued to look straight ahead through the windshield. "What makes you think that? Just because the only people you ever pass on the freeway are Cal-Trans workers . . ."

She punched his arm. "Very funny. Well, don't say I didn't offer."

"Offer noted," he said. "And declined."

Leah smiled. She'd rather he drove anyway. Her favorite way to take long drives was asleep, though she imagined they'd dig into some of their mom's turkey sandwiches somewhere along the way.

She noticed Jonathan's smile disappear, replaced by a frown, though he didn't say a word. She closed the eye that had been watching him and spoke from behind heavy eyelids. "I'll just take a nap then," she said, "while you drive. Let me know if you get sleepy or hungry."

"I will."

Leah sensed that her brother had more on his mind than eating or even getting back to school, but she also sensed that he wasn't ready to talk about it. Though she opted to leave him alone until he was ready to open up to her, she knew without asking that Sarah was at the center of his thoughts. Whatever was going on between them didn't feel right to Leah, and she imagined that's what was bothering her brother too.

She sighed. Time for that later. For now . . . naptime.

Jonathan headed north on Interstate 5, wishing he had more time to cruise up the coastal route where he could at least spot the ocean between the many beach towns that nearly ran together along the way. But the Sunday traffic and windy roads, stoplights and tourists would turn a six-hour drive into an all-night event, so he'd stick to the straight, fast, but oh-so-boring freeway that ran straight up the middle of the state.

At least the weather was good, just right for rolling the windows down and letting the slightly warm breeze blow in and help keep him awake. Though he doubted he'd have to fight his usual inclination to get drowsy after a few hours. All he had to do was rehearse the events of the last four days, and there was no way he'd risk falling asleep at the wheel — or, worse yet, giving in and letting his little sister drive for him.

He sighed. He should never have yielded to even one of Sarah's overtures — no hand-holding or eye-gazing or picnics at the beach. And certainly not a kiss! Why had he even agreed to come downstairs when she called him after he was already in bed for the night? He tightened his lips together, annoyed with himself at the obvious truth of it. He wasn't interested in Sarah the way she was with him, but she was cute, she flattered his ego — and he wanted that kiss. In fact, he'd enjoyed the entire weekend's events with Sarah. She was actually a lot of fun, but he knew from the beginning that it was wrong to encourage her, to give her false hope when there was absolutely no chance of anything ever coming from it. It was fun for a few days, period. But for Sarah, it meant so much more. And that's what made it so wrong on his part.

Squinting into the noonday sun, he snagged his shades from the dashboard and jammed them on. Yes, he would most definitely clear this all up the first chance he got once he was back at school. He wondered if a letter was the cowardly way out, and yet it would help Sarah save face, too, since she could read it in privacy. Then, after she'd had time to digest it, if she approached him while he was home at Christmas, he would deal with it head on. He would also deal with the issue of being just a few miles away from Mara for two weeks and wondering whether or not he should try one more time . . .

He shook his head. He still had a lot of miles to cover, and he was getting hungry. He hated to wake Leah, but he couldn't reach the sandwiches while he was driving. She'd just have to go back to sleep later.

# Chapter 25

Mara sat on her familiar perch on the seawall, watching the sun slip down to meet the ocean. She never tired of the site, as the sky shifted shades of dark blue, purple, red, and orange. She'd heard the sunsets in Hawaii were even more breathtaking, with the sky displaying a green flash at the instant the sun disappeared below the horizon, but Mara couldn't imagine anything more beautiful than what she was looking at right now.

The breeze was cool, however, and she shivered in her light windbreaker. It was amazing how quickly the temperature could drop this time of year. It had hovered in the mid-70s all afternoon, but now she imagined it wasn't much more than 60.

She smiled. People back east would probably think her quite a wimp, shivering in 60-degree temperatures at the end of November, when many of them were still digging out of snowstorms and expecting more for months to come. But since she couldn't imagine herself ever traveling much beyond California, she'd probably never know about cold weather firsthand.

The thought of travel teased her memory with the thought that one day she should return to the village where she was born and at least see if her parents and brothers were still alive. But why bother? Maybe her brothers hadn't been in on it, but her parents certainly had been when they accepted cash from her *tio* so he could smuggle her over the border and subject her to a life of torture and degradation. No thanks. There was absolutely no reason for her to return to the poverty of her hometown and the pain it would resurrect to see her mother and father again. Best to leave that part of her life buried.

But what of her life now? She stood to her feet, brushed off the back of her jeans, and tugged her windbreaker down. Jonathan had no doubt left already to go back to school, and though she'd done her best to discourage his attentions while he was home, she had to admit that she was more than just a little disappointed that he hadn't at least stopped by on his way out of town.

*Foolish,* she told herself, setting a brisk pace for home. *It's not like he cares or anything. He probably just feels obligated because he helped rescue me. No doubt feels sorry for me too. Well, that's the last thing I need, from him or anyone!*

As she reached the corner where she would turn onto the street where she lived, she shoved away the memory of the blue Beetle zipping by a couple of evenings earlier. Jonathan had spent the day with his little blonde girlfriend. No wonder he hadn't had time to contact her again while he was home.

*And that's just fine with me,* she fumed. *She's probably a lot more his type, anyway. Besides, I don't need some guy complicating my life. I need to concentrate on working and saving money and getting into school next semester.*

As she came into sight of the front porch where she often sat, trying *not* to think of Jonathan, she realized how much she would miss his brief letters. *I shouldn't even keep the ones I have,* she told herself. *I should just throw them away, burn them. . . .*

But she knew she wouldn't. Still, she was determined not to write to him again . . . unless, of course, he wrote to her first. The chances of that, as far as she could see, were pretty much nonexistent.

"Mommy, will Lawan be in my class, or will she go to the big school?"

Lawan's head snapped up at the question. She was sitting at the end of the couch in the family room, not paying much attention to the program that aired but believing everyone else in the room was, so Anna's inquiry surprised her.

Lawan looked to Kyle, who sat in an overstuffed leather chair with his feet up on a hassock, his shoes resting on the floor beside him. His gaze didn't even falter from the screen.

She turned to look at Nyesha, who sat at the opposite end of the couch, with Anna in between her and Lawan. Anna's face was turned upward toward her mother while she waited.

Nyesha smiled down at her. "Lawan won't be in your class, sweetheart. You're in kindergarten, and Lawan is much too old for that." She lifted her eyes to Lawan, transferring her smile to the older girl before returning her attention to Anna. "Your dad and I have talked about it and decided that, for now, Lawan can study at home. I'll help her."

"You mean, like home-schooling?" Anna asked.

Nyesha nodded. "Exactly. And I'll be her teacher."

Anna's shoulders slumped. "That's not fair. I want to stay home and have you for my teacher too."

Nyesha's laugh was warm. "Your dad and I have talked about that too, and we just may do that one day. But for now, we think you should have the experience of being in the classroom with your friends."

At the mention of friends, Anna perked up again. "You mean like Josie and Marianne?"

Nyesha nodded. "Yes, like Josie and Marianne. If you stayed home for school, you wouldn't get to see them or play with them."

Anna seemed to consider the option for a moment before shrugging. "I guess I'll stay in my school for now."

This time even Kyle joined in with Nyesha when she laughed, but Lawan wasn't exactly sure what her own response should be. So, as usual, she said nothing.

"What do you think of all this, Lawan?" Kyle asked, drawing Lawan's attention in his direction. "Your mother and I have made the decision about homeschooling for you, but maybe we should have consulted you first."

Lawan still had only a vague understanding of what homeschooling might be, though she squirmed at the reference to Nyesha as her mother. "I do not know," she said, her eyes dropping downward. "What you want, I will do."

A brief pause preceded Nyesha's voice. "We appreciate that, Lawan," she said, her voice thicker than it had been moments earlier. "I will do my best to help you catch up on your studies, and if you think you'd like to go school later — maybe a private Christian school would be best — we can work that out."

Her head still bowed, Lawan nodded. Did it really matter where she went to school? Though she'd longed to do so when she was trapped in the brothel in Thailand, she now wondered at the purpose of doing so here in America. Would she really be able to become something someday, someone with a good job and a respectable life? Even if these new so-called parents of hers managed to get her an education, what would happen if she applied for a job and her past became known? Who would hire such a girl?

She sighed. To please the Johnsons, she would do her best to study and learn, but her hopes for a bright future seemed dim at best, her light having been snuffed out in a dark, dingy room in the Golden Triangle where she had watched her sister die as a result of the life they were forced to lead.

*Phrae yaeh suu,* she prayed, *You are my only hope. You sent Klahan to rescue me from that terrible place, and now You have reunited me with my only living relative. I am very grateful, but . . . but how can I expect anything more in my life? You have already given me so much, and I am so undeserving.*

*Daughter.*

The word whispered in her heart, and warm tears spilled from her eyes onto her cheeks before she could stop them. However could she explain them to the three people who shared this room, this house with her?

Nyesha switched places with Anna and scooted close to Lawan without saying a word. The harder Lawan tried to stop the tears, the more they poured forth. In moments she once again found herself in Nyesha's embrace, sobbing against the woman's soft shoulder. This was not at all the way she wanted to act in front of others. What must they think of her?

Jonathan and Leah had rolled into the parking lot in front of Leah's dorm right around sunset, and by the time Jonathan helped his sister upstairs with her still overloaded bag, he was glad to drive to the other side of campus to his own dorm. Now, shrouded in darkness except for the artificial lights in the parking lot and at the front of the building, he sat in his car, his heart as heavy as when he and Leah first exited the church parking lot and began their drive.

He laid his arms on top of the steering wheel and lowered his head to rest on them. How could he have been so foolish, so weak, so . . . selfish? Because surely that's what he'd been. He'd been so concerned about his own feelings, his own needs, that he'd thrown Sarah's to the wind. There was no way out of this now but to tell Sarah the truth — and to break her heart in the process. Could he be any more disgusted with himself?

Probably not, he decided. He knew he'd asked for and received God's forgiveness, but forgiving himself was going to take some time and effort. *And lots of Scripture reading and meditation. I've got to keep reminding myself that I'm not under condemnation, but I don't want to pretend like what I did was OK either. Because it wasn't. Not even close!*

He shook his head. Just when he thought he was making progress toward becoming a mature Christian, he pulled a stunt like this. *Holding hands, going on a picnic with her, sharing ice cream . . . and kissing, for Pete's sake! Why didn't I just declare my undying love and then stomp on her heart? What a jerk I am!*

*You are My son.*

The reminder sparked hope inside, and Jonathan lifted his head. "Thank You that You are faithful," he whispered, "even when I'm not. Especially when I'm not. I need You to help me make this right, and I hate that Sarah will be hurt in the process."

*She is My daughter. I love her, and I will take care of her. I will work out My purposes for both of you through all this.*

Jonathan nodded. He knew he could trust God to do exactly as He said. If only he had trusted God earlier, before he set himself and Sarah up for such a fall. God could certainly redeem any situation, but Jonathan wanted to learn to be mature and obedient enough that he didn't set up such potentially destructive circumstances in the first place.

He sighed and opened the car door, stepping out as it creaked its familiar protest. The old car with as many miles on it as stars in the sky had gotten him back safely once again.

*Thank You, Lord,* he prayed silently, reaching behind the seat to yank out his overnight bag, which weighed about one-third as much as Leah's suitcase. *You got me back here safely and on time . . . in spite of myself. And I know You'll get me through this situation with Sarah.* He slammed the door shut and sighed again. *And with Mara too. You know I'd really like to write to her again, but should I even bother? Is there any point? It's not like she's given me any encouragement to stay in touch or anything. But still . . .*

He turned toward the dorm, determined to refocus. He had to be in class in the morning, with his mind sharp and ready. That meant getting these Sarah and Mara issues settled — at least as much as they could be for the time being.

*I'll write to Sarah tonight,* he decided, striding toward the front door, *and then mail it before class tomorrow — before I have time to chicken out. But Mara? I'm still not sure about what to do there.*

"Hey, Flannery!"

A familiar voice greeted him from an open window on the second story. "About time you got back here. Did you bring any food with you? We're starving up here, dude!"

Jonathan chuckled and shook his head. So much for the extra sandwiches and pie his mom had packed for him this morning. He and Leah had gone through at least a third of the home-cooked supplies, and then split the rest. He imagined Leah would end up sharing her portion with her roommate too.

"Food's coming!" he called out, grinning at the excited whoop that answered him. It was good to be back.

# Chapter 26

Monday morning had dawned chillier than usual, with a thick gray fog blocking out the sun. Jefe would have given anything to be able to roll over on his cot and pull the cover over his head for a couple more hours, but this dump he now called home didn't afford such luxuries. And so he had dragged himself from bed, choked down the prison's disgusting excuse for breakfast, and was now ready to head outside for a couple of hours.

*Not like the old days,* he thought, buttoning his jacket as the line of men shuffled toward the yard. *I had it made then. Girls of any age any time I wanted them—even boys once in a while to break the monotony. Two idiot guerillas to do my dirty work and a never-ending line of customers just waiting to fork over their hard-earned money to get a few minutes with one of my workers.*

He grinned. Workers? That was too nice a term for them. They were his slaves, and he loved it that way. But didn't he take good care of them? So long as they behaved and didn't give him any backtalk, he gave them three squares and a place to sleep. What else did scum like that expect?

*Except for Mara,* he thought, the pain of her betrayal still stinging his heart. He'd done everything for her—got her out of poverty, trained her himself, gave her the prime assignments. And how did she repay him?

He nearly stumbled over a deep crack in the sidewalk, jarring him back to the present. Every time he let his thoughts drift back to Mara, he knew he put himself at risk, and this was no place to take chances. There was always someone looking to take him out, and even with bodyguards sworn to protect him, he knew there were ways. If someone wanted to get to him bad enough, they'd do it. So it was up to him to be on guard all the time.

He settled into his favorite spot against the wall, leaning back and wishing for the sunshine that usually warmed his face at that time of the morning. But the sky was gray, with little or no promise of a change anytime soon.

The familiar sounds of the yard began to fade as his eyes drifted shut. Though he jerked himself back a couple of times, he ignored the warning in his gut to get up and walk around to keep himself awake. A few minutes of shuteye couldn't hurt. And besides, Feo was close by, standing watch. Not even El Gato would get past him.

It wasn't a particular noise that jarred him back from sleep, but rather the unusual quiet. Eerie. Dangerous. Something was wrong.

Jefe opened his eyes only slightly and peered out, unmoving as he hoped to evaluate the situation before letting on that he was awake. But when he saw two goons holding Feo back, a hand over his mouth so he couldn't yell, he knew it was too late.

Opening his eyes the rest of the way and looking up, he saw El Gato standing in front of him, sneering. The shank in his hand was barely visible, but Jefe knew he'd have to move fast if he was going to get away before his enemy plunged it into his heart.

Which way? His eyes darted from left to right. Neither direction looked promising, and there wasn't a correctional officer in sight. Why had he been so foolish, so careless to allow himself to fall asleep in the one place anyone would know to look for him at this hour? He'd made himself a sitting duck, and short of a miracle, he was going to pay a fatal price for it.

Letting out a stream of curse words, he jumped up and launched himself at the bigger man, hoping a surprise attack would work to his advantage. *The best defense is a good offense,* he reminded himself. But it wasn't good enough. As he threw himself against El Gato, pushing against the man's shoulders in hopes of knocking him backward, he felt the blast of the knife as it plunged into his stomach, just below his rib cage and upward, toward his heart.

The man knew what he was doing and had no doubt hit his mark. Even as Jefe heard the yells and the horn began to blow, signaling an emergency situation, he realized that help would not get there in time. He would die there in that stinking prison, surrounded by violent men who had wasted their lives much as he had, and ultimately no one would care that he was gone.

*But at least Mara will remember me,* he thought, as blackness slipped in and the pain in his chest crushed out the air that he desperately tried to pull in. *She will remember me and never be free.* He smiled. It was enough. So long as his traitorous niece was tortured by memories for the rest of her life, he could die in peace. His legacy was secure.

Mara shivered in the midmorning fog, as she hurried down the nearly empty sidewalk on her way to work. She was so glad to be working today—and a long shift, at that. One of the other waitresses had called in sick, so when Mara got the invitation to come in early and work a few extra hours, she gladly accepted.

Not only could she use the money, but she wasn't up for spending any more time at home than necessary.

*Yesterday was enough. I thought the day would never end! I hope they don't give me any more Sundays off. It was terrible hanging around my room or sitting on the seawall all day, thinking about Jonathan and that girl. . . .*

She cut herself off at midthought. *Stop it! You can't keep thinking about that or it'll drive you crazy. He's got a girlfriend. So what? Did you expect him not to? He's a good-looking guy, after all, and it's not like you're the only one who noticed that. Besides, you had your chance. He tried more than once to get you to talk to him, but you weren't interested.*

"*Aren't* interested," she said out loud, then shifted back to silence, hoping no one had heard her. But the sidewalk was nearly empty, unlike it had been over the weekend.

*You're better off this way,* she reminded herself. *What if he really did want to get to know you better, maybe even have a relationship or something? Sooner or later he'd get hung up on what you used to be, and then bingo. He dumps you for somebody like that clean-cut blonde he was with the other day. Better that he starts out with her and leaves you out of the picture entirely. Any hope you ever had of a normal life was taken away by your parents when they sold you to that slimeball tio of yours.*

*Tio.* She nearly spit on the sidewalk at the thought of him. Even though she knew he was in prison for life—"where he belongs," she whispered—it wasn't enough. *He shouldn't be allowed to live,* she thought. *He should suffer and die and burn in hell for what he did to me and the others.*

The lonely screech of a hungry seagull, circling overhead, caught her attention, and she shook off all thoughts of the man who had tortured her for so many years. How she despised him! But she couldn't allow him to control her any longer. He was in prison now, and she was free. She had to forget him and pursue her own life—alone. No *tio*. No Jonathan. No one. Just herself. Because when it came down to it, that was all she had.

By midafternoon the sun had finally burned through the blanket of fog that had kept the sky and even the landscape gray and gloomy for the better part of the day. Barbara felt at loose ends, now that the holiday was over and her family had gone home. She considered calling Mara to see if she might be off and the two of them could go to a movie or something, but before she could decide, her cell burst into song.

The caller ID read private. She frowned but flipped it open anyway.

"Hello?"

"Barbara?"

The voice was familiar, deep and warm. Detective Bradley. Why would he be calling?

They exchanged brief greetings, and then the detective got down to business, which she had sensed he would do quickly.

"I thought you should know," he said, "that Mara's uncle is dead. Stabbed with a shank by another inmate on the prison yard."

Barbara's heart froze, refusing to beat for a moment. Jefe, dead? The man was the scum of the earth, and yet . . . he had been created in the image of God, stamped with his Creator's likeness, as had all humanity. But he had chosen to trade away his godly inheritance for a life of deprivation, dragging others down with him.

As she processed the news, a part of Barbara wanted to throw her arm in the air and yell, "Yes!" After all, hadn't he gotten what he deserved? Sadly, yes he had. But then, what better did she deserve?

*It is only by God's mercies that we are not consumed.*

The Bible verse echoed in her heart, and she closed her eyes, ashamed. *Forgive me, Lord,* she prayed silently. *There but for Your grace . . .*

"Are you still there?"

The voice interrupted her thoughts, and she cleared her throat. "Yes. Thank you. I am. I just . . ." She tried to pull her thoughts together and control her voice. "When . . . did it happen?"

"This morning. He died before they could get him to the infirmary. The whole place is on lockdown until they sort it out. Of course, no one saw anything, and no one's talking."

"Of course." She knew how strong the code of silence was behind prison walls, and she knew the officials had their work cut out for them trying to get to the facts of what had happened.

"Anyway," the detective said, "I thought you should know."

She nodded. "I appreciate it. Thank you."

By the time she'd flipped the phone shut, she knew she'd have to tell Mara, but she wasn't sure where or when. First she'd have to compose herself so Mara wouldn't discern anything in her voice. And then she'd call and set up a time to meet with her young friend.

*Will she be relieved? How could she not be?* Barbara sighed, remembering how lovely Mara had looked when she sat at their dining table on Thanksgiving, and yet how uncomfortable she had appeared as well. The man she called *Tio* had caused her such deep pain and injury through the years. Could the girl ever find healing?

"Only with You, Lord," she whispered. "Only with You."

# Chapter 27

The first day of being back in the school routine had come and gone, at least so far as classes were concerned. Most of the guys in Jonathan's dorm were gathered in the TV room downstairs to watch Monday Night Football, but Jonathan had used the excuse of too much homework to head up to his room instead. Not that he'd escaped without some catcalls and taunts about spending way too much time with his nose in the books and not nearly enough having fun, but he'd long since learned to ignore the testosterone challenges that were a part of campus life. Right now, he really did have work to do, though little of it included poking his nose in his books.

Sarah, he thought, sitting in a wooden chair at his desk and staring down at the blank piece of paper and the pen he held in his hand. *How do I tell you what a selfish jerk I am and that you should look for someone who will appreciate you?* He shook his head. There was no way, and certainly no easy way, to do it without hurting her. He was just going to have to say it, period. But he sure wished he could find a way around it.

*You're not just a jerk, Flannery. You're a coward too. You told yourself you were going to do this last night, and you didn't. No more stalling, dude. You created this problem, and you're not going to make it go away by ignoring it or putting it off. Now get busy writing.*

He ran his fingers through his short, wavy hair and sighed. How to start? At the beginning, obviously.

*Dear Sarah,* he wrote. *I hope you're doing OK and . . .*

He dropped the pen, wadded up the paper, and threw it in the trash. Sure, he was going to tell her he hoped she was doing OK so he could drop a bomb on her and make sure she wasn't doing OK anymore. What an idiot!

Maybe he should just text her. No, that was even more cowardly. The least he could do was send her the bad news in his own handwriting.

With a fresh piece of paper in front of him and determined to get to the point, he wrote, *Sarah, I'm sorry to have to tell you this but . . .*

He tossed the pen down again and dropped his head into his hands. Why didn't he just shoot her? It would be kinder.

"Lord," he whispered, "please show me what to say."

He picked up the pen again and, with a sorrowful but determined assurance, wrote, *Sarah, I've been thinking and praying about this past weekend, and I believe there are some things I really need to say to you.*

Occasional shouts, cheers, and muted laughter drifted up from the gathering below, but Jonathan scarcely noticed as he continued to write. By the time he signed his name to the bottom of the page, he knew he had written what needed to be said . . . and the rest was up to God. Though that thought didn't take away his apprehensions about how Sarah would react to his letter, it certainly made it easier to fold it up and place it in the already stamped and addressed envelope. He would mail it first thing in the morning, before classes began . . . and before he had a chance to change his mind. Meanwhile, he would continue to ignore the text messages she sent him every couple of hours. He'd answered once and told her he was sending her a letter;

that would have to do for communication until she got his note in the mail.

❧

Mara had been pleasantly surprised when she looked up from where she stood at the cash register, ringing up a couple of customers, and spotted Barbara walking through the front door. Their eyes met, and they exchanged smiles. Had they made plans and Mara forgot? She didn't think so.

She placed the change into the woman's outstretched hand, thanked her, and looked back at Barbara, who was already making her way to an empty stool at the counter.

"Hey," Mara said, stepping over to where her friend sat. "I didn't expect to see you tonight."

Barbara's smile seemed strained. "I tried to call," she said, "but I got your voice mail and I didn't really want to leave a message. I thought I'd just take a chance and drop by to see if you were working." She paused and raised her eyebrows. "Will you be off anytime soon?"

Mara glanced at her watch. "In about thirty minutes, actually. If you want to wait, we can go do something. Have you eaten?"

Barbara shook her head, and Mara noticed that the gray in her friend's hair seemed to have multiplied since she saw her on Thanksgiving. Was that even possible? She doubted it. Must just be the lighting.

"No, I haven't," Barbara said. "Shall we go get something when you're off?"

"Sure." Mara smiled and nodded. "I'd like that. You want some coffee while you're waiting?"

Barbara agreed, and Mara poured it before getting back to work. But her mind wasn't on her customers.

Why had Barbara come? True, she'd dropped by unannounced a few times in the past, but this seemed different somehow—as if Barbara had some specific reason for being there.

Mara took orders and delivered them while her thoughts bounced around in her head. What could it be? Had something happened?

Jonathan. The thought nearly knocked the glasses of water she carried from her hands. Surely nothing had happened to him . . . had it? Would Barbara even be the one to come and tell her?

*Who else?* she thought. *His family sure wouldn't do it.* She delivered the water and focused on taking deep breaths. This was going to be the longest half hour of her life. If something really had happened to Jonathan, how would she cope with such news? Jonathan was the only man who had ever really shown her any kindness. And how did she repay him? By rejecting his friendship without even giving him a chance. Oh, how she wished she had a chance to change that! What if Barbara told her something that meant Mara would never have that chance? It was all she could do to keep her hands from trembling as she took another order.

By the time Mara finally slipped off her apron and went to the back to let everyone know she was leaving, Barbara had gone through three cups of coffee and her nerves were even more jittery than when she'd first come in. Though she knew Mara despised her uncle and would no doubt feel a great sense of relief that he was finally gone and could never hurt her again, the news was still going to hit her hard and stir up lots of old memories and feelings, most of which she'd worked hard to keep buried.

The early winter darkness had settled in over the coastline by the time the two women exited the café and headed for Barbara's car. It was obvious Mara sensed there was more to Barbara's visit than a casual dinner with a friend, but at least the girl hadn't asked about it yet.

"How about that Mexican place we like so much?" Barbara asked as they belted themselves in.

"Sure," Mara said. "Sounds great to me. But I'm buying this time. You paid last time, plus you had me over for dinner on Thursday." Her laugh sounded only slightly forced. "I'm just now digging out from under those wonderful leftovers you sent home with me."

Barbara chuckled. "My kids always called me the 'leftover queen.' I've been known to stretch one Thanksgiving turkey right up to the Christmas ham. We've had hot and cold turkey sandwiches, turkey hash, turkey soup, turkey chowder, turkey gumbo . . . Well, you get the picture."

"I do," Mara agreed as Barbara pulled out of the lot and headed for *La Cocina del Cielo*. Barbara imagined "The Heavenly Kitchen" would be as good a setting as any to break the news.

By the time they were seated and munching on chips and salsa, Barbara caught the inquisitive look in Mara's eyes and knew she'd better dive in before Mara started interrogating her. She sighed, crunched a final chip, and then folded her hands in front of her as she fixed her gaze on her young friend.

"I got some news today," she said. "From my detective friend at the police department."

Mara raised her eyebrows but otherwise showed only a flicker of interest before going stoic and waiting in silence.

"It was about . . . your uncle."

A flash of fear darted through Mara's hazel eyes as they widened and her lips pressed together.

"He's dead," Barbara said. "Murdered by another inmate, though they haven't got all the details yet. The other prisoners have clammed up, so it may take some time to get to the bottom of it, but the prison authorities suspect it was some sort of rivalry thing."

She watched the movement in Mara's throat as the girl swallowed. At last she opened her mouth. "He's . . . dead? You're sure?"

Barbara nodded. "Positive. Died before they could get him to the infirmary."

Another pause, and then Mara reached for another chip and dipped it into the salsa. "Good," she said. "I hope he's burning in hell right now."

Barbara watched as Mara popped the chip in her mouth and chewed. Was she really taking it as easily as she appeared? Barbara doubted it, but she wouldn't push her to talk about it if she wasn't ready. Sooner or later she would be, and Barbara would make it a point to be there for her. Meanwhile, she knew it would be pointless to bring up Mara's need to forgive her uncle if she was ever going to be free of his hold on her. First the girl had to find her own forgiveness with God.

# Chapter 28

Mara thought she should be nominated for an Oscar, the way she'd played the part of the happy friend enjoying dinner with another friend after dismissing some surprising news. But surprising was hardly the word for it. When Mara heard Barbara say that Jefe was dead, it was all Mara could do not to fall to the floor and weep with joy, and . . . something else. But what?

She'd wrestled with that question throughout dinner and the ride home, but when she'd finally closed the car door behind her and waved at Barbara, Mara had climbed the stairs to her room as if there were huge weights attached to her feet. She recognized that it was actually her heart that felt so heavy, but why? Why did she feel such conflicting emotions? Why not just jump in the air and shout "hooray" at the top of her lungs? Hadn't she dreamed of this day, even wished she could personally make it happen, for ten long years? The thought that the man, who first befriended her and convinced her he loved her and thought she was special and wanted her to have a better life, had actually been planning all along to betray and torture her had nearly driven her over the edge of sanity many times. This man who was her own flesh and blood, her father's brother, her tio, had lived off her suffering for a decade and would have continued to do so until she died in the process if Jonathan hadn't come to her rescue.

Jonathan. A delayed sense of relief washed over her as she realized her worst fears about something happening to him had not come true. But what about before she knew he was all right, when she thought he might not be and she wished she could have a second chance? Now that she knew nothing bad had happened to him, was it possible she just might get that second chance? And if she did, how would she respond?

She shook her head as she turned the key in her lock and let herself into her room, flipping on the light as she did so. Who was she kidding? She'd been so rude to him when he was home at Thanksgiving that he'd probably never write to her or talk to her again. Besides, he had that blonde girlfriend now. Mara might never see or hear from him again.

*And that's for the best,* she thought, as the pain of it slashed at her already ragged heart. *I don't need any more confusion or problems in my life. Jonathan's better off without me, and I'm better off without him. And I'm for sure better off without* Tio!

Tears seemed to explode from her eyes then, and she crossed the room in three steps and threw herself onto her bed, stuffing a corner of her pillow into her mouth so she wouldn't wail aloud and bring her landlady or one of the other boarders to her door. The last thing she wanted at that moment was someone invading her space and trying to ease her pain. Mara was still trying to make sense of that pain, and she sure didn't want to share it with anyone else.

*Not even Barbara, she thought. As much like a mother as she's been to me, I'm not up to talking to her about this . . . not yet anyway. Maybe if I had a real mother —*

She scrunched her eyes shut, squeezing out more tears as she pushed down the dim memory of the woman she had once called Mama. If only she had been a good mother and protected her, loved her enough to stop her father from selling her to her

186

tio, then maybe she might have had a happy life, a normal one, with friends and family. . . .

No. She sobbed at the finality of it. She did not have a good mother, and that was that. Her life was what it was, and there was nothing she could do about the past except leave it buried. At least she could take comfort in knowing that the horrible man who had tormented her for so very long was finally dead and rotting in hell, where he belonged. What she couldn't understand was why that knowledge brought tears instead of laughter. Why was she mourning when she should be celebrating?

Perhaps one day she would understand. For now she would cry her tears and then get up tomorrow and go on with her life. There was nothing in her past that she wanted to think about ever again.

187

Cecelia Jimenez was exhausted. It had been a long and exceptionally busy day. Rudolfo had invited a half dozen of his friends over to play cards, and of course that meant Cecelia had to cook for them. It also meant they would all be drinking heavily throughout the afternoon and into the night.

Her stomach had felt twisted and hard from the moment Rudolfo told her his friends were coming and that he expected her to feed them. Cecelia knew how to tune out the rowdy behavior and lewd conversation that always became the centerpiece for such an event, but it wasn't so easy to figure out how to make her meager food supplies stretch to adequately satisfy such a large gathering of men. Yet what choice did she have? Rudolfo did not ask her to do this; he told her. And what Rudolfo commanded, she obeyed — or paid the price.

Now, as the last drunken visitor stumbled out the door and

down the street toward home, Cecelia forced herself to clean up as best she could. Despite the ache in her shoulders and feet, and the heaviness of her eyes, she washed dirty plates, gathered up trash, and even scrubbed the floor where one of the revelers had vomited before leaving.

At last she was done. Rudolfo had gone to their tiny bedroom ahead of her and, she hoped, was already sleeping soundly. If she crept in quietly and didn't wake him, she might get away with falling asleep before he accosted her. If not, she would tolerate his rough treatment of her as she always did—as silently as possible so as not to arouse his anger and make the situation worse.

Her heart sank as she entered the room and saw her esposo lying on the bed, wide awake. "Come here," he growled, holding out a hand to her.

The knot in her stomach grew tighter, as she fought the urge to turn and run. Where would she go? She'd tried to run from him once, when she was younger, but he had found her and beat her until she lay unconscious for two days. When she finally awoke, he had warned her that if she ever ran from him again he would kill her. She had no doubt that he would do as he said, and so she never ran again.

Resigning herself to yet another painful episode at her husband's hand, she determined to try to please him so he wouldn't hurt her quite as badly. But the minute she lay down next to him on the bed, he shoved her away and snorted in disgust.

"You smell like a goat," he declared, his dark eyes gleaming. "Do you think I want to sleep with a goat?"

When she didn't answer, he grabbed the back of her hair and yanked her head backward. "Do you?"

As much as she was able, she shook her head. "No," she squeaked.

He leaned in close to her, and the smell of alcohol and rotted teeth was rancid, nearly causing her to gag. "No, *señor,*" she answered, remembering that he liked to be addressed with respect.

Rudolfo let go of her hair. "That is better," he said. "Now go wash yourself and come back to me — quickly, do you understand?"

Forcing back tears, she nodded. "*Sí . . . señor,*" she said, rising from the bed and hurrying outside to where she always kept a bucket of fresh water. With trembling hands, she splashed her face and then washed as best she could before returning to the bed where her husband waited.

The sound of his snores made her heart leap and her shoulders relax. He was asleep. *Gracias a Dios!* She would be spared, at least for tonight.

She turned out the kerosene lamp and lay down beside him as quietly and gently as possible. He didn't move. Closing her eyes in the darkness, her thoughts went to her grown children, as they so often did. Her life had been so much worse since her sons got married and moved out to start lives of their own. And yet, Rudolfo had always treated her badly, even when the children were little. Did their sons now beat their own wives? Cecelia imagined they did. But at least Maria had escaped . . . hadn't she? Oh, how Cecelia prayed that she had! If only she knew for certain that her precious daughter had indeed found the good life that her *tio* had promised the child . . . and them. Though Cecelia would give anything to have her little girl back, she was glad Maria had not been subjected to this sort of treatment. Surely whatever had happened to her was better than this. But why hadn't her *tio* reported back to them as he promised?

Or had he sent word to Rudolfo, who chose not to pass the news on to Cecelia? It was a terrifying suspicion that the woman had long since harbored because, if it were true, there could be only one reason. Maria had not escaped such a horrible life after all. And it was that conclusion that pushed the tears from the knot in Cecelia's stomach to her eyes and out onto her cheeks. It was a hard thing being a woman, even harder being a woman with a daughter who was taken away at such a young age. But the hardest thing of all was wondering what that daughter must think of her as a mother.

Nearer the Texas border, in the violence-torn city of Juarez just across the river from El Paso, Francesca struggled to find a comfortable position on her narrow bed beside the open window. The nighttime crickets sang their familiar song, as the ever-growing baby rolled and kicked inside her. Why did the little one have to sleep during the day and toss and turn all night, jamming tiny feet into already sore ribs?

The teenager who had been forced to grow up far too quickly and under such hideous conditions now smiled as she rubbed her swollen belly. *"Mijito,"* she whispered, long since having decided her infant was a boy, "you must rest so I can sleep. You are wearing me out."

Another sharp jab was the only reply, and Francesca sighed. How would she take care of such an active baby if she decided to keep him, particularly if he was determined to stay up all night? When would she sleep? How would she go to school and study?

And yet . . . could she bear to part with this little one who had already become such a part of her life? Reason told her it would be best for all concerned to give her baby a chance at a better life, but the closer the time came for the birth, the more she resisted what seemed to be the best choice.

"Is there no other way?" she prayed, closing her eyes as she continued to rub her stomach. "*El Señor,* please show me what to do. What do You want? Make it clear, and I will do it. But whatever it is, You will also have to give me the strength. I am just a child myself . . . and I am so scared."

A warm peace seemed to flow over her then, and she smiled. God would not let her go through this alone, and He would guide her to the right decision. With that she allowed her mind to drift, and soon—despite continued kicks and flips inside her—she was sound asleep.

# Chapter 29

Lawan woke up early Tuesday morning, pleased that she'd finally found something that excited her. Yesterday she had ridden with Nyesha to take Anna to school. During the next three and a half hours until they had to pick her up again, Lawan had Nyesha to herself, and the two went shopping for school supplies.

"We'll get you started on some basic studies first thing tomorrow," Nyesha had told her. "I have friends who know all about homeschooling, so I'll make some calls and we'll get this thing rolling so you can catch up with your schooling. How does that sound?"

Lawan thought it sounded fine, though she wasn't sure she understood everything the woman had told her. But she liked the idea of studying again. She'd attended school briefly and sporadically in Thailand before she was kidnapped, but her parents were too poor to send her on a regular basis. And neither her *maae* nor *phor* read very well, so they hadn't been able to help her much at home. Now it seemed she was finally going to get to learn to read, and she couldn't wait to get started.

*It was fun being alone with Nyesha too,* she thought. Though she wasn't anywhere near ready to consider the woman a replacement mother, Lawan imagined they might at least become close friends, the way she had been with Joan.

The memory of the orphanage tugged at her heart, particularly as the first rays of morning peeked in through the bedroom window. All she had to do was close her eyes and she could hear the sounds of children and animals waking up around her. She especially missed the trumpeting of the elephants and screeches of the monkeys, not to mention the calls of the mynahs and countless other birds that inhabited the jungle that surrounded the compound where she had come to feel safe after a few weeks of living with Joan and the other workers and children.

*BanChuen.* What had become of the little girl whose love and acceptance had made Lawan feel welcome? Her heart squeezed at the memory, but then she opened her eyes and looked across the room at Mali, tangled in the covers and still sound asleep. Lawan was growing to care for her sister, much as she had for BanChuen and the others. But would it be enough? Would she ever be able to feel at home here in this strange land?

She sighed, pulling her thoughts back to the studies Nyesha had promised would begin today. Lawan knew that if she was ever going to transfer her heart and loyalty from Thailand to America, she would have to do well in school. That would at least be a start.

*But even if my heart moves from Thailand to America, how can it ever leave my true parents behind and become loyal to the ones Anna calls Mom and Dad?*

Tears threatened at the thought, but she brushed them away. *Studies first,* she told herself. *Learn about America and this way of life. But I can never forget my real parents. I will try to be friends with this family here, but I don't think my heart can ever break away from my maae and phor — or Chanthra. If only she could have come here with me. . . .*

She threw back the covers and hopped up from bed before the tears could push past her determination to keep them back. An early shower would get her mind back on track with beginning her studies, and right now that was all she wanted to think about.

By the time Leah woke up on Tuesday morning, her roommate was already gone. Her eyes widened at the brightness of the room, and her heart raced. Had she overslept? Was she late for class?

The digital clock on the stand beside her bed said eight-thirty. Mentally she ran through her schedule, and then relaxed. Of course. That was why she hadn't set her alarm last night; she didn't have a class until ten that day. Still, it was a good thing she woke up when she did.

She stretched and resisted the urge to roll over for a few more minutes of luxuriating in bed. After all, she'd had to be in class at seven yesterday and would have to do that again tomorrow. Today was such a rare treat for a school day, but she didn't dare risk falling back to sleep, so she climbed out from under the covers and headed for the bathroom. A shower would get her blood moving and her endorphins kicked in so she'd be ready to concentrate once she got to class. If she didn't spend too much time in the bathroom, she might even have time for a quick breakfast between her dorm and the classrooms on the opposite side of campus.

The memory of the thoughts that had plagued her before she finally fell asleep the night before came to the forefront as she peered into the mirror at her puffy eyes. *Jonathan. He wouldn't talk to me much about Sarah on the ride back up here, but I know he was thinking about her. But exactly what was he thinking? Did he miss her? Is he glad they seem to be heading in the direction of becoming a couple . . . or is he regretting it?*

She turned on the water and grabbed her toothbrush. *I guess I should be glad if the two of them hit it off and actually become an item someday, but . . . why does that just not seem likely?*

Leah loved Sarah. They'd been best friends for years, more like sisters, actually. But was she really a good match for Jonathan? There was a time Leah might have been concerned about their relationship because Sarah wasn't a very strong believer and Jonathan wasn't at all. He might have pulled her away entirely. But now, Jonathan was very serious about his relationship with the Lord, and Leah knew he had every intention of going into some sort of fulltime ministry. Sarah would have to make a lot stronger commitment in her faith walk before she'd be ready for the sort of life Jonathan was planning.

She rinsed her mouth and wiped it dry before turning on the shower and testing the water. *Brrr!* It was going to be a few seconds before it warmed up enough for her to subject herself to that.

"Father, I spent way too much time worrying and wondering about Jonathan and Sarah last night," Leah said. "Help me to stop worrying and start praying. If this relationship is of You, then help me to accept it and be happy for them. If not . . . well, Lord, please stop it before it gets any more serious."

With that perspective, she pulled her nightgown up over her head, tossed it on the floor, and stepped into the shower, pulling the curtain closed behind her.

Mara had Tuesday off, though she wished she didn't. She even considered calling in to see if they needed any extra help, but she knew they wouldn't. Tuesdays weren't that busy, and they already had a full crew. It was nearly noon, and if someone had called in sick, they would have asked her to sub by now.

So what was she going to do with her day? She supposed she could head to the beach like she usually did, since she never tired of walking the shoreline or just sitting on the seawall and people watching. But today just didn't seem like a beach-going day to her. It was if she had unfinished business that she just couldn't identify.

The picture of the compound, long since raided and shut down, floated into her mind. What would it be like to hop a trolley and head over there to take a look at it, now that she knew her *tio* could never touch her again? The thought intrigued her, though it also terrified her. Would seeing the place under these new circumstances help her overcome the fear and the nightmares and put the past in the grave where it belonged, along with the monster who had terrorized her for so long?

It was worth a try. Taking a deep breath and jutting out her jaw, she grabbed her purse and cell phone and headed out the door into the hallway. Though the thought crossed her mind that it might be easier to ask Barbara to come along with her, she somehow knew this was one excursion she would have to make on her own.

As the trolley neared the stop a couple of blocks from the remains of the compound, Mara was having serious second thoughts. She hadn't been back to that area since Jonathan rescued her—not even during the trials. Yes, she had rejoiced when *Tio* and his two assistants, Enforcer and Destroyer, were convicted—all of them sentenced to life without parole—but she had still been too traumatized to even consider going to look

197

at the place where she'd been held captive and tortured more times and in more ways than she could count.

The trolley drew to a stop, and despite her misgivings she hopped off. She'd walk in the general direction of the compound and stop when she felt she couldn't go any farther. If she made it, fine. If not . . . maybe some other time.

The afternoon sun shone warm on her head, and she was glad for the breeze that blew in off the Pacific. Her hands were clammy, and her feet felt like cement blocks. But she continued on, wondering suddenly if she might have trouble finding the place. After all, *Tio* never allowed the slaves to leave the compound during daylight hours, and when they went out at night they rode in the back of a van with darkened windows. Still, she knew the area and the address, so if she really wanted to locate the place, she could.

Mara turned yet another corner, and fear clutched her throat. She couldn't swallow and was having trouble breathing. How could she have imagined she wouldn't be able to find the compound? There it stood, the fence that had always surrounded the three buildings that covered the two full lots now reinforced with another fence and boards besides. She'd been told that the buildings where they'd lived and been forced into unspeakable acts with their so-called customers had been condemned, and to date no buyers had stepped forward to purchase and refurbish the property.

*Just as well, she thought, as she stood on the sidewalk, staring at the macabre sight. Condemning the place wasn't enough. They should have blown it up. No one should ever set foot on those grounds again — ever. It's a place where demons live, just as they did when Jasmine and Jolene and I were there. Demons. Yes! Those men were too evil to be human.*

The thought of Jasmine and the little girl who had died in the box almost immediately after arriving at the compound nearly knocked her to her knees. Yet she stood her ground, faced her memories, and swore that she would walk away from this spot and never let it haunt her again.

But even as she turned her back on that dark place and set her mind on the trolley and the return ride home, she knew she would never be free. The memories of the site of her captivity would surely follow her for as long as she lived on this earth.

# Chapter 30

Joan's eyes flew open, and she was greeted by her husband's soft snores and the muted darkness of a predawn Wednesday. Had she heard something unusual that jarred her awake? The night noises of the jungle, particularly the ever-present hum of insects, continued unabated, so it seemed unlikely. Still, something had yanked her from her slumber.

She closed her eyes again. *What is it, Lord? The children? Is something wrong with one of them?*

Lawan's lovely face took form in her mind, and she felt herself relax. Of course. Her ties to the woman-child whom she had so recently escorted to her new home in America ran deep, more so than she would have expected with the short time the girl stayed at the orphanage. But from the moment Joan had laid eyes on the child, her heart had felt the tug. It wasn't that Lawan's life was so much different than many others in the orphanage. Most had been born in poverty and either ended up there because parents died or other circumstances left them with no one to care for them. Joan and Mort, as well as the other workers, had dedicated their lives to caring for such children.

Still, Lawan's case seemed even more tragic because she had been kidnapped from a loving home, however poverty-stricken, and forced to serve her perverted masters and their customers in a filthy brothel. Others in the orphanage had experienced similar tragedies, but Lawan had watched her sister die as a result of the torture she endured at the brothel. Then Lawan had been rescued by a man she believed loved her, not realizing he had his own perverted pleasures in mind.

Joan smiled then. *But God . . .*

Yes, God had intervened in such a miraculous way at that point, bringing Lawan's rescuer to Himself and changing the man's heart. And so Lawan had been delivered at last, hoping to be reunited with her parents but quickly learning that would never be. The girl now lived thousands of miles away with people who no doubt loved her, but how long would it take the wounded child to understand and accept that? The fact that her younger sister lived in the home gave Joan hope, but her heart ached to think of the overwhelmingly painful and confusing challenges Lawan faced on a daily basis.

"Keep her on my heart, Lord," she whispered into the night. "I promise to pray for her each time You bring her to my mind."

As her husband and the children continued to sleep, Joan began to pray for a precious soul so many miles and heartaches away.

~❦~

By Tuesday night Jonathan was edgy. He'd been confident that he'd done the right thing when he dropped his brief but uncompromising letter into the mail to Sarah. But as Tuesday's sun had sunk below the horizon, he found himself having second thoughts.

*It was the coward's way out,* he told himself, as he walked briskly across the campus toward his room. *What was I thinking, writing a letter? I at least owed it to her to tell her in person.*

He nodded in greeting as he passed a small group of students heading in the opposite direction. *But what else could I have done? There was no chance to talk to her alone on Sunday . . . and I sure couldn't leave her hanging until I get home for Christmas break next month.*

Sighing, he turned up the lengthy walkway that led to his dorm. He could already hear the faint catcalls and laughter that epitomized college life, where teens worked hard at becoming adults but were still young enough to want to prolong the carefree days that would soon be left behind. *It isn't just your letter to Sarah that shows you're a coward,* he reminded himself. *You took the easy way out on that one. But Mara? You know you should write to her, even if you don't say anything personal. After all, the two of you exchanged letters after you came back to school in September. So why are you putting it off now?*

He mounted the steps to the cement porch that spanned the front of the building, ignoring a greeting that floated to him on the evening air. Could he feel any lower than he did right now? He doubted it. He'd opted for the easy fix with Sarah, sending her a letter that would no doubt break her heart, and yet he postponed writing one to Mara, which he knew he really should do.

*But what's my motive?* he asked himself as he stepped into the entryway and headed for the stairs to his second-floor room. *It's not like I just want to maintain a little level of chitchat with her. I want more than that, but she shuts me out every time I try. So what do I do? Try to ease my wounded ego by spending time with Sarah. I have no one to blame but myself on this one.*

Once inside his room, he was relieved to see that—at least for now—he had it to himself. Though he knew his roommate could walk in at any moment, he fell to his knees beside his bed, determined to settle things once and for all.

Lawan had ridden with Nyesha to drop off Anna at school on Wednesday morning, and now she sat at the table with her own books and study materials. There was something about being a "student," even if it was just in her new family's kitchen and with no one else her age present, that made her heart hurt a little less.

From the corner of her eye, she peered from her notebook where she practiced writing letters of the alphabet, as Nyesha had shown her, to the woman with the warm brown skin and ready smile. Lawan was careful to hold her heart in check with the kind woman, but she had to admit that she was beginning to feel close to her.

Unexpected tears pricked her eyes, as she realized it was more the fact that Nyesha seemed able to relate to her when she was sad, and even cried with her. The woman understood that more than anything, Lawan wanted someone to hold her when the pain and fear swept over her. God had provided Joan to be that someone, but now Joan was so very far away, and Nyesha would have to do.

She quickly brushed away her tears and tried to refocus on the paper in front of her. Nyesha was a nice lady. Kyle seemed nice too, but Lawan struggled with the idea of trusting him. With the exception of Klahan, who had rescued her from a life more horrible than she could even now let herself think about, Lawan had trusted no man since she was kidnapped from the safety of her parents' home and village. Would she ever be able to trust Kyle? She hoped so, but only time would tell.

And at least she had Mali. Though Lawan continued to make a real effort to remember to call her little sister Anna, she would always be Mali to her. She wrestled between a smile and tears at the thought. Chanthra was dead, living in heaven with their maae and phor. One day Lawan would see them again because of phrae yaeh suu, but until then she would have to learn to live with the new people who claimed to care about her—including a little sister who insisted on waking her up early every chance she got and loved peanut butter sandwiches with a passion.

Tucking her tongue between her teeth and gripping her pencil with renewed fervor, Lawan began anew to print the letters that seemed so awkward to her. Would she ever be able to think in English? She had learned to speak it well enough to communicate, but always she had to sort through the words in her mind, translating from Thai to English, before speaking them. It was an exhausting exercise, one that drained her after an hour or so until she found herself withdrawing and not entering into the conversations around her.

*I must learn English well,* she thought, her hand tiring at the repetitive discipline of filling line after line with similar markings. *If I can speak it, and even read and write it, maybe these Americans will forget my past. Maybe they will accept me and love me, the way they love Mali.*

*Anna,* she corrected herself. *If I want to be accepted, I have to remember to call her Anna. But she will always be Mali to me, just as my* maae *and* phor *will always be my real parents.*

She glanced up at Nyesha then, who had begun humming a song that somehow warmed Lawan's heart. The woman was slicing apples, and Lawan's mouth watered. Would she ever get used to the abundance of food that seemed to be constantly available everywhere they went? But it was the kindness of the woman who prepared it for her that most surprised Lawan. Why would such a fine lady do so much for someone like her? That was the part she imagined she would never understand, no matter how much English she learned.

# Chapter 31

"Sarah, there's a letter for you."

Lazing under the covers, Sarah ignored the midmorning announcement. Probably just another ploy to blast her out of bed. Why couldn't her mother lighten up a bit and let her enjoy the one day a week she didn't have any classes? If she wanted to spend it in bed, so what? Homework and studies could wait.

Her mother's call came again, this time snatching her from the warmth of her covers and jerking her to a sitting position. "I think it's from Jonathan."

Sarah scrambled from her bed and hit the floor running. She was downstairs and thumbing through the mail, stacked on the kitchen table, leaving her mother standing outside Sarah's bedroom door with her mouth open.

*Sarah Peterson.*

Seeing her name and knowing Jonathan's hand had written it weakened her knees, and she nearly fell into the nearest chair. With her elbows propped on the table, she resisted the impulse to tear open the envelope and devour every word. She could already hear her mother making her way down the stairs, and there was no chance Sarah was going to read her letter in front of anyone.

She smiled and resisted yet another impulse, this time to press the envelope to her lips. Jonathan had written to her! And since this was only Wednesday, he must have done it almost immediately upon arriving back at school. Oh, how she had hoped and prayed that the time they spent together the previous weekend had meant as much to him as it had to her! Jonathan's letter seemed to indicate that it had.

"I thought that would get your attention," Mrs. Peterson said, walking into the room and standing behind her daughter. "Aren't you going to open it?"

Sarah lifted her head and twisted around to look at her mother. As always, the woman was neat as a pin, though Sarah wondered if she grew more gray hair each day.

"Not down here I'm not," Sarah said, smiling to take the sting from her words. "This is private, you know."

Mrs. Peterson's eyebrows lifted. "Getting pretty serious, is it?" She harrumphed before continuing. "It must be, since your father and I had to celebrate Thanksgiving without you."

"Mom, I told you I was staying at the Flannerys all weekend. Leah and Jonathan were home from college, and I wanted to spend time as much time with them as I could."

Her mother's lips were tight as she spoke. "Jonathan? Sure. But Leah? Did you even talk to her or see her?"

Sarah felt her cheeks warm, and she swallowed the guilt that threatened to pop into view. "Of course I did," she said, her tone more defensive than she'd meant it to be. "We all spent time together. All of us."

Mrs. Peterson nodded. "Whatever you say. You know I like the Flannerys—all of them, including Jonathan—and if something comes of a relationship between the two of you, that's fine. I just don't want to see you get hurt, that's all."

Hurt? How could she get hurt? Jonathan cared about her as much as she did about him. Could life get any better than that? If only her mother weren't so old that she couldn't understand that.

"I appreciate that, Mom. Really, I do. But you don't have anything to worry about. Now I'm going to go up to the privacy of my room and read my letter."

She slipped past her mom and headed for the stairs but stopped at the bottom. Looking back at the woman whose forehead still crinkled with concern, she said, "Thanks for waking me up and telling me about the letter."

Her mother nodded, and Sarah abandoned all restraint and raced up the stairs to her room.

Mara didn't have to be at work until noon, so she'd slept in and was now taking her favorite walk along the beach before heading to the cafe. The sun was especially warm that day, feeling more like spring than the end of November. A light breeze tossed her short hair as she strolled beside the seawall, listening to the crashing of the waves and the screeching of the hungry gulls. She hadn't brought anything to share with them this morning, so they'd have to find someone else to feed them breakfast.

The daybreak surfers had already worn themselves out on powerful waves, and most had dragged their boards to shore and either gone on about their day or sprawled on the sand to catch a few rays. Only a handful of black-suited diehards remained in the water, bobbing like waiting seals.

She was about to claim a perch on the seawall when she spotted a petite blonde, sitting a few yards away, straddling the wall, her head bowed. Mara couldn't see her face, but the girl looked very much like the one she'd seen with Jonathan just days earlier, right in this very spot.

She edged a bit closer, careful not to move quickly and catch the girl's eye. She hoped to observe her unnoticed, at least for a while. Was she here, reliving her time with Jonathan? If so, the slight heaving of her shoulders and the sound of occasional sniffles did not bode well for their relationship.

Mara nearly smiled at the thought. Maybe the two of them weren't as much of an item as she'd suspected. Maybe . . .

The girl lifted her head then and turned in Mara's direction. Too late to move. She would just have to act nonchalant. After all, the girl didn't know her . . . did she?

Mara frowned. The blonde seemed familiar, more so than from just having seen her briefly with Jonathan a few days earlier. Had they met somewhere before?

"Mara?"

The girl's question stopped her in her tracks, and her heart skipped a beat. So they did know one another! How and where? Mara's mind raced, but she came up blank.

She stepped closer. "Yes," she answered hesitantly. "I'm . . . Mara. And you're . . . "

Sarah brushed tears from her cheeks. "Sorry," she said, sniffling. "I thought you'd remembered. I'm Sarah. Leah's friend." She paused, and when Mara didn't respond, Sarah added, "Leah is Jonathan's sister."

Of course. Now it all made sense. Jonathan was dating his sister's friend. Perfectly natural. But why was she crying?

The girl sniffled again, and Mara fished in her purse and handed her a tissue. "Are you OK?" she asked, using the transaction as a natural excuse to sit down on the seawall next to her.

Sarah wiped her face, blew her nose, and nodded. "I'm fine," she said, though Mara didn't believe her.

Mara waited a moment and then asked, "Can I . . . help?"

Sarah shook her head. "Nobody can help." She swallowed a sob and sighed, her body trembling visibly. "Thanks for offering, though . . . and for the tissue too."

Mara nodded. Maybe the girl was just missing Jonathan because he'd gone back to school. But Mara didn't really believe that. Sarah acted more like a girl whose boyfriend had just dumped her, and though Mara tried to deny the feelings of hope and joy that stirred in her own heart, it wasn't working.

"I'm an idiot," Sarah said, staring straight ahead as if she were talking to the ocean.

"No, you're not," Mara said, laying her hand on Sarah's. How could she feel compassion for the girl, even as she rejoiced in the possibilities that might result from her pain?

Sarah nodded. "Yes, I am," she insisted. "I thought he felt the same about me as I did about him. How could I have been so stupid?"

Mara fought the smile that pushed at her lips. So she was right! Jonathan didn't care for the girl after all. Could it be because he actually cared for Mara instead?

Another thought popped into her mind then. She'd seen Jonathan talking and laughing with Sarah, giving her every indication that he cared when, in fact, he had not. Just what kind of guy was this Jonathan Flannery? Was he the hero who rescued girls from captivity—or the creep who broke their hearts?

Sarah turned her eyes back to Mara. "I've got to go," she said, standing to her feet. "I've got studies waiting for me at home. School tomorrow, you know."

Mara nodded, though she didn't know at all. School had not been much of a part of her life through the years, though she hoped to change that when the new semester started.

"Thanks again for the tissue," Sarah said, turning toward the parking lot. She looked back at Mara one last time. "And thanks for caring."

Mara watched Sarah walk away, her parting words stinging her heart like a shearing shard of glass. As she too turned away from the seawall and headed in the direction of Mariner's, she felt like the biggest hypocrite who had ever lived.

How had she ended up here when she'd been heading for work?

The church was hushed and empty; Mara had made sure of that this time before settling into a pew near the back door. Only a few candles flickered in the semi-darkness of the room, sending a faint fragrance of incense her way. The wooden cross adorned the front wall, drawing her eyes toward its emptiness.

Isn't Jesus supposed to be hanging on it? she wondered. At least, the few times she'd gone to church with her family in Mexico, it seemed she'd seen Him there. But it was so long ago and so much had happened in the meantime that she probably just didn't remember like she thought she did.

And yet . . .

Her mind wandered then to the brief letters Jonathan had written to her when he was away at school. *Jesus.* The name echoed in her mind, tugged at her heart. She couldn't remember a lot of what Jonathan had said in those letters, but she knew it always seemed to center around Jesus. And despite the fact that she had told herself she didn't care about Jonathan or his Jesus, she had saved his letters. Maybe, if she wasn't too tired when she got off work that evening, she'd dig them out and reread them.

*He wrote a letter to Sarah too.*

The thought popped into her mind and brought back her feelings of guilt and hypocrisy over Sarah's words of gratitude to her.

*Thanks for caring,* she'd said.

Did Mara care about Sarah . . . really? She considered the question for a few moments and could come up with no answer except that she cared less for Sarah's feelings than she did for the fact that Jonathan might actually be interested in her instead. But why did that matter when she knew there was absolutely no chance of a future between them?

She sighed. Relationships were too complicated, and feelings too dangerous. Didn't Sarah's tears prove that to be true? Why should Mara subject herself to a similar heartbreak?

Mara squinted at her watch, lifting it to her face to be able to read it in the semidark sanctuary. It was nearly noon. Time to leave the church behind and get busy waiting on a hungry lunch crowd. Work meant relief to Mara, and she hurried out the back door into the bright overhead sunlight, slipping her sunglasses into place as she walked, anxious to replace her emotional turmoil with as much busyness as possible.

# Chapter 32

Barbara had been concerned about Mara ever since she gave her the news about her uncle.

*She took it too lightly. She has to be more upset than she let on,* she thought, running a dust cloth over the mahogany dining table. It was midafternoon and she'd started cleaning just after lunch—something she did when she was worried about something.

"I should be praying instead of cleaning, Lord," she said aloud, her voice sounding strange in the otherwise empty house. Her eyes took in the vacant chairs, evenly spaced around the oblong table. The room had been filled with laughter and conversation less than a week earlier, but now everyone had gone back to their lives, leaving her there alone.

"Except for You," she said, centering the fake floral arrangement that had graced the dining table for years. "I really don't mind being alone because You're always here. And besides, You know cleaning is what I do when something's bothering me. But I'm praying at the same time, so that's all right . . . isn't it?"

No words of agreement came to her, but she and the Father had been close friends for so long that she wasn't surprised when much of their communion time was spent in comfortable silence. Today, however, she had concerns to transfer from her shoulders to His.

"It's Mara . . . as You already know. She just isn't dealing with her past. Sweeping it under the rug doesn't cut it." Her own words drew her eyes to the plush carpet below her feet, and she knew that vacuuming was next on her agenda. "Of course I didn't expect her to grieve over the death of her uncle. He was a horrible man, despicable—though I surely do wish someone had gotten to him with the message of the gospel before it was too late." She sighed and checked to be sure all eight chairs were pushed in evenly around the table before turning toward the hall closet to retrieve the vacuum cleaner.

"Who knows? Maybe someone did. Either way, it was his choice to live the way he did, Lord. But to inflict such suffering on Mara and others . . ." She shook her head as she pulled the closet door open and snagged the vacuum handle. "I have to remind myself that You love us all, Lord, and that without You, I'm no better than Mara's uncle or anyone else. Still . . ."

She wheeled the machine into the dining room, plugged it in, flipped the switch, and began to push it back and forth over the carpet. "It's too late for that man now, Father, but it's not too late for Mara. Oh, how I pray You are working in her heart and drawing her to Yourself. She needs You, Lord, so very much."

*I know. And I love her more than you do.*

The words came then, silently but clearly, and Barbara stopped midsweep, her hand still gripping the vacuum handle. Tears bit her eyes at the same moment a smile warmed her lips.

"Thank You, Father," she whispered, nearly choking at the effort. "Why do I spend so much time worrying when You've had it under control all along?"

Her heart lighter than it had been in a while, she went back to her task, humming as she worked.

It was dark by the time Mara let herself into her room that evening. On the way upstairs she'd stopped for her mail and found only one piece waiting for her—a letter from Francesca.

*Interesting,* she thought, as she set her purse down on the bed and plopped down next to it. *Must be the week for letters—first for Sarah, and now for me.* The thought that she wished she'd had a letter from Jonathan teased the edges of her mind, but she shoved it away as she ripped open the envelope and pulled out the single sheet. She was grateful that Francesca was bilingual and wrote in English because Mara remembered very little of the Spanish she had once spoken so fluently as a child—and she could read or write none of it. She kicked off her shoes and began to read.

*Hello, Mara:*

*How are you? I think of you often and wonder how your job is going. Are you still planning to go to school soon? Have you decided what you want to study yet? I want to go back to school too, but I'm not sure how that will work out when the baby comes. Right now I am trying to study at home.*

*The baby is getting so big that I don't think it can be much longer until he comes. (I know he is a boy!) I have wondered and prayed so much to decide if I should keep him. My heart says yes, but my head tells me it is better to give him to a family who can give him a good life.*

*Last night I asked God what to do. I told Him I didn't want my baby to grow up without a father. Then I heard words—not with my ears but with my heart—that said, "I will be His Father." Does that sound crazy to you? Do you think God would talk to me like that? If He did, then I think I should keep my baby and let God help me raise him.*

*Please write to me and tell me what you think. I haven't told
this to my mama or papa yet.*
*Love, Francesca*

Mara's eyes burned with unshed tears. How could she answer
this girl when she had no idea if God had talked to her or not?
She wished she knew, for then she might be able to answer some
of her own questions, as well as Francesca's.

The memory of Jonathan's letters, stashed under her clothes
in the second drawer of her dresser, drew her gaze away from
Francesca's words. Fixing her eyes on the old four-drawer dresser,
painted white somewhere during its lifetime, she wondered if
those answers just might lie in the words Jonathan had written
her while he was away.

She took a deep breath and set the letter down beside her.
There was only one way to find out, she decided, and she stood
to her feet with her heart feeling as if it would beat right through
her chest.

Rudolfo slammed his fist into Cecelia's cheek, sending
her reeling into the flimsy wall of her tiny home. Stars
punctuated the darkness in front of her eyes, as she sank to the
floor, aware of broken teeth fragments in her mouth and warmth
gushing from her nose. What had she done to infuriate him
so? Would he truly kill her this time? If he did, would it be
such a bad thing?

How many years had it been like this? Nearly from the
beginning, even when she was pregnant with their children.
That was why they had only three children instead of five. Two
had come forth from the womb already dead.

*Both girls,* Cecelia thought, as the roar of her husband's voice faded into the background. *Daughters. They were the blessed ones. Not like Maria. Poor Maria! My poor little girl . . .*

The toe of her husband's boot connected with her ribs, forcing air from her lungs as she rolled into a ball, instinctively protecting her stomach as she had tried to do when she carried little ones inside her. At least when the boys got a little older and cried out to their father to leave their mother alone, the abuse wasn't so severe. Now Cecelia knew her esposo hated her enough to kill her, without regret or remorse — and there was no one left who cared enough to try to stop him.

*Ay, Dios mio,* she cried without words. *Ayúdame, Señor, por favor! Help me, Lord, please!*

As she braced herself for another kick or punch, she heard a thud and dared to open an eye. Rudolfo had either tripped or lost his balance — or passed out from the alcohol. Whatever the cause, he now lay on the floor, just a couple of feet away. His eyes fluttered shut and he moaned. As she watched, frozen in fear as his putrid breath washed over her, he began to snore, and she knew he would live through the night to terrorize her again. But at least now, for a few hours, she was safe.

Broken, bruised, and bleeding, she pulled herself away from the man who despised her and whose presence made her nauseous. Perhaps she herself would not live through the night as a result of his brutality, but at least she would not die in his presence.

# Chapter 33

Mara lay on her bed, the small stack of letters beside her. She had to admit that Jonathan had never written anything to her that would lead her to think he cared about her beyond a casual relationship. Oh, he wrote a lot about God's love and her need to know Him—as if that were possible!—but no hints at a romance between Jonathan and her. And yet . . . One of the letters lay open in her hand as she closed her eyes and rehearsed the times she'd seen Jonathan face-to-face since he helped rescue her. Though he'd never quite come out and stated how he felt or asked her on an actual date, he had indicated that he might like to spend time with her.

*But what's so unusual about that?* she thought. *Men have always wanted to spend time with me, from the time I was a little girl—beginning with my* tio. The memory of the first time he forced himself on her when she was barely eight years old, hurting her so badly she wished for death and terrifying her into never refusing or disobeying him, brought fresh tears to her eyes. How glad she was that the terrible man was finally dead! She just hoped he suffered in his last minutes, as the shank was shoved into his body and his blood drained onto the ground. If there truly was such a thing as hell, she wished above all else that the man known as Jefe had a place of special tortures reserved just for him.

Mara's thoughts returned then to the words Jonathan had penned in the letters, words of love and forgiveness. How could she ever be expected to forgive her uncle? He had tortured her, ruined her life, humiliated her over and over again, even as he forced her to declare her undying love for him.

*Love. Ha! I hate you, Tio, and I always will. I will never, ever forgive you! I hope you rot in hell where you belong. I don't care what Jonathan says about God's love and forgiveness.*

Tears began to pour from her eyes then, and she couldn't decide if it was because of all the horrible things her uncle had done to her—or because they were so very horrible that she would never be able to forgive him and find out if God's love was real after all. She wanted Jonathan's words to be true, and perhaps they were—for everyone else. But not for her. She could never let go of her hatred, and somehow she knew that meant she'd never experience God's love. It was a terrible tradeoff, but her tio—and her parents who had sold her to him—had left her no choice.

Wednesday night. Had it really been a week since she and Jonathan drove home for Thanksgiving? Leah lay in bed, her mind drifting between memories of that weekend and the need to get some sleep so she'd be alert for an early morning class the next day. Her roommate was already sacked out, and the entire dorm was relatively quiet. She closed her eyes, determined to get some sleep.

She must have been nearly there, because she jumped when her favorite song played in her ear. She'd turned her phone nearly off, yet it was close enough to get her attention. Alert now, she held the phone close to her face to read the caller ID.

Sarah? Why would she call this late? She knew Leah was usually in bed by now. That meant it was important.

She flipped open the phone as she sat up and slid her feet into slippers.

"Hello?" she whispered. "Sarah? Are you OK?"

The sound of her friend's crying gave Leah her answer, and she tossed a robe over her shoulders as she headed for the door.

"Hold on," she said, keeping her voice low but doubting that her friend heard her over her ongoing crying. "I need to get out in the hallway so we can talk."

"What is it?" she said, free at last to talk at a relatively normal tone once she was outside the room with the door closed behind her. "What happened?"

"Jonathan," Sarah whimpered between sobs. "He . . . broke up with me."

223

Leah frowned. "Broke up with you? I didn't even realize you guys were a serious item. I mean, I know you spent time together over the weekend, but—"

"That's why I thought he cared," Sarah whined. "He held my hand and even kissed me . . ." She hiccupped before continuing. "Well, I kissed him . . . but he let me. And he took me to the beach and spent the whole day with me. Doesn't that mean he cared?"

Leah was confused, unsure how to answer. Obviously Sarah had read more into the weekend than Jonathan had intended, but why had Jonathan encouraged her if he wasn't interested?

"So . . . why do you say he broke up with you? Did he call you or something?"

"He wrote me a letter." Sarah's voice had begun to stabilize as the sobs disappeared. "I just got it this morning. He apologized for giving me the wrong impression and took all the blame for everything that happened. He said he thinks I'm cute and sweet and everything, and that he cares for me, but . . . only as a friend." Her voice quavered and she sounded on the edge of tears again. "Leah, I don't want to be just his friend."

Leah sighed. "I know you don't. But if he doesn't feel the same way, there's nothing you can do about it."

After a slight pause, Sarah's voice grew small. "Do you . . . think you could talk to him? Maybe he really does like me and just doesn't want to admit it. Maybe he thinks it's wrong because I'm your friend or something. Maybe . . ."

Leah jumped in before Sarah could take it any farther. "I don't think so," she said, her heart wishing she didn't have to say what she knew she must. "Sarah, if he said he just wants to be friends, then he means it. I know my brother, and he wouldn't say that if it wasn't true."

After another pause, she heard a sob and knew the tears were flowing again. "But I . . . I think I love him, Leah. I think I've loved him for a long time. For years, maybe. He's everything to me. I think about him and dream about him." Another sob hit, this one stronger than the last. "What am I going to do? At least before . . . I had hope that we might get together one day. Now I don't have any hope left."

She burst into full-blown crying then, and Leah waited until she'd settled down a bit before answering. "Sarah, you're not going to want to hear this," she began, hesitant to go on but knowing she must. "But the truth is, you were wrong to pin all your dreams and hopes on Jonathan—on anyone, for that matter. It's the perfect prescription for a broken heart. And it's not what God wants for you."

She took a deep breath and pressed on. "Sarah, God loves you. You know that. And I know you're a Christian. But your relationship with God isn't number one in your life, and it needs to be. Maybe . . . maybe God allowed this to happen to get your attention. Maybe He's trying to tell you that He's the One you need to love above all else. He's the only One who deserves to hold your hopes and dreams in His hands."

Sarah didn't answer, but her crying slowed down.

"I'm going to pray for you now," Leah said. "Please listen — not just to my words but to God's words when He speaks to your heart. He won't make the pain go away, but He will carry you through it. And in the process, you'll learn to trust and love Him more than anything or anyone else."

Silence continued over the phone, but Leah knew Sarah was listening. And so she began to pray, not only out loud for Sarah to hear, but silently, as she asked God to give her the words to say — and to give Sarah the ears to hear.

Leah headed for class early the next morning, despite getting little sleep the night before. Her books, notebook, and laptop were securely tucked into her backpack, though her thoughts wavered between the imminent test in her eschatology class and her concern over Sarah.

*Did I come across as self-righteous when I talked to her? You know I didn't mean to, Lord, but You also know how I can do that sometimes. And it isn't like I have any experience in what she's dealing with right now. A couple of high school crushes that didn't work out don't even come close, I know, but —*

*You spoke the truth in love.*

The silent words nearly knocked her off the pathway as she trudged across the campus, squinting against the early morning rays that were just beginning to make themselves known. Yes,

225

the words she had spoken to Sarah were true, and she truly had meant them in love because she cared very much for her friend. But had Sarah understood that?

*That's not your concern. You spoke the words I put on your heart; now let me deal with Sarah.*

Leah's heart soared. What an amazing God they served! He guided her to what He wished her to do, gave her the strength and wisdom to do it, and then took the burden from her when her assignment was complete. If only she could remember that all the time!

Smiling, she pushed on to the classrooms, which were now in sight. She had a test to take this morning, and she was determined to do well.

# Chapter 34

By the time Thursday morning rolled around, Lawan was not only getting the hang of drawing her letters and even putting a few of them together to form simple words, but she was beginning to enjoy the routine of spending time alone with Nyesha every morning. As they headed back from dropping Anna off at school toward another morning of studies at home, Lawan was surprised when Nyesha turned off at a fast-food restaurant.

"I got a little bit of a late start this morning and barely had a chance to get breakfast down Anna before we left. I'm afraid I missed yours altogether." Nyesha smiled at her. "I thought it might be nice for the two of us to grab a bite together. Does that sound all right to you?"

Lawan raised her eyebrows. It was surprising enough that Nyesha wanted to have breakfast alone with her at a restaurant, but that she would ask Lawan's opinion was almost too much for the girl to process. Still, it was obvious that the woman was waiting for an answer, so Lawan shrugged. "Yes, please," she said. "That would be nice."

Nyesha's smile widened. "Wonderful," she said. "We might just go all out and have breakfast sandwiches and hash browns instead of the usual healthy fare of yogurt and fruit. Do you mind?"

Now the woman had asked her opinion twice, and Lawan was stumped. Why did she care what Lawan wanted? And yet she felt pleased to realize that she did. "I would like that," she said, not sure what a breakfast sandwich and hash browns might be but ready to give them a try, especially if they didn't contain peanut butter.

Together they walked from the car to the entrance, and when Nyesha took Lawan's hand, she did not pull away. Though she struggled with feelings of disloyalty toward her maae and even Joan, the feeling of her hand in Nyesha's was a good one. Safe, she thought. I feel safe.

She smiled as they walked up to the counter to place their order.

Grandma Stewart was a stickler about being up before the sun so she could spend time in prayer and Bible study before heading to the communal dining room for breakfast. Though she didn't think much of the gooey, lukewarm oatmeal and powdered eggs they offered there, she was grateful for the three meals God provided her, as well as the care of the staff and companionship of her friends. All in all, Peaceful Acres was a pleasant place for a widow like herself to spend her last years.

This morning, however, she knew she had an assignment from God, so instead of sitting out in the sunshine and visiting with her friends after breakfast, she went back to her room and gathered together a few things before signing herself out and heading for the bus stop, one block away. She usually called her daughter for a ride when she wanted to come over, but it was a lovely day, she was feeling well, and she decided it would be nice to get there on her own.

By the time the bus dropped her off and she had walked the two blocks to Nyesha's house, she realized it was a good thing she hadn't come earlier. Her daughter and newly adopted granddaughter, Lawan, were just pulling into the garage when Grandma Stewart came into view.

"Girl, don't you shut that garage door in my face!" she called, loud enough to turn both Nyesha's and Lawan's head in her direction. "I didn't walk all the way from the bus stop to end up standing out here on your porch, trying to get in."

The startled look on Nyesha's face quickly gave way to warm laughter, as she headed toward her mother with outstretched arms. "Mama, what in the world are you doing here? Why didn't you call me if you wanted to come over? I would have come to get you."

Grandma Stewart folded her only daughter into her arms and pulled her against her ample chest. "What are you talking about? Since when can't I surprise my own family and drop by unannounced?" She pulled back so she could look into Nyesha's eyes. "You think I'm too old to get here on my own?"

Nyesha's dark eyes widened. "No, Mama, of course not. It's just—"

Grandma Stewart laughed then and shifted her gaze from her daughter to Lawan. "And how are you, young lady? You don't mind that your grandma came to see you without calling first, do you?"

The child's eyes were even wider than Nyesha's as she slowly shook her head from side to side, the sunlight glinting off her hair and giving it an almost blue sheen.

"Good," Grandma said, bending slightly to hug the frail girl. "At least someone is glad to see me. Now can we please go inside? It was a long bus ride, and I need to use your facilities. I drank too much coffee at breakfast this morning."

229

The two women were chatting and laughing as they walked through the garage and into the kitchen, with Lawan trailing a couple of steps behind. Though Grandma Stewart was talking with her daughter for the moment, she had every intention of spending some alone time with the shy child with the fragile heart and tragic past. When God gave this senior saint an assignment, she took it seriously.

Sarah couldn't decide if she was mad at Leah or just hurt. She'd called her the night before wanting sympathy; instead, her friend had preached at her.

*Well, maybe not exactly preached,* she conceded, as she sat in her mom's car in the parking lot at school. She knew she really should be in the classroom right now, taking notes on a lecture, but what did it matter since she still had no idea what she wanted to do with her life, especially now that spending it with Jonathan was never going to happen? Still, she felt guilty taking her mom's car for the morning when all she was doing was sitting in it, feeling sorry for herself.

*Leah meant well,* she thought. *She always does. It's just her way. She really is one of those people who says what she means and means what she says. In a way that's good because I never have to wonder if she's telling me the truth. And besides, I know she cares and wants the best for me. But . . .*

She sighed, drumming her fingers on the steering wheel and refusing to let the tears start flowing again. There were times—lots of times, actually—when Sarah wished she could be more like Leah. The girl was so maddeningly mature for her age, and Sarah knew she wasn't. She tried to look like she was, especially with Jonathan, but she was embarrassed now as she thought back over the Thanksgiving weekend and realized how she had come across as exactly the opposite. She acted like a lovesick school girl—which she supposed was to be expected, since that's what she was—but she just wished she hadn't been so obvious about it. At least before she could dream that maybe someday Jonathan might look at her and see an attractive woman instead of just a dopey little girl that hung around his sister. Now she knew that was never going to happen.

"And it's all my fault," she said out loud. "I acted like an idiot and threw myself at him. I didn't even give him a chance to say no. Of course he took me on a picnic and let me hold his hand and even kiss him. But it wasn't like any of that was his idea."

She dropped her head onto her hands which clenched the steering wheel. "I am such an idiot," she moaned. "No wonder Jonathan doesn't want me for a girlfriend. Who would? What man is ever going to want someone like me?"

*I want you. And I love you.*

The feather light whisper in her heart was just strong enough to raise her head from her hands. Her eyes widened. She'd always believed in God and even accepted Jesus as her Savior when she was a child. But she was pretty sure He'd never spoken to her before.

"God?" She swallowed. "Is that You?"

No more words came to her, but something like a warm breeze touched her cheek, and she looked at the slightly opened window beside her. Could it have come from outside? Somehow she knew it didn't.

She swallowed again, afraid to move. What had God said? That He wanted her and loved her. Was that possible . . . just like she was?

The words to "Just As I Am," one of the hymns she'd heard countless times at church, stirred in her memory. How many times had she read the words from the hymnal and joined her voice in song with the congregation and yet never even thought about what she was saying?

*Just as I am. Just as I am.*

The threat of tears returned, and this time she let them flow. "Forgive me," she whispered, wondering how she could not have realized before that the very rejection she felt from Jonathan was the same rejection she had exhibited toward God. She knew He existed, and she was even willing to make Him her Savior so she could get into heaven one day. But spend time with Him? Get to know Him and learn to love Him? She'd always been too busy.

"Forgive me, Father," she said again. "I've been so selfish. All I've thought about is my own heart. I never once thought about Yours. I'm so sorry."

A feeling of peace, as warm and smooth as honey, seeped into her heart, easing her pain and infusing her tears with inexplicable joy. She might have missed the lecture she was scheduled for that morning, but she knew at that moment she had gained something much more precious—and her life would never be the same.

# Chapter 35

Lawan had a hard time concentrating on her studies. First she'd had an unexpected treat with Nyesha, eating something called a breakfast sandwich and hash browns for the first time — and being pleasantly surprised, even though she hadn't been able to finish it all. She still liked cereal for breakfast best, but the time alone with Nyesha had been nice.

Now she was trying to study with the sounds of talking and laughter drifting into the kitchen from the family room. Though she wasn't able to understand much of what was being said, she did catch her name once in a while.

*What do they think of me?* She focused on looping her capital *B*, as Nyesha had shown her. *They sound happy, but surely they know what happened to me before I came here. It's not like it was when Mali came. She was a baby . . . and innocent.*

The thought that a lot of bad men had taken her innocence away nearly caused her to burst into tears, but she forced the feeling back down, as she had done for so very long. There was no sense crying over what could not be changed.

"Lawan?"

The girl jerked her head up, unaware that anyone had come into the room. Nyesha stood in the doorway, watching her, with Grandma Stewart right behind.

"I know we got a late start, but Grandma Stewart came all the way over here just to spend some time with you. How about if we take a break from your studies for a while so you two can get to know one another better?"

Lawan raised her eyebrows. Nyesha's mother had come all this way just to see her? Why would she do such a thing?

The women seemed to be waiting for her response, so she shrugged and nodded. "Yes, please," she said, trying to keep her voice from trembling. Why did she suddenly feel nervous?

Nyesha smiled. "Good. I'll fix you each a nice cold glass of lemonade, and then I've got some things to do out in the yard while you visit."

Lawan watched Nyesha as she plopped ice cubes into glasses, filled them up, and then left the room after leaving the drinks on the table, one in front of Lawan and one in front of Grandma Stewart, who had taken a seat next to her. Lawan kept her eyes focused on her glass, watching tiny beads of sweat begin to form as the ice floated in the pale yellow liquid.

"I just love a good glass of lemonade, don't you?"

Grandma Stewart's question forced Lawan's attention away from her drink. She peered up at the woman, who was smiling down at her, her glass of lemonade in her hand.

Lawan nodded and watched as the woman took a hearty drink and then set it back down.

"So," Grandma Stewart said, "what are you studying?"

The girl felt her cheeks grow warm. "I'm learning to write the alpha . . ." Her voice trailed off, as she struggled to remember the rest of the word.

Grandma smiled. "The alphabet? Well, good for you! Nyesha tells me you're very smart, so you'll learn it in no time." She nodded. "I remember when I was learning the alphabet — way back in the Dark Ages, of course." She laughed, as Lawan wondered what the Dark Ages might be. "I loved learning anything new in those days," Grandma went on. She tapped the side of her forehead with one finger. "I had a sharp, quick mind back then, but not anymore. I forget everything now. Why, if I didn't write my name on a piece of paper and carry it with me, I'd forget that too."

She laughed again, and though Lawan couldn't imagine not being able to remember your own name, she smiled. Grandma Stewart was a nice lady. She made Lawan feel warm inside.

The woman leaned close to her then, still chuckling. "You know I'm teasing you, right?"

Lawan nodded, though she wasn't absolutely sure what teasing meant.

"Good. Then let me tell you something serious, something I believe the good Lord wants to remind you about."

Lawan felt her eyes go wide. The Lord, phrae yaeh suu, had something to say to her? Her heart raced at the thought, but she determined to listen carefully.

"You already know that God loves you," Grandma said, still leaning close as she spoke. "Nyesha told me you and Anna came from godly, Christian parents, and that you already accepted Jesus as your Savior."

She seemed to be waiting for a response, so Lawan moved her head slightly in a nod.

Grandma Stewart beamed at the wordless affirmation. "That just blesses my heart more than I can say. There's nothing that pleases a parent or grandparent more than to know that her children are Christians. You know that means we're related, don't you?"

Lawan frowned. Related? What did she mean by that?

Grandma put her finger in the middle of Lawan's chest and then moved it to her own chest as she spoke. "If you're a Christian, that means you've been born into God's family. I'm a Christian too, so I'm in the same family. We have the same Father, so we're related. Do you understand? We're part of the same forever family, along with your mother and father and sister who are already in heaven, waiting for us to join them one day."

Lawan sucked in a quick breath at the thought. Why had she not realized that before? Of course it was true! Her parents and Chanthra were not just family here on earth, but family in heaven—forever, as Grandma Stewart had said. And this kind woman sitting in front of her was family too.

A smile broke out on her face before she could stop it, and she threw her arms around Grandma Stewart's shoulders. The woman pulled her close and kissed the top of her head.

"Oh, sweet girl," the elderly woman crooned. "It wasn't just my words that showed you this truth, was it? God showed you. He opened your heart and showed you in a way you'd never forget."

Lawan's eyes were wet by then, but her heart felt full as she allowed the woman known as Grandma Stewart to cradle and rock her in her arms. Her lap was big enough and soft enough that Lawan thought she might just stay there forever.

Forever. A forever family. *Phrae yaeh suu* had sent Grandma Stewart to teach her something so much more important than how to loop her letters.

It had been a full day of classes for Jonathan, and by the time he got out of the last one he was more than ready to head straight back to his dorm room and catch a few z's before tackling the studying he needed to do for tomorrow's exam. The afternoon breeze was cooler than he'd experienced down in San Diego the previous week, and he shivered, wishing he'd thought to grab a jacket that morning. Now that it was nearly December, he'd have to start remembering to lay one out by his books at the end of the day so he wouldn't forget to throw it on or at least take it with him when he left in the morning.

A few brown and gold leaves flew past him as he zigzagged around a bush and took a shortcut across the lawn. Individual students and a hand-holding couple crisscrossed the campus in various directions, but Jonathan paid them little attention. He was sleepy and a bit cold, but his mind was where it had been most of the day — on Sarah. No doubt she had received the letter by now, probably yesterday. But she hadn't called. Though he felt like a coward even admitting it to himself, he was relieved.

*How's she doing with it?* he wondered as his dorm came into view and he picked up his pace. *Would it have been better if I called? But writing is so much easier. I can get my thoughts straight and not get tongue-tied and forget what I want to say. What I really should have done is tell her in person, before Leah and I left, but I just didn't have a chance.*

He took the three steps to the porch in one leap and reached for the door. *Who am I kidding? The best thing would have been to never let it happen in the first place. What was I thinking?*

The door slammed behind him and he sighed as he aimed for the stairs. *OK, I've asked You to forgive me,* he prayed. *And I know You have. Now I need to forgive myself. Help me with that, Lord, please.*

By the time he reached his room, his sense of guilt had dissolved once again, and he wished for nothing more than a quick catnap before tackling the books. That was one of the perks of rooming with a jock: the guy was sure to be at football practice for at least another hour or more, so Jonathan had little doubt that he would be asleep in minutes.

Mara had worked the afternoon shift and now had an hour break before digging in for the dinner crowd. Thoughts of revenge and feelings of hatred for her uncle continued to plague her as she left Mariner's and headed toward the church. She had argued with herself for the majority of the afternoon before deciding to go in that direction. After all, didn't it make more sense to go toward the beach and sit on the seawall, rather than spending the time at church? She could count on two hands the times she'd been in any church throughout the twenty years of her miserable life, so why go there now? And yet she couldn't seem to convince herself otherwise. It was as if the church knew her name and was calling her.

238

Within moments she was there, settled into the back pew, staying near the exit in case she needed to leave early. *The last thing I want is for anyone to see me here and come up and start talking to me. I'm just here to settle some things, to . . . to . . .*

Her thoughts trailed off. Exactly why was she here? She wished she knew. Hadn't she decided just the night before that if God's love was real, it could never be extended to her because of the hatred she held in her heart against her uncle? But what else could she do? Forgiving him would be impossible.

*There is nothing impossible with God.*

Mara gasped. Was someone here after all? She jerked her head toward the door, but the back of the church was empty. She scanned the front of the building. Had she missed someone when she came in?

She swallowed. No, she hadn't missed anyone, and no one was there. Just her—and God. In that moment she knew He was the One who had spoken to her. But why?

"Why would You want to speak to me?" she whispered.

*I love you.*

She'd known, even as she voiced the question, exactly what the answer would be. And yet it made no sense. How could God love her? She was spoiled, filthy, ruined. No one would ever love or want her. Hadn't *Tio* told her that all those years? He said he was the only one who would ever love her and want her.

*He lied.*

Yes. Mara knew that was true. *Tio* lied. He raped. He tortured. He murdered. And now he was dead.

*What is that to you? You follow Me.*

Mara's eyes widened. God wanted her to follow Him? How could she do that?

*I will hold your hand.*

But . . .

*I will even carry you. But you must let it go. The hatred. The anger. The hurt. It will destroy you.*

"But I can't," she whispered. "It's impossible."

*Nothing is impossible with Me.*

They had come full circle. Where did she go from here?

Her eyes darted toward the exit again, and she considered running away and never looking back. But where would she go? Her heart wanted desperately to stay, to connect with God's offer of love, but the pain she had carried for so long warred with that desire.

"Help me," she whispered. "Show me what to do."

The memory of Sarah, sitting on the seawall, crying, floated into her thoughts, and she remembered her feeling of hope that the end of Sarah's relationship with Jonathan might mean the beginning of one for her. A sense of selfishness and loathing washed over her then, and tears stung her eyes, quickly spilling over onto her cheeks.

"That was terrible of me to feel that way," she said, her voice hushed. "How could I be happy that someone else was suffering?"

And then she understood. Though she had been a victim nearly her entire life, she too needed forgiveness. She was indeed flawed, even as those who had victimized her through their own selfishness.

Selfishness. Was that what God was trying to show her, that at the root of humanity's evil was an absorption with self? Mara may not have acted on it to the extent that *Tio* and many others had done, but the same desire to serve self had motivated her feelings when she saw Sarah crying.

"I'm so sorry," she whispered, folding her hands on the back of the pew in front of her and laying her head on top of them. "I'm so sorry, God. I need You to forgive me . . . but how can I even ask when I refuse to forgive others?"

*Give it to Me—all of it. The pain, the suffering, the anger. All of it. I will carry it for you.*

Mara's shoulders shook as sobs rose up from deep within, seemingly splitting her heart with the pain of their release. And yet she let them go, soothed by invisible arms that wrapped around her, offering her a welcome she had only dreamed about but never imagined would be hers.

*Free.*

The word echoed in her heart, and she knew for the very first time that it was indeed true. Though Jonathan had set her free from her uncle's physical imprisonment more than two years earlier, it was God Himself who had come to deliver her from her own pain and bitterness.

She remembered then how she had sat in this very church just days earlier and wondered how to pray. She'd heard God say,

"What's in your heart?" And she had responded, "Show me what's in my heart, and then maybe I'll know how to pray."

"You knew all along what was in my heart, didn't You?" she whispered. "I wanted Your love and forgiveness, but my pain was in the way and I didn't know how to pray. Thank You for showing me. All I want is Your love, God. That's all. That's enough."

241

# Chapter 36

Jonathan dropped off even faster than he'd expected, and when he awoke an hour later, the room was nearly dark and he was still alone.

Flipping on the lamp beside his bed, he tried to blink himself into alertness so he could get to his studies. He'd had a late lunch, so dinner could wait a while.

Pulling himself to his feet, he snagged his books from the foot of the bed where he'd dropped them when he came in and transferred them to his desk, clicking on the light there as well. He'd no sooner opened a book and brought his laptop to life than Mara popped into his mind.

"Not again," he groaned. "If it isn't Sarah, it's Mara. How am I supposed to keep my mind on my studies?"

The reminder that Sarah had already received and read his letter stung his heart momentarily, but the thought of Mara was so strong that he allowed his mind to focus there. *Does she need me to pray for her?* he wondered. *Is everything OK with her?*

The fear that she might be in some sort of danger again nearly drove him from prayer to a phone call, but he thought better of it. *Sorry, Lord. Even if she is in danger, she needs Your help a lot more than mine.*

Closing his eyes, he bowed his head and prayed for Mara's safety, but most of all for her salvation, for he knew that was the most important thing. As he added a final amen to his requests, he refused to entertain the thought that if Mara did become a Christian, he could at least attempt a relationship with her.

*Not going there,* he reminded himself, turning back to his laptop. The peaceful ocean screensaver waited patiently, but Mara's face still dominated his thoughts.

*Is there something else I need to do, Lord? Call her, maybe?*

When he heard no answer, he touched the mouse pad and told himself to get to work, but the next thing he knew he had opened a new document and typed "Dear Mara." A letter? What in the world would he say . . . and why? What was the point? A relationship between them was impossible . . . wasn't it?

He sighed. OK, a letter didn't have to be a romantic invitation; it could just be a simple communication between friends. With that clarification in mind, he placed his hands over the keyboard and began to type.

---

Barbara was surprised when Mara called her fairly early on Friday morning and invited her to meet for breakfast.

"I don't have to be at work until noon," she'd explained, a lilt in her voice that Barbara wasn't used to hearing. "And I have some news to tell you. Can you come?"

Barbara had glanced at her calendar to confirm that she hadn't forgotten anything, and then agreed to meet Mara at nine. There were distinct advantages to having a flexible, part-time counseling schedule, and one of them was the ability to meet with a friend for an occasional meal.

"I wonder what this is all about," she mused, as she took one last look in the bathroom mirror after applying her makeup and running a comb through her hair. No answer came from the image that still shocked her each time she saw it staring back at her. *Where did the years go? When did I start turning gray?*

She shrugged at all the unanswered questions and hurried out to her car, excited to hear what her friend had to tell her.

The coffee shop was busy that morning, but Barbara arrived first and managed to find a vacant table with two chairs in the back. Mara had insisted she would order and pay, so Barbara waited, knowing Mara would automatically order two chai lattes and two raspberry scones, as those were their favorites at this particular establishment.

When the door opened and the bell tinkled, announcing Mara's arrival, Barbara raised her eyebrows at the girl's appearance. It wasn't that she was dressed differently or had changed her hair in some way; it was that she glowed in a manner that exuded freshness and energy, as well as excitement and joy. What had happened to the girl to light her up that way?

She watched as Mara stood in line and ordered, then waited to collect their food and drinks before joining her at the table. Mara's smile as she sat down was contagious, and Barbara thought she would burst with curiosity. But she restrained herself, graciously accepting the cup and scone Mara handed her, waiting for the girl to make her own announcement.

"I went to church last night," Mara said, her voice almost a whisper as she leaned toward Barbara, her hazel eyes twinkling. "Something happened to me while I was there."

Barbara blinked. Mara had gone to church? Had she missed something? Had someone invited her? Was there a church near Mara's home or work with a Thursday night service? Of course that was more than slightly possible, but . . .

Mara set her own cup and scone down, and then laid her hand on top of Barbara's. "I could hardly keep from calling to tell you about it last night," she said, "but I had to finish my shift at

Mariner's and by then it was too late. I hardly got any sleep last night, just thinking about it."

Barbara forgot about her breakfast, as she uttered a silent prayer, daring to hope that she was about to hear the best news anyone could ever deliver. She smiled and listened as Mara began to talk.

Francesca had been especially tired the last couple of days, so when she first awoke to the rising sun and the crowing of the family rooster, she rolled over as best she could and drifted right back to sleep. But by midmorning she was jolted awake by a pain that ripped through her stomach right into her back, turning her belly to stone even as lava seemed to shoot through its very center.

"Mama!" Her scream echoed the terror she felt, as a warm wetness gushed from between her legs, soaking her sheets. "Mama, help me!"

Her mother burst into the room, her eyes wide. "What is it? What happened?" she cried, as she rushed to her daughter's bedside.

"My baby," Francesca moaned. "I think . . . he's dying."

A look of terror flitted across the woman's face, quickly replaced by a knowing look as she laid her hand on her daughter's stomach. After a moment she smiled, though concern still dominated her expression. "Your baby is not dying, *mijita*," she said. "He is just letting you know that he is tired of being in your womb; he is ready to come out into the world."

Francesca gasped. She had known this time was coming, and she'd been warned that it would be painful. But never had she imagined something like this! Was her child going to rip her apart to get out? Though the initial pain had subsided, her back still ached and she knew enough to realize the pain would return—again and again until her little one was born.

And then what? She had thought and prayed about what to do, but always there was time to decide later. Now there was no more time. Her baby was coming, and her decision had to be made now . . . before she saw him. For once she did, it would be too late.

"I will send for the doctor," her mother said, interrupting her thoughts. "The one who said he would help when your time came. If he thinks we need to take you to the hospital, we will find a way. If not, we will bring your baby into the world ourselves, right here in our own home." She smiled, touching Francesca's cheek and then brushing a stray strand of hair from the girl's eyes. The feel of her mother's hand encouraged Francesca. So long as her mother remained by her side throughout the ordeal, she knew she would be all right.

"There is only one thing," the woman said, her dark eyes serious now. "The doctor will want to know what you have decided. Will you keep the baby, or give him up for adoption? The doctor said he has a family lined up to take him, but you must decide now so we will know what to do when the baby arrives."

Francesca knew what her mother was trying so hard not to say. If Francesca opted to give her child up for adoption, he would be whisked away the moment he came forth from her body, and she would never see him. And she needed to tell her mother right now whether or not that was her choice.

# Chapter 37

As excited as Mara was in her newfound faith, she was equally nervous about going to church with Barbara. She trusted her friend implicitly, and the two of them had enjoyed a wonderful time together celebrating the news of Mara's newfound faith. But even if Mara could accept the fact that not only Jesus but also Barbara loved her just the way she was—forgiven past and all—she still couldn't imagine that the people at church could do the same.

*Of course, it's not like they have to know,* she reminded herself, as she and Barbara walked up the steps to the church's entrance. For a moment she wished she had chosen instead to go to the church where she'd met Jesus a few nights earlier, particularly as the congregants closed in around her as they entered the sanctuary. *Then again,* she thought, *that church wouldn't be empty now either. I just happened to go there when it was.*

Sticking close to her friend, who thankfully hadn't dressed up so much that Mara felt uncomfortable in her dark slacks and long-sleeved peach-colored blouse, Mara edged into the pew, following immediately behind Barbara. She was relieved when they sat down and Mara found herself near the end of the pew, next to the center aisle. Maybe no one would sit on that side of her.

She watched Barbara thumb through her Bible and place a marker on a certain page. Peering down at the brand-new Bible Barbara had presented to her just that morning and caressing the dark leather cover, she wondered how she would ever know where to turn in such a massive book.

Glancing around, she noticed that nearly everyone arrived with a Bible in hand, so apparently it was normal and even expected to bring your own Bible to church. She would make a note of that and not forget—assuming she decided to come back, of course.

Mara was anxious to learn what was in this wonderful book, which she already knew would teach her more about Jesus, whom she'd already come to love. But gathering together with other people on a regular basis—people who had no clue what sort of life she'd led and would no doubt be appalled if they did—that was another question entirely. For now, she was here because her good friend had invited her and told her it was important to come.

Though pockets of hushed conversation and even an occasional laugh continued throughout the sanctuary, most halted as a group of six people standing onstage began to play their instruments and sing. Mara was surprised to see people using guitars and drums in church, as the little exposure she'd had to organized religion of any sort had led her to believe that the only acceptable instruments for a church service would be an organ and possibly a piano. Still, the music was lively, and she had to admit that she liked it.

The reassuring warmth of Barbara's hand covered Mara's then, and the younger woman felt herself relax. Barbara was such a good friend, and she seemed to understand Mara's needs and accept her shortcomings. That meant a lot to the apprehensive girl.

*Help me, Lord,* she prayed silently. *I don't know if I belong here or not, but as long as You want me here, just show me and I'll keep coming, whether I'm welcome or not.*

People began to rise to their feet then, Barbara included, so Mara joined them. Some clapped their hands, others raised theirs in the air, while nearly all joined in the singing. Mara wasn't familiar with the songs, but she did her best to follow along by reading the words on a screen on the back wall, just above the musicians' heads. She decided she'd work on the clapping and other gestures later, once she understood what they meant.

When at last the singing was done, someone in the front invited them to greet one another. Mara's stomach clenched at the thought. What should she say?

"This is my friend Mara," Barbara said, jumping in before Mara had to make the gesture herself. "Mara," Barbara continued, "these are my good friends, Celia and Monica."

The two women shook Mara's hand and welcomed her, but it was the warm smile and attractive features of the red-haired woman named Celia that caught Mara's attention. A look passed between them, and Mara froze. Did she know? How could she?

Mara nodded her greeting and withdrew her hand, glad to sit down once again, but the connection had shaken her. Perhaps she would ask Barbara about Celia later . . . or not. First Mara would see how the rest of the service went.

Her eyes widened as she lifted her gaze to the podium at the front of the stage, where the musicians had stood only moments earlier. She knew the man who stood there now, his friendly expression taking in the people that sat before him. It was Jonathan's father. She'd seen him a couple of times during the trials after she was rescued from her uncle.

Mara blinked. She remembered now that Jonathan had mentioned in one of his letters that his father was a minister, but it never crossed her mind that he would be at the very church Barbara attended.

*And why not?* she thought. *You know Jonathan's family and Barbara are friends. Why would this surprise you?*

As the man she now knew she should think of as Pastor Flannery explained to the congregation that the senior pastor was gone for the weekend and he was filling in, she couldn't help but think how much farther out of reach Jonathan was than she'd realized. They were like night and day—absolute opposites. Jonathan was a good person, from a good family, who grew up in a good neighborhood and lived a good life. She was . . .

She shuddered and cut off the thought before allowing it to pull her any farther from her newly discovered joy. After her encounter in that empty church the previous Thursday night, she'd imagined that nothing could ever suck her back into the darkness of her former life, but now she wasn't so sure.

Sarah walked behind her parents as they merged with the rest of the foot traffic heading for the back door of the sanctuary. It was surprising how much more meaningful church had been to her today. She had even dug out the dusty old Bible her parents had given her as a child when she first received Jesus years earlier. For a short time then she had made an attempt to read and understand the Scriptures, but she had been young and soon lost interest, even though her parents encouraged her to grow in her faith. In the past couple of days, those beloved pages had seemed to come alive as she read them, and she carried it now with a renewed passion.

*If only Jonathan's father hadn't given the sermon today,* she thought, sighing as she shuffled along, careful not to block others who were still trying to exit the pews. *Not that I didn't need to hear the message on forgiveness, especially when it comes to forgiving myself. That's the hardest part. Still, seeing him up there and remembering Thanksgiving weekend with Jonathan . . .*

She shook her head and blocked out the memories that threatened to tear at her heart and start the tears afresh. Sarah had accepted that she was going to hurt for a while, but she was also excited about reconnecting with God in a more serious way. Who knew what He might have in store for her in the future?

Stepping through the doors into the bright midmorning sun, she lurched to a stop, nearly causing the people behind her to stumble. "I'm so sorry," she mumbled, stepping aside where she wouldn't block anyone else but where she could still watch the backs of the two women she'd picked out of the crowd, heading for the parking lot. One she knew for certain was Barbara Whiting, a friend of her parents and someone who'd been in the church for years. But the other one, the young one . . . was it possible? From behind she certainly looked like Mara.

253

She pulled her sunglasses from her purse, hoping to see better without squinting into the glare. As the two women turned to walk down a row of cars, Sarah caught a side view of the younger woman's face and nearly gasped.

*It really is Mara,* she thought, feeling her eyes widen in surprise. *What's she doing in church? I know she's friends with Barbara, but . . . I never expected to see her here.*

Her heart raced at the implications. Had Mara come out of curiosity? Maybe she'd just felt pressured to accept Barbara's invitation. She blinked at the third possibility. Maybe Mara had made a commitment to the Lord and become a Christian. The thought nearly took her breath away. Sarah had been in church all her life, and she knew God could, and absolutely would, forgive anyone who truly repented. But Mara? After all she'd been through?

*She was a victim.*

The thought stung her heart, as she realized again how far she'd strayed away from God all those years that she could be surprised by the magnitude of His forgiveness. And hadn't Jonathan's father just preached on that very topic? His words came floating back to her. "If someone, no matter how vile or reprehensible their sin, turns to God in true repentance, He graciously forgives and welcomes them into His family. If He did not, then His Word would not be true, His promises would not be trustworthy . . . and you and I could never be forgiven, for we all need His forgiveness as surely as the worst criminal who ever lived."

Sarah swallowed and nodded, as she heard her parents calling. She had promised to go out to brunch with them, and they were waiting. It was time to leave. She just hoped she could process the morning's events without dissolving in tears—at least not until she made it home to the safety of her room.

It was the first day Francesca felt strong enough to get out of bed and move around the house, though she did so slowly. She'd heard that women in some countries gave birth and went right back to work hours later, and she had even heard her great-grandmother tell a neighbor that she had all nine of her children at home, with no one to help her.

Francesca shook her head. How was that possible? She thought she had endured the worst pain possible while she was in the clutches of El Diablo, but bringing her baby into the world had magnified her understanding of agony. It had been a long, difficult delivery, and even the midwife had encouraged her parents to take her to a hospital. At last they had, and oh, what blessed relief Francesca had experienced when the nurse gave her an injection to relieve her pain!

She was still tired, though, even two days later, as she padded softly across the floor to the kitchen to get a drink of water. The rest of her family had gone to church, wanting to worship and thank God for rescuing their daughter and bringing her through this latest ordeal safely. Francesca knew that next Sunday, when the family once again walked the five blocks from their home to the church, she would be with them. She had so much to be grateful for, and surely she would be strong enough by then to join her family and offer her thanks.

*You don't have to wait until then.*

The reminder was a loving whisper to her heart, with no condemnation in the tone. She smiled. "*Sí, Señor*," she whispered. "And though I have thanked You already, I will continue to do so, again and again." Tears stung her eyes as she realized where she might be at this very moment if she had not been rescued with the help of the young woman named Mara, who had since become her friend.

She smiled as she headed back to her room. *I will write another letter to Mara today, she decided. I must tell her of my decision . . . and about little Antonio.*

Francesca stopped beside the tiny, hand-carved wooden cradle where her son slept peacefully, his fist pressed against his mouth and his thick, dark hair lying in gentle waves around his sweet face.

"I love you, *mijito*," whispered the young mother.

*And I love him, too,* whispered the child's heavenly Father.

# Chapter 38

It had been a quiet Sunday so far, with Leah attending chapel services on campus, where she spotted Jonathan on the opposite side of the sanctuary but didn't have a chance to talk with him.

*I'll catch him later,* she told herself as she'd headed for a late breakfast with her friends. Now the pleasant, lengthy meal was over and Leah had peeled off from her companions as they left the restaurant, wanting to call her parents to check in since she hadn't talked with them since she and Jonathan phoned home to let them know they'd arrived safely from their drive back to school the previous week. She picked out a vacant bench under the spreading branches of a huge oak where the sunlight peeked through the leaves that still managed to hang on and punched the 2 on her cell phone.

"Hey, Mom," she said as soon as she heard her mother's greeting. "How are you?"

Leah was sure she could hear the smile in her mother's voice. "I'm fine, sweetheart. How about you and Jonathan?"

"I'm good. We both are," she added. "I spotted him at chapel service this morning but didn't get a chance to talk to him. How about you and Dad?"

"We're fine, too. Your dad preached this morning."

Leah smiled. She could hear the pride in her mother's voice. She just wished she'd been there to hear her father's sermon and to cheer him on. "That's great," she said. "Was there a big turnout?"

"Not quite as full as last Sunday's service, but attendance is always higher on holidays."

Leah nodded. She'd been around the church long enough to know that was true, except perhaps on Memorial or Labor Day when many of the parishioners took off for a few days.

"The Johnsons were there, of course," Rosanna continued, "with their two adorable daughters."

Leah laughed. "I can just see that little Anna, showing off her big sister to everyone like she did last week. She sure is proud of her."

"That's for sure. I just hope Lawan is able to make the transition. It must be incredibly difficult. Anna came when she was just a toddler, but Lawan . . . with all she's been through . . ."

Her mother's voice trailed off, and Leah knew exactly what she was thinking. She'd thought the same things, many times, and had prayed accordingly.

"I saw Sarah . . . with her parents."

Leah sighed. Once again, she and her mother were undoubtedly thinking the same things. They'd prayed about that relationship, and now they waited to see how God would resolve it.

"I . . . saw someone else too." Rosanna's voice was hesitant as she spoke the words, and Leah frowned. Distant chatter of students crisscrossing the campus buzzed in her ears, but she ignored it. Her mother's statement wasn't a random one; she was sure of it. There was a purpose in her bringing it up, and Leah was certain she was about to find out what it was.

"Barbara Whiting brought a very special guest this morning."

Leah raised an eyebrow, curious but still waiting for her mother to finish.

"It was Mara."

Leah nearly dropped her phone. Mara? At church? Now that was a major surprise!

"Wow," she said at last. "I almost don't know what to say. That's wonderful, though, isn't it?"

"It sure is," Rosanna agreed. "And there's more. I saw Barbara in town yesterday, and she told me Mara has accepted Christ as her Savior. So I was thrilled when I saw her at church this morning, but not really shocked."

Hot tears pooled in Leah's eyes. Mara had received Christ. She was a believer, a sister in the Lord. Wait until she told Jonathan about this!

Jonathan. Leah had always suspected her older brother had a thing for Mara, which was all the more reason Leah had been surprised when it appeared that Jonathan and Sarah were developing a closer relationship. Though Leah didn't doubt that Jonathan would rejoice at the news about Mara, as any Christian would, she did wonder what other emotions the news might stir up.

259

<hr>

Mara picked at her salad as she sat across from Barbara. Her emotions roiled within her to the point that she was almost afraid to eat her lunch, despite the fact that she and Barbara had picked a beautiful spot outside on the patio at their favorite Mexican restaurant, where they could watch the sun glint off the Pacific and hear the waves *whoosh* up to shore.

"So . . . what did you think of the service?"

Barbara's question jerked Mara back from her thoughts. She'd known her friend would ask this very thing sooner or later, but she still wasn't sure how she should answer.

She forced a smile. "It was nice," she said, wishing she sounded more convincing. "I really liked the music."

Barbara returned her smile and nodded. "Yes, I love our worship team." She took a sip of iced tea and drew her brows together. "But what about the rest of it? The people, the sermon . . . ?"

Mara swallowed and shrugged. "Fine," she said, stretching her smile wider. "Really. It was fine."

Barbara studied her for a moment. "Something bothered you. What was it?"

She sighed, trying to buy herself a little time before answering. She knew she owed it to this woman who had treated her better than anyone else in her entire life to at least tell the truth . . . but how could she? The memory of the red-haired woman named Celia gave her an idea. Maybe she could get away with telling part of the truth, and skipping the rest. That wasn't really lying, was it? It was worth a try.

"That woman," she said, trying to sound nonchalant as she poked at a cherry tomato with her fork. "Celia, I think you said. Why did I . . . feel like I knew her . . . or had at least seen her, or . . . I don't know, connected with her somewhere before?"

Barbara set down her own fork and folded her hands in front of her. Her pale blue eyes grew serious. "I can't say whether or not the two of you ever crossed paths," she said. "In fact, I doubt it very much. However . . ." She took a deep breath. "You do have a lot in common."

She paused, as if waiting for the words to settle in. Mara tried to digest them, but they didn't make sense. What could anyone from that church possibly have in common with someone like her?

"Celia was a human trafficking victim too," Barbara said. "Though she wasn't enslaved nearly as long as you were, she knows. She understands."

Mara felt her face flame. How was this possible? Another one — like her — right there in that church? Were there others? Of course! The Johnsons. Barbara had told Mara about their older daughter, Lawan, the one who had just arrived from Thailand, and how she too had escaped human trafficking. Sooner or later the two of them would have to talk, though she doubted if either of them was quite ready yet. Just the thought of it sent her mind reeling.

Barbara reached across the table then and laid a hand on Mara's. "You're not alone," she said. "You have God now. You're in His family. And that means everyone else who is also in His family is related to you. We take this family-of-God thing seriously because we know that none of us gets into the family without first being forgiven. We all come to the Father with the same need — forgiveness for turning our backs on His unconditional, undeserved love." She smiled. "I've received it, and now you have too. So has Celia, and almost everyone else who was in that church this morning. If there is anyone there — or anywhere, for that matter — who feels you're unworthy of God's love and forgiveness because of what's happened to you in your past, then I would venture to say that person has never been born into God's family." She paused again and patted Mara's hand. "Do you understand what I'm saying? The past is past, period. It's over, done with. Under the blood, as we Christians often say. And that's where we need to leave it. We're all on equal ground at the foot of the cross."

Tears overflowed from Mara's eyes as the impact of her friend's words infiltrated her heart. Was it possible? Could it be true that not only God but also His people would love and accept her . . . just as she was?

And did she dare to dream or imagine that love and acceptance would go so far as Jonathan and his family? Her heart nearly burst at the thought, but oh, how she prayed it might be true!

Jonathan had found a quiet spot behind the dorm—not as attractive as the more popular places in front, on the spreading lawn or under a shade tree, but private and peaceful, and that's what he really wanted. No matter how hectic college life got during the week, he was determined to honor the the Lord's Day and get some much needed rest, even as he communed with his Creator.

With that in mind he had spent the last hour lying on his back on top of an old blanket from his room, his Bible beside him. The sun had begun its afternoon descent, but still he wore his dark glasses. Other than a few distant sounds of cars or students coming and going, he'd succeeded in protecting his seclusion. Until now.

"Hey, Bro."

His sister's familiar voice snagged his attention just as the warm afternoon sunshine had begun to lull him to sleep. He removed his shades and squinted up at the figure who stood over him, her curly hair appearing to be on fire.

"Hey," he answered. "What are you up to?" He indicated the blanket. "Have a seat."

She did, plopping down next to him and folding her legs in front of her as she continued to look down at him.

"I have some news," she said.

He had been about to replace his sunglasses, but he stopped, frowning at her while he waited. "From home? Everything OK?"

"Everything's fine. Dad preached this morning."

Jonathan smiled. "Wish I'd been there."

"Me too."

He put the shades back on and waited. She hadn't searched him out just to tell him that. There was more.

"Mara was there."

Jerking off the sunglasses, he sat up. "What? At church?"

Leah nodded. "Yep. With Barbara Whiting."

"Wow."

She smiled. "That's what I said. Wow. And that's not all."

Jonathan caught his breath, afraid to hope.

"Barbara told Mom yesterday that Mara accepted Christ."

The air nearly exploded from Jonathan's chest, as a rush of joy and relief washed over him and he barely held back a shout. Mara was saved! She was a Christian now—and oh, how that changed things!

"Wow again," Leah said. "I knew you'd be pleased, but . . . like I said, wow. I'd also say you're more than pleased, aren't you?"

Jonathan felt his cheeks flame. What a jerk he was! Leah gives him the greatest possible news anyone can ever hear about anyone, and his first thought is that now he has a chance at a relationship with Mara.

*First,* he told himself, *that's a selfish way to think. And second, just because she's a Christian doesn't mean she'll suddenly be interested in you.*

"Sorry," he said, remembering that he owed his sister an explanation—as if she needed one. She probably saw right through him—had probably seen it all along. He sighed. "You're right. Busted. Royally. I'm crazy about her. But you know that already, don't you?"

Leah cocked her head to one side. "I thought I did," she said. "But then I saw you with Sarah last weekend, and I wasn't so sure anymore."

Jonathan's cheeks flamed again, and he shook his head. "Big mistake. I figured I had zero chance with Mara—which is probably still true—so I thought maybe Sarah and I . . .

He hung his head. "That was so wrong. I gave her false hope, and now she's hurt."

"I know. She told me about the letter."

Jonathan looked up. "Is she OK?"

Leah shrugged. "Mom said she was at church with her parents this morning."

"Sarah and Mara both?" He sighed. "I sure do make a mess of things sometimes, don't I?"

"Who doesn't?" Leah smiled. "But hey, we know the One who can bring good out of our messes, don't we?"

Jonathan's smile was weak but hopeful. "We do," he said. "And I'm praying like crazy that He'll do that—with Sarah and Mara, and all of us."

Leah nodded. "He will. For sure, He will."

# Chapter 39

By the time Monday rolled around, Mara was feeling better again. Her joy had returned, and she was facing the new week at work with optimism. She didn't have to be there until just after lunch, since she'd be working straight through dinner to closing, so she lazed around in bed for a while before showering and heading out for a morning jaunt along the beach.

She threw a light windbreaker over her T-shirt and jeans and nearly jogged down the stairs, anxious to experience the morning sun before it settled directly above in its noonday peak. The small mailboxes in the entryway caught her eye. They'd already been loaded up for the day, so she took her key from her pocket, where her cell phone also rested, and opened the box marked "M. Jimenez." A phone bill and a personal letter awaited her, and she pulled them out and shut the mailbox door.

She shoved the phone bill in her pocket, along with the key, and read the address on the letter before opening the front door and stepping outside onto the vacant porch. Her hand trembled as she considered ripping the envelope open right away, but she pressed her lips together and determined to wait until she had her morning cup of coffee in hand and was comfortably situated in her favorite spot on the seawall.

*Almost the same place I saw Sarah sitting the other day, crying,* she thought, a stab of guilt nicking her heart as she considered again how selfish her initial reaction had been. She reminded herself that God had forgiven her and pushed the letter into her already full windbreaker pocket and continued down the walkway toward the sidewalk, setting a brisk pace as she went.

The late morning breeze was light, not enough to cause a chill but just enough to ruffle Mara's short brown hair as she walked. The usual weekday traffic passed by, punctuated by an occasional horn blast from an impatient driver or a burst of laughter or conversation, though she wasn't close enough to decipher the words.

A short line at her favorite coffee spot enabled her to get her hot drink and cruller quickly and then take them outside where she could enjoy them while listening to the surf and enjoying the wonderful Southern California winter weather. Her perch awaited her, and she settled down on it before taking her first sip of coffee.

A few sips and a bite of cruller later, and she set them down on the seawall beside her so she could read her mail. Pulling the two pieces from her pocket, she glanced at the phone bill first. Any point in opening it? Not really. It was the same exact amount each month. She never went over her minutes—never even came close to using them, in fact. Other than an occasional call from Barbara, she seldom used it at all.

She replaced it in her pocket and stared down at the remaining envelope, the handwriting familiar, causing her heart to race. Jonathan had written to her before, but his letters were always casual and light, despite the fact that Mara suspected he wanted something more.

*Wishful thinking,* she told herself. *What would he want with you? Men are only interested in you for one thing, so you're just imagining things because Jonathan's not that way . . . is he?*

The flash of doubt stung deeply, as she had been so determined to keep Jonathan's image perfect. He was her hero, after all, the one who had rescued her from a life that, in her mind, truly was worse than death. Was it possible that he wasn't perfect after all?

*He's just human,* she reminded herself. *Maybe he's interested in you for the same reason other men are. It's not like he could be serious about someone like you — not with girls like Sarah around.*

She pushed the memory of Sarah, sitting on the wall crying, from her mind and tore open the letter. No sense staring at it and wondering any longer. There was only one way to find out what was really on Jonathan's mind.

*Hello Mara,* it began. *I'm really sorry we didn't get a chance to spend any time together while I was home for Thanksgiving. I wanted to find out how you were doing. I hope everything is going OK for you, with work and all. Are you still planning to start school after the first of the year? Have you decided yet what you want to study?*

Mara sighed and lifted her eyes from the letter to gaze out toward the sea. Only a few wet-suited surfers bobbed on the fairly quiet waves, and a mere handful of people dotted the beach. It was peaceful here, and yet peace eluded her at the moment. Jonathan's words gave no indication that he was interested in anything more than a casual friendship with her. Still, he did say he was sorry they hadn't had a chance to spend time together while he was home.

*My fault. If I'd given him just one hint of encouragement . . .*

But she hadn't, and that was that. She dropped her eyes back down to the letter.

*Things are going well for me at school, though I have to admit I'm really looking forward to a couple of weeks off at Christmas time. Please forgive me if I'm out of line for asking, but is there any chance we can get together while I'm home this time? Just to talk and get to know each other a little better. What do you think?*

Tears threatened at the thought, but Mara squeezed her eyes shut, determined not to give in to them. What did she think about getting together with Jonathan when he came home again? She thought it would be wonderful. But she couldn't say that to him, since he had made it clear he only wanted to talk, nothing more.

She wiped away the tears and read on.

*On a different topic, I can't help but wonder if you've thought about some of the things I wrote to you before — you know, about Christianity. About the universal need for forgiveness, for a Savior, and how God has provided One — only One — in His Son, Jesus Christ. I won't push it or preach at you, I promise, but I really would like to discuss this sometime, either in letters or, better yet, in person. Think about it . . . and let me know.*

She looked at the signature: *Praying for you. Jonathan.*

At that moment, more than anything, she wanted Jonathan to know that she had indeed thought about the things he'd told her about Jesus. She wanted to tell him what had happened to her in that little church last week, and also how she had heard his father speak on forgiveness the previous morning.

And then she remembered. He always scratched his cell phone number at the bottom of his letters — "Just in case," he wrote beside it — and sure enough, it was there now.

Before her courage could wane, she reached in her pocket and pulled out her phone. Maybe it was about time she took advantage of some of those unused minutes.

Ten more minutes until class ended. Jonathan was counting the seconds. It had seemed like the longest morning of his life, with little sleep the night before and way too much on his mind to concentrate on his teacher's droning lecture.

*Indigenous people groups and the need to get the gospel to them should not be a boring subject, he thought. But even if my eyelids didn't weigh ten tons right now, I'd still be snoozing through this class. They must have sent this guy to school just to master being boring because he sure has nailed it.*

The vibrator on his phone sprang to life and pushed his eyes open. No one called him during class unless it was important. He frowned and slipped the phone from his pocket. The area code was from home, but he wasn't familiar with the number.

Pushing the receive button as he grabbed his backpack and slunk from his desk to the back door, he whispered, "Just a minute," and slipped out into the hallway. It was close enough to the end of class anyway, and besides, how much could he miss? He hadn't heard more than a few words the instructor had mumbled in the past forty-five minutes anyway.

He pressed the phone against his ear. "Hello?"

"Jonathan?"

The voice was familiar, though strangely so. He knew it, but not over the phone. His heart raced. "Mara?"

After a pause, she answered, "Yes. I'm sorry if I bothered you, but—"

"Oh no, you didn't bother me," he rushed to assure her, making quick time to the end of the hallway and then out the door into the thin sunshine. The wind was cool, scattering leaves around his feet, but he ignored everything around him,

269

concentrating only on the voice at the other end of his little black phone.

"Are you sure?" she asked. "Because I can call back later . . . or something."

"No, no, this is fine. Perfect, in fact." He smiled, knowing it would come through in his voice. "In fact, you saved me from death by boredom. I couldn't have lasted another minute."

She giggled, and his heart soared. He didn't think he'd ever heard Mara laugh before, and he was glad he'd been able to make her do so now.

"Tough class?" she asked.

"Deadly. Worse than deadly."

"Then I guess it's a good thing I called when I did."

"Beyond good. Seriously. No one should have to endure an hour lecture from someone with a monotone voice."

He waited, but she didn't laugh again, so he decided he'd better get the conversation rolling before she changed her mind and hung up. Something about Mara always made him feel tenuous, fragile, even though he knew she must be incredibly strong to have lived through what she'd endured at the hands of her uncle.

The reminder of the news his mother had sent via Leah popped into his mind then, and he shot up a silent prayer for wisdom.

"I . . . heard some great news about you yesterday . . . from Leah."

"Really?" She sounded genuinely puzzled. "I haven't talked to Leah, or even seen her. Isn't she there at school, with you?"

Jonathan nodded, then reminded himself that she couldn't see him. "Yeah, she is. But . . . she called home yesterday, after church, and Mom told her she'd seen you at the service with Barbara Whiting."

The pause was brief before she responded. "There's a lot I want to tell you, and most of it can wait until you're home for Christmas, like you said in your letter."

He'd nearly forgotten the letter he'd sent her before hearing the news from Leah, but his heart raced at the realization that Mara had not only received and read it, but planned to take him up on his suggestion of spending time together when he was home in a few weeks.

"Still," she said, "I wanted to at least let you know now, before I see you next month, that . . . I received Jesus as my Savior. And . . . I went to church with Barbara on Sunday, just like your mom said, and heard your dad speak on forgiveness." She paused briefly before adding, "His words meant a lot to me."

Jonathan swallowed. So it was true. Mara had become a Christian, as he'd hoped and prayed for the last couple of years. On top of that, she was willing to spend time with him. What else could he ask for?

271

"And your words mean a lot to me," he said, his voice husky. "More than I can tell you. I'm so glad you called, Mara."

He waited, his heart suspended, until at last she said, "So am I. It just seemed too important to put in a letter. And since you always put your number at the bottom of your letters, I figured it would be OK to call."

"OK?" Jonathan nearly laughed. "It's better than OK. It's great! But now I have your number on my phone, so you'd better know that I'm going to be calling you back now and then."

This time he could hear the smile in her voice. "I'm counting on it," she said. "And make it as often as you want."

A gust of wind blew leaves across Jonathan's feet, and he realized he was still standing right outside the door where students would be pouring out momentarily. Clutching the phone, he hurried to a secluded spot under a towering pine tree and did his best to make himself invisible. He just wasn't ready to let her go yet.

"So . . . what are you doing the rest of the day?" he asked.

"I have to go to work in a couple of hours. What about you?"

"An early lunch," he said, "and then more classes. But I'm going to have an even harder time concentrating now."

"Why is that?"

Jonathan swallowed and took a deep breath. "Because I'll be thinking about you. About how great it is that you're a Christian now . . . and that I'll be seeing you in a few weeks."

"I'll be thinking about that too," she said. "Maybe even counting the days."

He smiled. "I'll count them with you."

And just when he thought things couldn't possibly get any better, she said, "Will you . . . pray for me too?"

This time he couldn't keep the laugh inside; the joy of it was just too strong. It burst out, brief but excited, and he answered, "I sure will, Mara. I promise. And you pray for me too. Please."

Sarah was back in class that Monday, determined to do whatever was necessary to get herself back on track—not just in her relationship with the Lord, but with school as well. It was time to get serious about her future, especially now that she had accepted the fact that it would not contain Jonathan Flannery.

The thought still hurt, and probably would for quite a while. But she'd worked through a lot of the pain and realized she'd brought most of it on herself. She'd pursued Jonathan shamelessly, giving him little choice in the matter, and then been shocked when he rejected her. It was a mistake she wouldn't make again, not just because she didn't want to be hurt or humiliated by someone else but because she realized that her priority needed to be a love relationship with Christ. She had left that somewhere at the bottom of her priority list for far too long, but now her priorities were realigned. Whatever God had for her, that's what she was going to go after with all her heart.

She typed notes into her small laptop as the teacher spoke, reminding herself that she needed to pay attention and ace the upcoming test. Who knew where her newfound dedication to the Lord might take her? Wherever or whatever it was, she wanted to fulfill it honorably.

The buzzer rang then, catching Sarah by surprise. How had the hour flown by so quickly? She shook her head and turned off her computer. Time for lunch. Maybe one of the other girls in the class would want to share it with her. She smiled at the thought.

# Chapter 40

Kyle was tired by the time he got home from work on Monday evening, but he was determined to spend some special time with his new daughter. He'd noticed that Nyesha and Lawan were beginning to bond, and he was thrilled. But he didn't want to be left out of that bonding process.

Nyesha greeted him at the door with a kiss. "Lawan is ready for your date," she whispered, "though I think she's more than slightly nervous."

"Poor thing. She probably hasn't a clue what to expect." He stepped inside and loosened his tie. "Do you think I should leave my suit on, or dress down a bit?"

She smiled and refastened his tie. "Leave it on," she said. "I took her shopping this afternoon, and she's wearing her new dress."

Grateful to his wife for remembering the details that never even crossed his mind, he turned to head down the hall to the girls' room.

"Wait," Nyesha called.

He turned back.

"Lawan got a letter from Thailand today . . . from her friend BanChuen at the orphanage. Joan translated it into English so I could read it to her." She paused. "Lawan said it made her sad to hear from her friend and to know that BanChuen was sad too.

But she let me hold her while we talked about it, and I think that means she's making progress."

Kyle nodded before turning back toward the hallway. He breathed a silent prayer as he knocked on the door. In seconds, Anna pulled the door open and squealed with delight when she saw her father, reaching up as he lifted her into his arms and hoisted her up for a hug and kiss.

"How's my princess today?" he asked, relishing the feel of her tiny arms around his neck.

"I'm fine, Daddy," she said, planting another wet kiss on his cheek. "Are you taking us out for dinner tonight?"

From the corner of his eye, Kyle spotted Lawan sitting stiffly on the side of her bed, her hands folded in her lap. She was dressed in white ruffles of some sort, and her hair was pulled back with a flowered clip. Gently he set his youngest child on her feet and smiled down at her.

"Not tonight, Princess," he said. "You remember we all talked about this yesterday, right?"

The little girl's smile faded, and her lips trembled slightly as she nodded.

"You and I have had lots of date nights, and we'll have lots more," he said. "And sometimes we'll all go out together. But tonight is date night for Lawan and me."

He directed his smile in Lawan's direction then, but her eyes were downcast. This was going to be more of a challenge than he'd anticipated. But he knew Nyesha would be praying the entire time they were gone, and he imagined God would move others to do the same.

With that assurance he crossed the room to stand in front of the young girl who had so recently joined their family. "That's a lovely new dress you have on, Lawan," he said. "May I have the honor of your accompaniment to dinner?"

Slowly the girl raised her head, her wide almond eyes slightly damp. Her nod was nearly imperceptible, but he accepted it and held out his hand. Lawan's eyes grew wider, but obediently she placed her hand in his and rose from the bed. It was time for their date.

Morning spread across the bamboo-forested valley, heralded by the calls of babblers, mynahs, and trumpeting elephants. Another day had started.

Joan yawned and stretched, knowing she needed to get up and get moving. There were several hundred hungry mouths to feed before the compound's activities began in earnest. A new girl had arrived just the day before, and Joan had been pleased to see BanChuen take her under her wing the way she had done with Lawan a few months earlier. That meant BanChuen was beginning to heal from her pain at having been separated from Lawan.

As so often happened, Joan's heart tugged at the reminder of Lawan. The girl's sweet smile hovered in her memory, tainted by the tragedy of the child's tortured life. Oh, how Joan hoped she was adapting to her new environment and that she would find healing from the countless wounds that had been inflicted upon her!

*Breakfast will just have to wait a few minutes,* she thought, slipping to her knees beside her mosquito-netted bed. Mort was already up and about, so she decided to take advantage of a few moments of solitude and pray for the children in their care—and for the one she had left across the sea in the care of others. Something told her that God was listening . . . and that He was working it all out in that faraway land of America that had once been Joan's home and now belonged to little Lawan.

The restaurant was just upscale enough that Lawan would feel special without being intimidated—at least, that was Kyle's hope and obviously what Nyesha had in mind when she made the reservations. He and Nyesha had eaten here before, on several occasions, so he knew the food was good and even offered some Thai specials, which might please Lawan.

She sat across from him now, looking up only when spoken to, and otherwise seemingly fascinated with her plate as she stared down at it. So far she hadn't touched the spring rolls the waiter had left as an appetizer.

"Aren't you hungry?" Kyle asked, his voice gentle.

Lawan looked up, a trace of fear in her dark eyes. It was obvious she didn't know how to answer him, so he intervened, using a serving spoon to scoop a roll onto her plate.

"These are very good," he said. "Try it. Please."

She nodded then and used her fork to break off a piece.

"It's OK to use chopsticks if you prefer," Kyle said. "You can even pick it up and eat it with your fingers." He smiled. "I don't mind, and we don't care what anyone else thinks."

A trace of a smile touched her lips, but only for a second, as she continued to use her fork, lifting a bite to her mouth.

*Help me, Lord,* Kyle prayed. *Help her!*

Lawan's face brightened slightly.

"Do you like it?" Kyle asked. "Is it good?"

She nodded, a surprised but pleased look spreading across her face.

Kyle continued to pray silently as they worked their way through the meal. Though their conversation remained limited, she did appear to relax a bit as the evening wore on. By the time the waiter brought her a glass bowl with a scoop of mint chocolate chip ice cream in it, Lawan's smile was as close to full as Kyle had seen it since she arrived.

"Good," Lawan said after her first bite.

It was only one word, but it was the first she'd offered of her own accord and not in response to a direct question. Kyle felt his shoulders relax.

"Very good," he agreed. "Should we get some of this ice cream to take home for you?"

Her eyes lit up, and this time her nod was vigorous. "Yes," she said. "I like it!"

Kyle laughed. "I like it too. OK then, mint chocolate chip ice cream it is, stored up in the freezer just for you."

Lawan was still smiling when she said, "But not peanut butter." Her eyes widened then, and her smile disappeared. She seemed to be holding her breath while she waited for Kyle's reaction.

Puzzled, Kyle frowned. "No peanut butter? You don't like peanut butter?"

Her face still somber, Lawan shook her head slowly from side to side.

Kyle remembered then how much Anna loved peanut butter and how often she lobbied for peanut butter sandwiches, no doubt subjecting Lawan to repeated offerings of the sticky food. And Lawan would no doubt have been too shy to say anything.

*Until now,* he thought, his smile spreading across his face. She had trusted him enough to tell him, even though the words had escaped before she'd realized what she was saying.

He reached across the table and laid a hand on hers. She flinched but did not pull away. "If you don't like peanut butter, you never have to eat it again," he assured her. "You're our daughter too, Lawan, and we care about you. It's all right to tell us if you don't like something."

For a moment she didn't move, but then a slow smile once again touched her lips, as the mist returned to her eyes and she nodded. "*Kop koon,*" she said. "Thank you."

"*Kop koon,*" Kyle repeated. "Thank you, Lawan, for telling me . . . and for coming to live with us and being our daughter."

# Chapter 41

Mara had almost hoped her boss would tell her she had to work late that evening and that would be her perfect excuse to skip the Wednesday night service. As it turned out, that didn't happen. The day was so slow that her boss actually told her to take off early, so she'd had plenty of time to walk and pray and think between the time she left Mariner's and arrived at home.

"I want to go, Lord," she whispered, as she checked her image in the mirror one last time before heading downstairs to wait for Barbara. "It's just . . ."

*Just what?* She narrowed her eyes and peered more closely at herself. "You're a coward," she said out loud. "You're afraid of what people will think if anyone realizes who you are—or, at least, who you used to be." She took a deep breath. "But it wasn't your fault. You were a child, a victim. You did not choose what happened to you, and you couldn't escape. Besides, you're forgiven now, and you need to remember that."

She forced a smile, but it looked wobbly. For now, though, it was the best she could do.

She stepped out of the bathroom and retrieved her Bible from her bed, grabbed a light jacket, and headed for the door. Barbara said she would pick her up at seven, and it was nearly that now.

*Why am I so nervous? I survived Sunday service; what's so different about this?*

But even as she arrived at the bottom of the stairs, she knew the answer. Barbara had told her the Wednesday evening service was much more informal. "More intimate," she'd said. "A better chance to get to know people."

And that was Mara's hesitation. Just how well did she want to know the people at church? More specifically, how well did she want them to know her?

She took a deep breath and stepped outside onto the porch just as Barbara's familiar sedan pulled into view. One way or the other, she was about to find out.

~§~

By the time the service was over and Mara and Barbara had piled back into the car for the drive home, Barbara sensed that the tension she'd felt coming from her younger friend earlier had dissipated.

"You in a hurry to get home?" she asked.

Mara turned toward her as she buckled her seatbelt, her eyebrows raised questioningly. "Not really. Why?"

Barbara shrugged and grinned. "Oh, I don't know. I thought maybe you might want to go with me for a quick bite." She leaned toward her and lowered her voice. "To tell you the truth, I'm starved. I skipped lunch and didn't have time for anything before we came tonight."

"You haven't eaten since breakfast?"

Barbara shook her head. "Nope."

Mara laughed. "Well, then I guess it's my duty to make sure you don't pass out from hunger before the night's over. By all means, let's go get something."

They exited the parking lot laughing, and Barbara felt a warm sense of gratitude wash over her. What a delightful friend Mara was—and what an amazing work of grace and healing God was doing in her life!

"So where are we going?" Mara asked, interrupting her thoughts.

Barbara shrugged again. "I don't know. I'm so hungry I hadn't even thought about it. Anywhere is fine with me."

"The usual?"

Barbara grinned and nodded. "Sounds great to me—unless you think we're getting into a rut."

"Hey, if delicious Mexican food is a rut, I'm all for it."

They laughed again as they drove the few blocks to the restaurant where they'd almost become regulars. In moments they were seated across from one another in a back booth, dipping chips in a bowl of salsa and chatting about their day.

"So how did you enjoy the service?" Barbara asked between mouthfuls of chimichanga.

Mara paused as she swallowed, but Barbara thought it was intentional so she could consider her answer. Then she nodded. "I liked it," Mara said. "To be honest, I was afraid I wouldn't. Seriously, I thought it would be uncomfortable because you said it was more intimate. And when we broke up into small groups for prayer, I nearly panicked, especially when I found myself standing next to Celia." She leaned forward and lowered her voice. "I couldn't help but think of what you told me about her past, and how she talks about it to help people understand the problem and to get them involved in helping to rescue people like . . . like Lawan and Francesca and . . . me." Her eyes flicked away briefly before returning to rest in Barbara's gaze.

Barbara reached across the table and patted Mara's hand. "I've long since come to believe that God doesn't deal in coincidences.

283

I am instead a firm believer in divine appointments. There is a reason — probably more than one — that you and Celia were standing exactly where you were tonight."

Mara nodded as her eyes misted over. "I think you're right. I don't know if I can ever speak about my past life the way Celia does, but I do want to do something to help if I can."

"Of course you do," Barbara agreed, squeezing Mara's hand. "And you will — in God's time."

Mara watched the taillights of Barbara's car disappear around the bend. The evening had turned out so much better than Mara had anticipated, but she was tired now and ready to go to bed. She had to be up early to work the morning shift at the restaurant, and the breakfast crowd usually kept her hopping.

She stepped into the entryway and spotted the mailboxes on the wall, realizing she hadn't checked her mail that day. She did so now and was pleased to find another letter from Francesca. Smiling, she tucked it inside her Bible and took the stairs at a fast clip, anxious to read her friend's news in the privacy of her room.

Once inside she plunked down on the edge of her bed, kicked off her shoes, and tore open the envelope. She nearly laughed aloud at the news that greeted her the moment she began to read:

*It's a boy! His name is Antonio Eduardo Calderon, after mi papa and mi abuelo. And yes, I have decided to keep him. My parents*

*will help me raise him, and I know that God is my* bebito's *true Father, so He will help me too.*

Tears pooled in Mara's eyes and spilled over onto her cheeks as she continued to read, and her heart felt as if it would burst with joy. A baby! Francesca had a baby, a beautiful little boy to love and raise—and her family would help her do so. How wonderful that the girl had such a family, people who cared for her and supported her.

*Not like my family,* Mara thought, and then immediately banished the words. This was no time for self-pity. A new life had come into the world, and it was cause for rejoicing. Maybe tomorrow Mara would invite Barbara for dinner again, this time to celebrate.

And then she read the closing lines, and her joy nearly dissolved to ashes.

285

*You must come to Mexico and meet Antonio. It is because of you that he lives—and that I live as well. Please come soon, Mara. I would truly love to see you again, and to thank you for all you have done for us.*

Mara set the letter down in her lap, as her hands began to tremble. Return to Mexico? No. Not even for a day—or a moment! Her parents were there, only hours from Francesca's home. Mara had no desire ever to set foot anywhere near them again. They had sold her into slavery, and the one thing she could never do, despite God's great mercy to her, was to forgive them.

The thought of what that could mean to her relationship with the Lord she had met so recently sent a chill down her back, and she threw herself onto the bed and buried her face in the pillow as she sobbed.

# Chapter 42

Sarah had been surprised but certainly not shocked to see Mara at the Wednesday night service two days earlier. After all, why shouldn't she come? She was a believer now—assuming she truly had received Christ as her Savior, and Sarah had no reason to think otherwise—so it was nearly expected that she should start attending services somewhere as regularly and often as possible.

*It's what I'm doing now,* she reminded herself as she strolled along the packed, damp sand, her bare feet flirting with the remnants of the waves that rolled onto the shore. *Now that I've finally made a real commitment to my faith.*

She smiled, even though tears stung her eyes. The pain eased a little with each passing day, though she knew it would be awhile before it disappeared completely. Still, she understood better now that she had pushed for something God had not intended, and that was never the best for anyone.

*Two weeks,* she thought. *Just two short weeks ago I was right here, at this very beach, enjoying a picnic with Jonathan and imagining a relationship I had dreamed up in my own mind. No wonder he felt awkward. He's been so apologetic to me, when I should be the one apologizing to him. Maybe next time I see him . . .*

*That would be for Christmas,* she reminded herself. *When Jonathan and Leah come home again.* Sarah doubted she was ready to see him at that point, but she saw no way to avoid it.

Jonathan's sister was her best friend, and they all went to the same church. She took a deep breath. She would just have to hang on to God and trust Him to get her through it, especially during church services.

*Mara will be there too.*

The thought pierced her heart, but she kept walking, her feet leaving water-filled impressions behind her. Yes, no doubt Mara would be at the same services as she . . . and Jonathan. Christmas Eve would be the hardest.

*I will just have to stay focused on why we're there, she thought. Help me do that, Lord. Please. I know it won't be easy, but I know You won't let me walk through it alone.*

Even now she felt the assurance that He walked beside her, as she remembered the famous "Footprints" poem about the two sets of footprints left in the sand as God walks beside the lonely pilgrim.

*Except in the worst places. Then there's only one set of footprints because You carry us.*

She sensed God smile, and it warmed her more than the sunshine overhead. Yes, He would carry her, as He had promised. And one day she would look up to find that He had brought her through the pain and into a place of joy once again. Despite the ache in her heart, she felt that promise of joy permeate her—even now.

Barbara and Mara had not been able to reconnect for dinner on Thursday or Friday due to their conflicting schedules, but Saturday evening was free for both of them. Opting for Chinese food that night, they sat inside on a rare rainy evening, sipping steaming hot tea and munching on eggrolls while they waited for the rest of their meal. Mara had handed her letter from Francesca to Barbara as soon as they sat down, and now they discussed its contents with enthusiasm.

"I just can't get over how well this has worked out for that precious girl," Barbara said, pouring herself another cup of tea and silently offering one to Mara as well. When Mara nodded, Barbara filled her cup and then set the pot down before continuing her comments.

"When I think of how things could have turned out for her if you hadn't intervened when you did . . ." Her voice trailed off and she shook her head.

Mara smiled. "I've thought of that myself—many times. It's a lot like my own situation. If Jonathan hadn't stepped in and taken a chance when he did, I might still be trapped in that horrible compound." She dropped her gaze for a moment and then looked back up. "Or worse," she said.

Barbara sighed and nodded. "Or worse. Yes. I've considered that, especially since you told me of what happened to that poor girl—Jasmine, was it?"

Tears immediately stung Mara's eyes, as they always did at the reminder of the young girl who had died not long before her uncle's "business" was busted and his slaves rescued. "Yes. Jasmine." She shook her head. "She was such a sweet girl. But she wasn't the only one. There were others, some as young as five or six." Her voice broke and she paused, breathing deeply as Barbara covered her hand with her own. "Sometimes I can't think about it. It's just too . . . brutal."

"I can't even begin to imagine," Barbara said. "I know God will bring healing, Mara, but I also know it will take time."

Mara nodded, waiting until Barbara removed her hand when the waiter came with shrimp chow mein and fried rice. Enough about her past. Time to change the subject.

"So," she said as she scooped some rice onto her plate. "How is everything going with you?"

Barbara smiled. "All is well on the home front," she said. "Kids and grandkids fine, personal life fine, work fine . . . you know the drill."

Mara laughed. "Yes, I do. I know you well enough by now to know you don't allow circumstances to control your life. You trust God, no matter what happens. That's what keeps you so even-tempered, isn't it?"

"Oh, I have my moments," she laughed. "If you ever get my kids alone, they'll tell you that, just as my husband would have before he died all those years ago. But yes, for the most part, I've learned that despite what's going on around me, Jesus Christ is the same yesterday, today, and forever, just as the Scriptures say He is. And that's the Rock I stand on when everything around me is bucking and rolling with the winds."

290

Mara sighed. "I sure hope I can get to that point some day."

Barbara smiled. "You just keep your eyes on Jesus, and you will. I promise."

The women worked their way through half of the chow mein and rice before they found themselves moaning about how full they were and decided to split up the leftovers and take them home for another time.

"They always give us way too much here," Barbara said, signaling for the waiter to bring some cartons. She retrieved her purse from the floor beside her, picking up Francesca's letter as she did so.

"Oh, I must have dropped this," she said, handing it back to Mara. "I wouldn't want to lose it. Have you answered her yet?"

Mara took the letter and shook her head. "No, not yet, but I will. Probably tomorrow after church."

Barbara nodded. "And what about her invitation to come to Mexico and see little Antonio? Are you going to take her up on that?"

Mara felt her eyes widen. "No," she said quickly. "I'm not going back to Mexico."

Barbara's eyebrows raised. "You sound quite definite about that."

"I am."

"Any particular reason?"

Mara felt the tears return to betray her, and she tried to blink them away. Before she could, Barbara once again reached across the table and took her hand. "It's your parents, isn't it? Your family and . . . what they did to you."

Mara wanted to deny it, wanted to scream and tell Barbara that it was none of her business. But she couldn't do that to the one person she trusted more than anyone else in the world. How could she tell Barbara that she meant more to her than her own mother, that she never, ever, wanted to see her real mother or father again?

She realized then that she didn't have to tell her. Barbara already knew. And God knew too. So why didn't He just let the subject lay where it belonged—dead and buried? Why did He have to keep niggling at her heart with the thought that . . . ?

No. She couldn't do it. Not now, not ever. She simply could not go back to Mexico and see her parents . . . and forgive them for what they had done to her.

Or could she? Was this truly what God required of her? And if so, would He help her do the impossible? Jefe was gone now—dead and no doubt in hell, where he could never hurt her again. But her parents were still alive. Maybe she could somehow, someday, really and truly let go of the anger she felt toward her *tio* simply because she would not have to face him to do it. But her parents . . . So far as she knew, they were still alive. And though she longed to deny it, she realized she would have to face them in person if ever she was going to forgive them and find the freedom she so desperately needed to move on with her life.

---

Jonathan had kept his promise to Mara to pray for her, though it hadn't been hard to do. He thought of her nearly all the time, and shot up a prayer for her each time the memory of her wide hazel eyes invaded his consciousness. How his heart soared at the thought that Mara had come to know Jesus as Savior . . . and he prayed daily that she was growing in her relationship with Him. What a difference it would make in their own relationship—if God indeed had purposed that they have one.

He continually reminded himself of that, using God's purposes and not his own to keep his feelings and dreams in check. Just because he and Mara were both believers now didn't necessarily mean that God intended for them to have a future together. But at least it was a distinct possibility.

A crisp wind blew across campus that morning, as Jonathan zipped his jacket and headed for class. The first two weeks of December had passed in a blur of studies and exams, and in less than a week, he and Leah would be piling into the old blue Beetle and heading south again, toward home . . . and toward Mara.

He shivered, more with anticipation than from the cold, at the thought of finally seeing her again. This time he wouldn't take no for an answer. Though he would bow to God's purpose regarding his relationship with Mara, he was certain they needed to spend time together to discover that purpose. And oh, how he hoped and prayed that God would give them a green light!

Jonathan smiled as he remembered their last phone conversation. It had taken great restraint to limit his calls to a couple of times a week, as he really wanted to talk with her every day—more than once. But the last thing he wanted to do was scare her off, so he took his time and didn't push. As a result, she was opening up more, talking to him about topics other than just work or the weather.

"I saw your parents at church last night," she'd said when they spoke on Thursday. "The Bible study was really good," she'd added, warming his heart. And the way she'd said his name when they ended the call had stayed with him for hours.

Yes, they were indeed making progress. And in a few more days, he would see her face to face. Where would God take them from there? His heart raced at the possibilities as he turned toward his next class and determined to pay attention to his studies.

293

# Chapter 43

It almost felt like winter this morning, even in Southern California. The sun barely warmed Mara's face as she walked from her home to the little beachside café where she was to meet Barbara for a light breakfast. As she neared the seawall, and the vast expanse of sand that stood between her and the rolling gray waves came into sight, she realized she wasn't the only one who felt the chill wind. Only a couple of brave souls, bundled up in jackets, dotted the landscape, and they were walking at a brisk pace—no casual strolls today.

She stepped up to the little café and pulled the door open to the sound of tinkling bells, announcing her arrival. Barbara was already seated at one of a half-dozen little tables that filled the tiny room. All the other tables were empty.

Barbara looked up and smiled in greeting. "I ordered your coffee," she said. "I knew you'd be on time."

Mara nodded. Punctuality was definitely one of her strong points. Did she have any others? She hoped so.

She settled into the chair across from her friend. "Thanks," she said, taking her first welcome sip. "I needed this."

"I didn't order anything else yet," Barbara said. "Do you want a menu?"

Mara shook her head. "Not yet—unless you're in a hurry."

"Not at all. So what's up? You said you wanted to talk to me about something."

Mara's grip on her coffee cup tightened. The only reason she'd told Barbara ahead of time that she had something specific she wanted to talk to her about was so she wouldn't chicken out. The thought still drew her stomach into knots, but she felt so certain that she had to do it. Might as well plunge in and say it now; it wasn't going to get any easier later.

"I'm going back," she said, her voice cracking. "To Mexico. To my family."

Barbara's eyes widened and her mouth opened, but before she could speak, Mara continued.

"Not to stay," she explained. "Just to see them. To see if they're still there, still alive, still . . ." She shrugged. "I don't know. Just . . . to see them."

The silence hung between them for a moment, until Barbara reached across the table and covered Mara's hand. Her voice was nearly a whisper. "To tell them you forgive them?"

Mara swallowed. She nodded. "Yes. At least . . . I'm going to try." She dropped her eyes, willing away the tears.

"That's a very brave thing to do," Barbara said at last. "How will you go? By bus, or . . . ?"

Mara lifted her head. She hadn't even thought about the details. Just making the decision to go had taken all her strength. "I . . . don't know," she said. "I guess a bus is the most likely . . . maybe the only way to get there. They don't exactly live in a major city."

Barbara nodded. "That's what I thought. So . . . when will you do this?"

"Soon," Mara said. "Very soon. Before I change my mind."

Barbara squeezed her hand. "My passport's at the ready. Just let me know. I'm going with you. We'll drive."

Mara felt her eyes widen. What was Barbara saying? Was she crazy?

"You can't do that. I can't let you. It's not safe. I mean, you know how much violence and corruption goes on down there. We'd be driving straight into it."

Barbara smiled. "We won't be going alone. I believe with all my heart that God is directing you to do this, and He's directing me to go with you. Therefore, we can rest assured that He too will be with us. And if God is for us, as the Bible says, who can be against us?"

Mara's heart began to hammer against her ribs. It was the craziest thing she'd ever heard of . . . and yet, she knew it was right. God was indeed directing them to do this—together—but she'd had no idea until this instant that she would have company on her trip.

Her best friend, the woman who had become like a mother to her, and God Himself, would go with her. The power of that great truth melted the fear in her heart, and she raised Barbara's hand to her lips and brushed a kiss against it.

"Thank you," she whispered. "Thank you for being the very best friend anyone could ever hope for."

"Thank you for letting me be that friend," Barbara said. "Now, let's make our plans. How soon can you get away from work, and how long do you think we'll be gone?"

When Jonathan called a couple of nights later, Mara talked with him about everything imaginable—except her trip to Mexico. She and Barbara were leaving the next morning, and she didn't want to give Jonathan a chance to talk her out of it. It would be so easy to change her mind, even now—especially now, knowing that she would be gone when Jonathan and Leah arrived at home for their Christmas break from school. But if all went as expected, the two women would be back in San Diego, safe and sound, before Christmas.

"Leah and I are really getting excited about coming home," Jonathan said, cutting into her thoughts. "We'll be there the day after tomorrow, in time for dinner. Do you . . . would you . . . consider joining us? Or do you have to work?"

Mara swallowed and cleared her throat before answering. "I . . . won't be able to make it that night," she said, hoping she didn't sound as evasive as she felt. "But you're going to be home for a couple of weeks, right?"

Jonathan's answer was enthusiastic. "Oh, absolutely! And I totally understand that you have your own schedule, so I'm not trying to push. I just thought it would be nice . . . Anyway, can I plan on getting together with you while I'm home? More than once, I hope . . . ?"

Mara paused, wondering how to explain that she wouldn't be available by phone for a few days after he arrived. If she told him now, she'd have to tell him why, and she wasn't ready to do that.

*A text. That's it. Once we're on the road tomorrow, I'll send him a text, giving him just as much information as absolutely necessary, and promising him I'll contact him in a couple of days. That should keep him from worrying.*

"I'm looking forward to it," Mara said, meaning every word. "I'm glad you're going to be here for a while."

"Me too," Jonathan said. "It'll be nice to spend some time together—in person."

Mara nodded and sighed. He had no idea how much she looked forward to getting the next few days behind her so she and Jonathan could get to know one another better. It was her reward, something to anticipate, after doing something first that she dreaded with all her heart.

The morning of December 20 dawned bright and sunny, warmer than it had been for the past few days. Jonathan and Leah had the blue bug loaded and ready to go by midmorning, and Jonathan knew he was going to have to remind himself more than once to observe the speed limit.

*Probably a good thing I don't have a decent car, or I'd really be pushing it to get home,* he thought, shoving his sister's two overstuffed suitcases into the tiny back seat and wondering where he was supposed to put his. She always packed nearly everything she owned when they went home, even though Jonathan had reminded her that their mother had a washing machine and dryer that she was more than happy to let them use. "She'd probably even do our laundry for us if we asked nice," Jonathan had told Leah, but it made no difference. She still packed enough for six people, and Jonathan had just learned to accept it and fit whatever he could of his own things in the teeny space allotted to him.

By 10:30 they had waved good-bye to their campus in the rearview mirror and chugged onto the freeway, windows down and a breeze ruffling their hair. Jonathan was always glad to break away from school and go home for some much needed family time, but never before had he been as excited as now.

They hadn't gotten far when Leah announced that she needed a restroom break, so Jonathan decided to combine it with a drive-through lunch stop. While he waited for the burgers and fries at the pickup window, Leah ran inside and Jonathan decided to check his phone for messages. His heart leaped when he saw a text from Mara. Was it possible she'd rearranged her schedule so they could see each other that evening?

299

*Jonathan,* it read, *please don't be concerned, but something has come up and I've had to go out of town for a few days. I'll be back by Christmas, and we'll still have time to get together. Please continue to pray for me, as I know you always do. Mara*

Jonathan's heart raced at the implications. He'd never known Mara to go out of town before, so where did she go? And why didn't she include that information in her text?

Punching the letters as fast as he could, he wrote: *Where are you? Is everything OK?*

He hit send just as the window opened and the lady handed down the bag of food and two drinks. Reluctantly Jonathan set his phone down and collected his change at the exact moment that Leah rejoined him.

"Mmm, that smells great," she said, snatching the bag and rummaging through it. "Did you get ketchup?"

"Too messy in the car," he mumbled, putting the car in gear and tapping the accelerator before exiting the drive-through lane. It was going to be a lot longer drive home than he'd imagined, with nonstop praying involved all the way.

# Chapter 44

Mara still couldn't believe she was actually returning to the home of her childhood—such as it was—or that Barbara was driving as the two of them bumped and jolted over the pothole-riddled back roads of northern Mexico. It had seemed such a long ride when her *tio* was taking her away from her family and toward what he promised would be a wonderful new life in the United States of America. Little did she know at the time that she was headed straight into a living hell that would last for an entire decade.

The barren desert landscape looked only vaguely familiar, but even the tiny villages and remote houses that interspersed their journey looked frozen in time. She doubted that much of anything had changed since she'd taken that fateful ride as an eight-year-old child.

*People grow old and die,* she reminded herself. Who was to say that when she arrived home her family would still be there? But she had to find out. She had to know for sure. She had to at least try if ever she was going to be free of the memories.

She glanced at Barbara. The woman's short salt and pepper hair was the only thing that gave away her age. Her skin was clear and unblemished, her gaze steady as she concentrated on the rough road ahead of her. What courage her friend had shown to accompany her on this trip into the unknown! Mara owed her more than she could ever imagine.

"You need a break?" Mara asked.

Barbara turned and flashed her a smile. "Sure," she said. "Why not? To be honest, I was just thinking about stopping and grabbing some water out of the cooler in the back seat."

She eased the car to a stop, kicking up only a slight stirring of dust. When it had settled, the two women got out of the car and stretched a bit before grabbing cold drinks out of the back, and climbing back inside. Mara removed the light jacket she had donned that morning after breakfast and tossed it into the back seat, next to the cooler. It was nearly 11:00, and already the thermometer had climbed to a comfortable temperature.

"According to the map and directions, we're only about an hour away," Barbara commented, unscrewing the lid from her water bottle.

Mara nodded, a familiar knot clutching the pit of her stomach. An hour away—from what? Her family? It was hard even to think of them that way. They had sold her, after all. What sort of family—parents—did that to their own child? Mara knew they had been poor, but was that an excuse to consign your own flesh and blood to a lifetime of torment and degradation? If Jonathan hadn't come along when he did, Mara knew she would probably still be enslaved in her uncle's brothel.

*Or dead,* she thought. *Like Jasmine . . . and the others.*

A shiver shot up her spine, and she shook her head, determined not to dwell on a past that was too ugly to contemplate. She was on a mission. If her parents were still alive, she would find them and offer her forgiveness. What they did with it was up to them. Then she would climb back into the car and head home, where she belonged.

"May I ask you something?" Barbara said.

Mara turned toward her and raised her eyebrows. "Sure. What?"

"You name," Barbara said. "*Mara.* It means *bitter,* doesn't it?"

Mara hesitated, deciding just how much information to include in her answer. Then she remembered how much Barbara had done for her, and she decided to hold nothing back.

"It does," she said. "And it fits me—or, at least, it did for many years. But . . ." She dropped her eyes and then raised them again, staring into her friend's blue eyes and willing her to understand. "But it wasn't my real name. Before my uncle bought me from my parents and took me across the border, my name was Maria. But he said Maria was too common. He liked to give his girls what he thought of as meaningful names. So he changed my name to Mara. He said it was prettier than Maria and a lot more unusual. He also said it was a reminder to me to be grateful to him for all he had done for me, for rescuing me from a wasted life where I would one day have become a bitter old woman."

Tears bit her eyes then, and she quickly brushed them away. "I was too young then to realize the name would become prophetic. For the exact opposite reasons my uncle used to name me Mara, I became bitter toward him. I despised him—hated him and dreamed of killing him someday." She took the tissue Barbara handed her and wiped her eyes again. "And now someone else has killed him instead. At first I was glad that he finally got what he deserved. But now . . ." She swallowed. "Now I know God wants me to forgive him." Her voice dropped to a whisper. "I want to, Barbara, but . . ."

Barbara reached across the console and took Mara's hand in both of hers. "God wants you to forgive your uncle," she said. "That doesn't mean He wants you to say that what he did was all right because it wasn't. It was a hideous crime. Depraved, cruel, and, horrible. If he didn't repent before he died—and we have no way of knowing that—then he is even now paying the ultimate

303

price for his sin." She paused, and Mara saw that Barbara too was fighting tears. "You must understand that, dear girl. Jesus paid the price for your uncle's sins, as surely as He did for yours and mine. Forgiveness is there for anyone to receive. But offering forgiveness does not condone the sin. Do you understand?"

Mara's eyes widened and her heart raced as the implications of her friend's words began to wash over her aching heart. Why hadn't she seen it before? No wonder she was having trouble forgiving her uncle and her parents! Somewhere inside she had clung to the mistaken idea that if she forgave them she was also saying that what they had done to her was not such a terrible thing after all. But it was! And she needed to understand that, even as she offered forgiveness in much the same way God offered it to her—and to all mankind.

*An hour away.* Suddenly she no longer dreaded the reunion, whatever it held. She smiled and released her friend's hands, then turned back to look out the front window as Barbara started the car. It was time to deal with her past, once and for all. Then, perhaps, she could move forward with her life.

The noonday sun warmed Cecelia's face as she lifted the wet clothes from her basket, clipping them one at a time to the single line that spanned the two wooden poles next to their house. She was grateful the wind wasn't blowing, as it often kicked up the fine dirt and dust of the yard and resoiled the clothes she had just scrubbed in the old tub in the kitchen. One of the things that seemed to make Rudolfo maddest was dirty clothes, though Cecelia couldn't imagine why since their house, their yard, and nearly everything else they owned was almost always coated with a thin layer of dirt, no matter how hard she tried to keep them clean. More than once Cecelia had experienced Rudolfo's wrath over the inevitable dirt that pervaded their lives.

Her most recent beating had come as a result of something else entirely: last night's dinner that had grown cold before he arrived at the table to eat it. Cecelia had cooked it exactly as he liked it, precisely at the time he had requested it, but then he had taken his time coming to the kitchen. Now, as Rudolfo slept off the drunken stupor he'd fallen into after beating Cecelia until she begged for mercy and collapsed in exhaustion, the battered woman tried to ignore the pain in her ribs and her swollen eye and lip. It was bad, but she'd received worse at his hands, many times throughout the years. And she imagined she would continue to do so in the future until at last he beat her to death and she would be free.

A cloud of brown dust in the distance caught her eye, and she stopped in the middle of clipping a shirt to the line. They didn't often get visitors, and she certainly hadn't expected one now. Should she risk waking Rudolfo? She didn't want to greet anyone in her broken condition, but she decided it was better to risk humiliation than to waken her husband and risk another beating.

She waited, watching the dust cloud grow closer. Soon she could make out the light colored four-door car bouncing along slowly as it drew nearer. Though she clung to the hope that the car would pass her by, she somehow sensed that it would not.

And then it stopped, directly in front of their house. Cecelia's heart raced as she realized the car was fairly new and had US plates, much like her brother-in-law's from years ago when he took Maria away. Cecelia squeezed her eyes shut, trying as she so often did to blot out the memory of watching that car drive off with their only daughter inside. How she'd prayed the girl would have a better life and that they hadn't made a terrible mistake by letting Rudolfo's brother buy her from them. Then again, what choice had Cecelia had? The deal was brokered between the brothers, and she'd had no say in it whatsoever.

She heard two car doors slam and she opened her eyes. A woman stood on each side of the car — a middle-aged lady next to the driver's door and a younger one, a beautiful one, on the passenger side. The young woman's short hair gleamed brown with golden highlights in the overhead sun. She was slim, her face serious and . . .

Cecelia caught her breath. The age was right. And those eyes! Even from where the young woman stood, nearly twenty feet away, Cecelia could see her eyes, the shape of her face, the high cheekbones . . . The cry escaped before she could capture it, and she threw her hand over her mouth as if to stop another sound from flying out into the air. She felt her knees buckle as darkness blotted out the sun, and she thought surely she was about to breathe her last.

Mara dropped her purse and raced to her mother's side. She had suspected that's who she was when she first spotted her, but when she heard the woman's cry, she knew.

Why? The question brought back a flood of memories she'd kept buried for years, memories of a battered, beaten woman, crying out in pain, curled up on the floor or on the bed, weeping. How could Mara have forgotten? Why didn't she remember the many beatings her father had inflicted on her mother? If she had, surely that would have changed her perception of all that had gone on in her life before her uncle took her away.

But there was no time to think of that now. As Mara knelt at the woman's side, with Barbara kneeling right beside her, she heard a groan. Her mother was coming around, but as she turned her head, Mara gasped. The woman's face was bruised and swollen, no doubt from a very recent beating. The realization brought tears to Mara's eyes, as she leaned over and scooped the woman gently into her arms.

"Mama," she whispered. "Mama, I'm here. It's me, Mara." She swallowed. "I mean, Maria. I'm here now. I'm back. You're going to be OK, Mama. You're going to be OK."

Cecelia's right eye fluttered open, but the other one was swollen shut. "Maria?" she croaked. "*Mijita*? You are here?"

"Sí, Mama," Mara whispered, stroking her mother's dark hair back from her face, being careful not to exert too much pressure. "I am here. I am with you. You're OK, Mama. You're going to be OK now."

The woman's chest heaved, as tears poured onto her cheeks. "Maria," she whispered between sobs. "Maria. Maria!"

Mara opened her mouth to reassure her again, but before she could speak she felt hands grab her from behind, yanking on her arms and lifting her from the ground to her feet. She heard her mother moan as she fell from Mara's grasp onto the ground.

Before she could catch her breath, Mara was spun around to face a man whose foul breath assaulted her as he leaned into her face. "You," he growled. "So you have come back at last." Still grasping her arms, he nearly spit his words as he spoke. "Who do you think you are, coming back here after all these years? You have no right. No right! I sold you to your tio. He promised I would never see you again. Why have you come back? Why, after all this time?"

Mara's breath came in gasps, but she was determined not to be cowered by this man who so resembled his now dead brother, the one who had tormented her for so many years. She had come here to offer forgiveness, and she would do so—regardless of how it was received.

"I came," she said, drawing herself up and shaking herself free of his grasp, "to forgive you. That's why I'm here, Papa. To forgive you for selling me to my *tio*." She took a deep breath. "He is dead now, murdered in prison."

Her father's red eyes widened briefly before returning to a squint. "Dead? *Mi hermano* is . . . dead?"

Mara nodded, their gazes locked in a battle that went back for many years. How was it possible that she had once thought her father was a handsome man? Deep lines etched his bloated, unshaven face, and what was left of his black hair stuck up in tufts as if it hadn't been washed or combed in days.

At last he broke eye contact and turned away, his shoulders hunched and head drooping as he shuffled back toward the house, murmuring a string of profanity that Mara had become all too accustomed to hearing while enslaved by her uncle. When he was safely back inside, Mara turned to her mother, relieved to see that Barbara now cradled the woman's head on her lap.

"Maria," her mother whispered. "Maria."

"Sí, Mama," Mara said, kneeling down once again and taking her mother's hand in hers. "I am Maria. And I have come home. I'll take care of you now, Mama. I won't let him hurt you anymore. We'll find a way to get you away from here, I promise."

Cecelia's right eye opened wide and she shook her head from side to side. "No," she moaned. "No, Maria, this cannot be. I cannot leave your father. He is my husband. I married him and promised to stay with him. Who would take care of him if I left?"

Mara glanced at Barbara, whose eyes were wide. "She doesn't know what she's saying," Barbara whispered. "She'll come around when she's had time to think about it. Don't worry, Mara."

"Maria," Cecelia said. "My daughter's name is Maria."

Mara turned her eyes back to her mother and nodded. "Sí, Mama. You're right. My name is Maria."

Cecelia smiled and nodded, then closed her eyes, as Mara wondered what she and Barbara would do next.

*Pray,* she thought. Of course. It was the only thing they could do, for the situation was truly beyond their own capabilities.

*You brought us this far, Father,* she prayed silently. *Show us what to do next.*

# Epilogue

"Any news?"

Leah's voice cut into the silence of Jonathan's one-sided conversation with God. He'd been talking to the Lord nearly nonstop since receiving Mara's text about being out of town, but so far he'd heard nothing in response. He had, however, had one more text from Mara—just that morning, as a matter of fact, when she had explained more about her trip.

He shook his head. "Not since she said she and Barbara were heading for the border and expected to be home soon." He glanced at his watch. I keep hoping she'll text again, or call, and let me know they made it back across safely."

Leah nodded, concern evident on her face. "Traveling in and out of Mexico isn't a pleasant, simple experience anymore, is it?" Crossing the family room to join Jonathan on the couch, she added, "And to think she actually went down there to see her family, her parents, and to forgive them for what they'd done to her. I'm so proud of her, but . . . wow, it took some serious courage."

"It sure did," Jonathan agreed. "Not to mention some serious faith. But I'm glad Barbara went with her."

"Me too." Leah glanced at her watch, a habit Jonathan had practiced nearly every few minutes since hearing from Mara. "Six-thirty. Only another hour until the Christmas Eve service. You ready?"

"I guess so," Jonathan answered, swallowing the words that would have revealed how desperately he was hoping to hear from Mara before they had to leave. He just wanted to be sure they were back on US soil before he and the family headed off to church.

"Because you know Mom and Dad will insist we be there on time—early, even."

Jonathan sighed. He knew what Leah was saying, which meant she knew what he was feeling. And they were both hoping for the same thing—that Jonathan's phone would beep, indicating that he had a message, and that it would be from Mara.

"At least she texted you this morning, so you know they were OK then," Leah said, a positive note in her voice. "It sounds like it was a long message, too."

He nodded. "Yeah, it was. They had just come into cell phone range, so Mara took the opportunity to explain where they were and what they'd been doing." He shook his head. "I just can't imagine how it must have felt to see her parents again after all these years—and under such sad circumstances."

"You said she remembered how her dad used to beat her mom."

Jonathan nodded again. "I guess hearing her mother cry out reminded her of it. And then she saw her mom's battered face." He shuddered. "That must have been beyond-words terrible."

"And then her father came out and grabbed her."

Jonathan felt his eyes blaze and his cheeks flame, and he had to utter a silent prayer and take a deep breath to dispel the righteous anger that threatened to overwhelm him. "It's probably a good thing I wasn't there," he said. "It would have been hard not to thrash the guy."

Leah laid a hand on his arm. "Don't be too hard on yourself. It's not like he doesn't deserve it, you know."

"I know. But it stuns me when I realize how easily I forget what I deserve—where I'd be without Jesus."

After a brief pause, Leah asked, "So . . . what do you think will happen with Mara's parents? It sounds like her mother refuses to leave her husband, even though it might be the only way to save her life."

"That's what Mara said in her text. She begged her mom to reconsider, and both she and Barbara promised to do anything they could to get her away from there and find somewhere safe for her. But the woman is determined to stay. It's so hard to understand, but I've heard that about battered women before."

"So have I," Leah agreed. "We'll just have to pray for protection for her, or that she'll change her mind."

"That's what Mara said. But at least for now she's reestablished contact and accomplished what she went down there to do. She offered both of them her forgiveness, and her mom gratefully accepted it. Who knows about her dad? Maybe she at least gave him something to think about. And she said she had a chance to tell her mom about receiving Jesus and how that totally changed her life."

"Did she . . . tell her about what happened to her during those years she was with her uncle?"

"Only briefly. She said she thought too many details would destroy her mom."

Leah nodded. "She's probably right. And it wouldn't serve any purpose."

Jonathan glanced at his watch again. What was taking so long? They should have been back by now. It didn't take that long to cross the border, even in the holiday traffic. Why didn't she call . . . or text . . . or something?

"At the risk of being repetitive," Leah said, her voice soft, "we're going to have to leave soon."

"I know. I just keep hoping."

The doorbell rang then, and Jonathan sprang to attention, leaping to his feet, his heart hammering as he rushed to the front door. Was it too farfetched to hope that . . .

He tore open the door and caught his breath. There, standing on the porch in the glow of the Christmas tree lights that surrounded the door frame and hung from the eaves, were Barbara and Mara. Jonathan thought his heart would explode out of his chest.

Unthinking, he threw his arms around Mara and pulled her close. "You're here," he exclaimed. "You're safe!"

Mara returned his embrace and then pulled back. "Yes, we're here. And I'm so sorry I didn't call again, but phone reception was spotty at best—especially in Juarez."

Jonathan frowned and stepped back to usher them inside. "Juarez? What were you doing there?"

Mara greeted Leah who had come up behind Jonathan, and then turned back to him while Leah and Barbara hugged. Mara's smile warmed Jonathan's heart like warm honey, and he forgot everyone else as he got caught in the sparkle of her wide hazel eyes.

"We stopped to see Francesca and her baby," she said, "just after I sent you the text. It was wonderful! Her family made us breakfast while we visited, and then we headed out and drove straight through. I was so excited about seeing them and about getting back home, I'm afraid I just didn't give you an update." She laid her hand on his arm. "Forgive me?"

At that moment he would have forgiven her for anything, but he just smiled and nodded, not trusting himself to speak. He heard his parents come down the stairs and greet everyone, but he still couldn't tear his eyes away from the beautiful young woman standing in front of him.

"We need to get going to church," his mother said. "Are you two going to come with us, or are you too tired after your long drive?"

Mara turned toward Rosanna and smiled. "Absolutely we're going to come with you. We talked about it all the way home. That's one of the reasons we were so anxious to get here on time."

Jonathan smiled as he shot up a silent prayer of thanks. God may have been silent throughout the day, but He had just answered Jonathan's prayers, loud and clear.

Mara slipped her arm through Jonathan's as they all pushed toward the front door and back out into the night. "I've never been to a Christmas Eve service," she whispered.

Jonathan whispered back, "And I've never been to one that meant as much to me as this one, Mara."

She squeezed his arm. "By the way, I've officially changed my name back to Maria." She smiled up at him. "Merry Christmas, Jonathan Flannery."

Tears bit his eyes as he returned her smile. "And Merry Christmas to you . . . Maria Jimenez."

# The End

Use the QR reader on your
smartphone to visit us online at
NewHopeDigital.com

If you've been blessed by this book, we would like to hear your story.
The publisher and author welcome your comments and
suggestions at: newhopereader@wmu.org.

# FREEDOM SERIES BOOK #1

*Deliver Me From Evil*
ISBN-13: 978-1-59669-306-7
$14.99

## *Praise for Deliver Me From Evil...*

"Macias tackles one of our world's most perplexing social issues with intense realism and hope. *Deliver Us from Evil* reveals depth, honesty, and grace to guide readers toward a deeper faith and a heart challenged to make a difference in our world."

  —**Dillon Burroughs**, activist and coauthor of *Not in My Town*

"*Deliver Me from Evil* will grip your mind and heart from the opening chapter and refuse to let go till you reluctantly close the back cover. Kathi Macias tackles a dark and difficult issue with compelling, complex characters and vivid prose. This novel will change you.
"—**James L. Rubart**, best-selling author of *Rooms, Book of Days,* and *The Chair*

Available in bookstores everywhere.

For information about these books or any New Hope product,
Visit NewHopeDigital.com

# FREEDOM SERIES BOOK #2

*Special Delivery*
ISBN-13: 978-1-59669-307-4
$14.99

## *Praise for Special Delivery...*

"*Special Delivery* by Kathi Macias handles a tough subject with compassion and an intriguing story that sweeps you from the United States to Thailand. The three-dimensional characters make you care what happens to them in this hard-to-put-down book."

—**Margaret Daley**, author of *Saving Hope*

"In *Special Delivery*, Kathi Macias explores the troubling realities of human trafficking in a powerful and emotional new novel that puts a face on the women and children involved in this all-too-real world."

—**Lisa Harris**, author of *Blood Covenant*,

Available in bookstores everywhere.

**NEW HOPE**
PUBLISHERS
Gospel-Centered. Missions-Driven.

For information about these books or any New Hope product,
Visit NewHopeDigital.com